# Giving Back One-Hundred-Fold

人生の百倍返し

## Volume 2

Hummanity

The Joys and Sorrows of Life

生きる 喜びと 悲しみ

### YAMAGUCHI Katsumi

Translation & Localization
**Harley Emmons**

## *Synopsis of Previous Work*

Naoto Yamamoto joined Marunouchi Bank in 1976 and gained experience with accounting and taxation at his first position at the Fukuoka branch–the foundations he laid there would continue to show in all of his later work. At the Motosumiyoshi branch, Naoto built his 'site-first principle' with Sugayama, the president of a non-ferrous metal recycling business and a close business partner and mentor.

After working at two business sites, he was transferred to the Planning Department at the head office, where he worked for eight different presidents over a quarter of a century. During that time, Naoto was initially in charge of the Ministry of Finance (MOF), and raised questions about the long-established 'convoy system' (controlling the entire fleet according to its slowest ship), and endeavored on his own to find a potential solution.

After that, he was involved in getting Marunouchi Bank onto the New York Stock Exchange. Later, he took advantage of that experience to introduce an information disclosure system in the financial industry, and to face the debt crisis following the 'burst' of the Japanese bubble economy and try to break down the outdated constitution of the banking industry. However, in the midst of repeated business mergers, he was forced to retire due to tax problems associated with the largest and final

Mitsuwa Bank bailout merger.

Naoto looked back on his life as a bank employee too absorbed in his work to look after his family for 35 years. He was once again grateful that his wife, Yoko, raised three wonderful children, even with a nursing career.

As soon as he arrived at the Accounting Education Foundation, which became his second workplace, he somehow managed to avoid the Foundation's disbandment crisis due to excessive liabilities. After that, he participated in practical accounting education for assistants who passed the Certified Accountant Exam, corporate accountants, and such.

Meanwhile, around this time, the Japanese government launched a nation-wide project to encourage Japanese companies to introduce International Financial Reporting Standards (IFRS) in an attempt to attract foreign investments, and ordered the Accounting Education Foundation to act as its leader.

Naoto struggled as the secretary-general of the Foundation, and just as he was on the verge of persuading Japanese companies to adopt the IFRS, Yoko was hit by an incurable disease. He retired halfway through his work at the Foundation to help her recovery. The two of them returned to their familial homes in Nagasaki and concentrated on assisting at the hospital. However, the true nature of Yoko's illness was soon revealed, one that was impossible to cure completely. They decided on at-home care in Kawasaki, where they continued to live.

At that time, Takeshi Terada, a business student who admired Naoto and joined the Tokyo Marunouchi Mitsuwa Bank mid-career, died in an accident. Naoto was furious with the insecure response at his funeral service and asked himself, "Who do I have to thank for my climb up to the top bank." Thus, I realized it was because of many exceptional, dedicated employees who sacrificed for the organization, only midway through their dreams.

While providing long-term care for Yoko at home, Naoto resolved to devote his life to the children of such employees, and to children fighting for their lives with diseases like Yoko. He found himself reflecting on the bonds that tie together families as he dutifully cared for his wife.

One day, his family's 16-year-old black Labrador Retriever named 'Great', passed on. Kumi, his eldest daughter who was taking care of the dog in Zushi, sent a message saying, "This morning, Great laid on my lap and was called up to heaven. I'm sure he's playing with Aki and Pokke (other beloved pets who had passed away) now."

The night before, Naoto had felt a sign, as if Great had come to his home, even though the dog had been in Zushi. Great may have come back to say goodbye to his owner, Yoko, who he had taken care of for a long time. At that time, Yoko shouldn't have been able to speak due to her illness, but she still called out, "Great, Great," as if he had been right next to her.

Great had no doubt given back 'one hundred times' to her beloved family.

# Giving Back One-Hundred-Fold  Volume2
Humanity The Joys and Sorrows of Life

# CONTENTS

## *Main Characters*

**Part 1 Bank Volume (Planning Department)**
- Yamamoto, Naoto – Investigator/Deputy Chief in the Planning Department, Tokyo Marunouchi Bank
- Sugayama, Toshikatsu – Former Business Owner/Close Business Partner
- Hiroaki, Ogi – Marunouchi Bank Fukuoka Branch Employee (Same Orientation Class as Naoto)
- Ishikawa, Takemi – Marunouchi Bank Planning Department (Naoto's Senior)
- Yamanouchi, Katsuto – Marunouchi Bank Fukuoka Branch Manager
- Seriyama, Tadashi – Managing Director, Marunouchi Bank
- Yamano, Takeshi – Managing Director, Marunouchi Bank
- Yabuki, Kazuo – President of Marunouchi Bank
- Wakata, Tsuneo – President of Marunouchi Bank
- Kishimoto, Akira – President of Tokyo Marunouchi Bank
- Itsuki, Shigeru – President of Tokyo Marunouchi Bank
- Kuroyama, Nobuo – President of Tokyo Marunouchi Mitsuwa Bank
- Nagai, Katsunori – President of Tokyo Marunouchi Mitsuwa Bank
- Wada, Toru – Managing Director, Tokyo Marunouchi Mitsuwa Bank
- Osaki, Shunichi – Ministry of Finance Bank Manager, MOF Inspection Bureau Manager, Financial Services Agency Bank Manager

**Part 2 Education Volume (Education Foundation)**
- Yamamoto, Naoto – Education Foundation Director /Secretary General
- Osaki, Shunichi – Financial Services Agency Certified Accountant/ Examining Board Secretary-General
- Morita, Kensuke – Chief of Education Foundation (Transferred from the National Association of Accountants)
- Terada, Takeshi – Tokyo Marunouchi Mitsuwa Bank Investigator (Practical Trainee)

**Part 3 Nursing Volume (At-Home Caregiving)**
- Yamamoto, Naoto – Retiree (At-Home Caregiver)
- Yamamoto, Yoko – Naoto's Wife (Registered Nurse)
- Motoyama, Yuko – Miyamae Care Center Visiting Nurse
- Ueki, Kinichi – Deputy Director of Nagasaki Roadside Psychiatric Hospital
- Asai, Jiro – Nagasaki Tozai Hospital Neurologist
- Takegami, Masako – Nagasaki Tozai Hospital Chief Nurse
- Sugiyama, Saburo – Sakuradamon Hospital Neurologist

**Part 4 Family Volume (Familial Bonds)**
- Yamamoto, Naoto – Retiree (At-Home Caregiver)
- Yamamoto, Yoko – Naoto's Wife (Registered Nurse)
- Yamamoto, Aiko – Naoto's Mother
- Yamamoto, Masao – Naoto's Father
- Yamashita, Suma – Yoko's Mother
- Yamashita, Yu – Yoko's Younger Brother
- Muto, Kayo – Yoko's Older Sister
- Muto, Ikuo – Kayo's Husband/Yoko's Brother-in-law
- Hiratsuka, Tadashi – Naoto's Friend (Same Orientation Class as Naoto)
- Hiratsuka, Ai – Tadashi's Wife (Yoko's Coworker)

# Part 1
# Bank Volume
## (Planning Headquarters)

# Prologue  The Pride of the Top Bank

After retiring from his second workplace at the Education Foundation, Naoto went to see all of the people who had helped him and to update them on the latest situation.

The first person he visited was Mr. Sugayama, president of a non-ferrous metal recycling business and a close business partner at the Motosumiyoshi branch. Naoto headed for the president's home while taking a nostalgic stroll through the shopping district outside Motosumiyoshi Station on the Toyoko Line.

When he pressed the intercom at the entrance, the president's cheerful voice asked, "Yes, who is this?"

"It's Yamamoto from Marunouchi Bank. Thank you again for all your help at the Motosumiyoshi branch."

"Oh, Mr. Yamamoto? This is a special visit indeed. Go ahead and come in."

Naoto climbed the stairs to find Sugayama waiting for him with the door wide open. "It's been a while, Mr. President. You're looking well." However, Naoto hid his surprise at how the man had aged, and promptly calculated his age. Naoto had transferred from the Fukuoka branch to the Motosumiyoshi branch at age 27, and the president had to have been in his mid-forties then. Nearly forty years had passed since then–the man was already in his mid-eighties.

Incidentally, the president's wife was Naoto's age, 64 years old. Sugayama had lost his first wife to illness before marrying his current one. She had been a teller at the Motosumiyoshi branch, working directly with regular customers, and there had been about a twenty year age difference.

Naoto tried to joke and gloss over his shock so Sugayama wouldn't notice. "You're looking as great as ever. By the color of your tan, you've already been golfing with that single-figure handicap."

"What are you talking about?" the president replied, "I've already moved on from golf. This is a truck-driver sunburn. Our industry is in a recession, it's tough out there. Thanks to that, I'm working hard everyday to keep out of poverty. By the way, what in the world happened today? I was just watching the news on your bank this morning and telling my wife you must already be an executive."

Naoto answered with a bitter smile. "No, no, the executives are ridiculous. Actually, I retired from the bank and started at the Education Foundation. Though I also retired from there last month. So, I came to say hello to you, my first mentor."

"What? Did you just say you retired before you were an executive?" The president asked with a bewildered look. "That couldn't be the case, that's not the Yamamoto I know.

You should have at least been a department head, what the hell happened there?"

"No, it's nothing. I retired from the bank right at retirement age."

"Huh, I wonder if that was my misunderstanding. No, that's not it–something must have happened in the Planning Department."

"You're as persistent as always. It was an amicable resignation."

"I scc, if you don't want to tell me, I won't pry anymore. But I can tell something happened. I heard about how much effort you put in."

Apparently the president knew some executives in the Human Resources Department and kept up on all the gossip.

Sugayama abruptly changed the topic. "By the way, Mr. Yamamoto, don't you think your bank has been a little odd? When you were there, everyone at the Motosumiyoshi branch was so full of energy, but now it's not the same. Everyone from the executives to the new-hires all operate on autopilot, not thinking about the customer at all. My bank finally told me that I was banned from frequenting the bank and its business too much anymore."

"What, what does that mean? How can a bank cut ties with one of its previously important clients? Is that what happened for us?"

"I didn't do anything, it's the banks that have changed. The Motosumiyoshi branch has apparently gone from an individual-centric store to a corporate-centric store, so individual business owners like myself are no longer dealing with them. The time has finally come for banks to screen and carefully select their partners. After all, your bank is a top bank with an established reputation, it's a trend of the times."

"That's absolutely ridiculous. Dealing with a private business owner like the president is the most profitable deal a bank can make. That can't be right, I need to look into it." Naoto frowned.

"Well, we've already been tossed aside," Sugayama bit out, "so we switched to a local credit union."

"I'm so sorry for that."

"Don't be sorry, it's not your fault. It was decided by the people in the bank that are too good for us now. For a small business like us, a local credit union is now the best match. By the way, Mr. Yamamoto, what are you planning to do next?"

"Actually, my wife developed a disease called 'progressive supranuclear palsy' seven years ago and was bedridden, so now I'm devoting my time to taking care of her at home."

"Oh really? That's a shame, let me know if you ever need anything. I only met your wife when you helped me after the cataract surgery at Kawasaki Rosai Hospital, but I know she was a tall beauty."

"What, how did you know she's beautiful if you couldn't see?" Naoto raised a brow.

"I only had the operation on my left eye, my right eye could see just fine. Back then, a nurse brought me a bouquet. When I asked, 'Who are the flowers from?' the nurse said, 'It's from my husband, thank you for always looking out for him'," Sugayama explained. "I was surprised and wondered who the husband of such a beautiful woman was, and then I saw her nametag with 'Yamamoto' on it and realized she was your wife. However, at that time, my wife came in and saw the bouquet, and asked, 'Who did you get this from? From a snack mom?' I immediately pointed to your wife and said, 'She's Yamamoto's wife, from the Motosumiyoshi branch.' My wife apologized in embarrassment. Both of our wives must be the year of the Dragon–it's rough always being under their thumb."

"I hadn't realized that. My wife is so talkative, but I don't talk much about my work. From now on, I want to be more vocal about thanking all the people who have taken care of me at the bank, the Foundation, and now during my wife's care. But now that I've heard about this ban on small businesses, I want to start making noise in the banking industry again. Correcting their current mistakes is really the best tribute I could make for all of my years there," Naoto finished, his breath ragged. "I'll keep you updated on how it goes, sorry for the intrusion."

As soon as Naoto returned home, he called Takeshi Terada to confirm what Sugayama had told him. Terada had retired from the Thomas audit company midway through his career to get a part-time job at the Accounting Education Foundation. However, once Naoto had to retire from the Foundation, Terada passed the mid-career entrance examination for Tokyo Marunouchi Mitsuwa Bank, Naoto's old stomping grounds. He even worked in the same Planning Department.

"Hello, it's Yamamoto. Thank you for hosting the farewell party the other day when I was busy. I'm sorry I couldn't get there until late."

"What are you talking about?" Terada responded. "Actually, I had tried to get more practical trainees who studied under you to come, but for some reason everyone suddenly declined with some obvious excuse. It sounds like someone from the Association was spreading a rumor to not go to any drinking parties with Mr. Yamamoto."

"I don't really care about that," Naoto said. "That's my own fault, not Terada's."

"Anyway, I bet you didn't call me just to say thanks. There's something else, isn't there?" As usual, Terada's intuition was clear.

"Actually, I went to see the president of Sugayama Shoten, one of my old clients from the Motosumiyoshi branch, to say hello after my retirement, and he said that the bank cut off business with him. According to Sugayama, the Motosumiyoshi branch was upgraded from an individual store to a corporate store, and it's no longer doing business with Sugayama Shoten, a sole proprietor. This organizational reform must lead back to the planning department, doesn't it? Was the same reform also done at the larger branches recently?"

"That's right. The purpose of this branch organizational reform is to separate corporate transactions and individual transactions to streamline their business operations. Specifically, corporatc transactions will continue at our pre-existing stores, but for personal transactions, like personal deposits or loans for individual business owners, we'll establish new, smaller stores focused on that purpose alone. As a result, branches that handle both corporate transactions and individual transactions will split, so the number of small branches that specialize in personal dealings will increase. It was more of the HR Department's plans, working behind the scenes."

Terada continued to explain, "As Mr. Yamamoto knows, the business integration with Mitsuwa Bank made it necessary to consolidate and abolish duplicate stores, and it made the battle for branch manager positions even more fierce. The deputy managers are all working hard to get promoted, and the section managers can't get promoted, so there's more and more complaints. The HR Department had been struggling, so the organizational reform was proposed to increase the number of branches. Though, the branch manager of these newly established branches is just a title, they don't have much more power than a deputy or section manager. It was all to appease upper-management."

Naoto was furious. "So they prioritized the made-up pride of the employees at the expense of the individual business partners? As you should know, dealing with these small business owners is a very profitable transaction for banks. Is it okay to spurn such an important business partner?"

"I agree, at first the Planning Department was against this measure," Terada stumbled for an excuse. "I also think we could easily lose these profitable business partners to rival banks now. However, Managing Director Wada, who transferred to the HR Department, led the charge to pass this measure, since it would make his job easier. There were no officers who specifically opposed the president or vice-president, and we didn't have any more HR employees who were familiar with the profit structure of the banking operations, so no one saw a problem with it."

"But the Planning Department controls the profits of the entire bank and should have more say in the matter than HR. Why didn't they stop such a bad idea? Could nobody come up with a clear explanation against it?"

"I'm sorry, Mr. Yamamoto. I didn't have the knowledge or experience to convince the officers with any concrete estimation results of how the measures would affect the entire bank's profits."

"I'm not blaming you, Terada, I'm blaming all of the seniors in the department that should've known better. Why aren't they taking this problem more seriously?" Naoto remembered something and advised Terada as follows. "Let me give you a helpful hint. I remember telling you this several times during your studies. This actually happened once at the Fukuoka branch where I was first assigned. Two newcomers– my roommate Hiroaki Ogi and myself–went to Shin-Nippon Airlines, one of our main business partners, to collect money every Monday and Friday. I used to go with a senior employee in charge of funding. From 9 AM to 3 PM, we went around to several offices in the airport to collect money– over 100 million yen each time. I had to carry smaller bills too to make change, so the bag would get huge. When I think about it now, it was all ridiculously high-risk, we could have been robbed at any time. Ogi and I wondered if this method of collection was actually profitable. So I calculated the labor cost for this collection, plus any additional costs like car insurance, liability insurance, depreciation, and gasoline prices. Meanwhile, Ogi investigated where the collected cash was sent afterwards, and then how much it contributed to the cash flow of the entire bank. So, we took about three months to analyze how the bank as a whole was profitable in terms of cash flow."

"By the way," Naoto continued, "that analysis method later became the basis of the bank's profit management. Until then, the profitability with business partners was negotiated only by the loan interest rate and the deposit balance. The 'comprehensive profit management method' was leagues better than the previous 'real money method' (an agreement with business partners using real interest rates) since it also included personnel expenses. The results found that the Shin-Nippon Airlines' collection was bleeding out money, and there was almost no overall transaction profitability. In other words, the name recognition of the airline made everyone assume it was good business. So they decided to cancel this collection business and the person in charge, Takemi Ishikawa, was impressed by our approval form. He consulted with the Sales Department deputy manager at the head office, which was in charge of Shin-Nippon Airlines account. Then, the deputy manager apparently scolded Ishikawa, 'What are you doing, canceling the airline account? Shin-Nippon Airlines is a great company!' and complained to the section manager. This all led to the head of the Sales Department yelling at the Fukuoka branch manager.

At that time, the Fukuoka branch manager decided to take a page from the old samurai Bushido code and 'lose a battle to win the war'. He called us to his office and said, 'New Japan Aviation is an unrivaled company in the aviation industry, while we are one of the lowest ranking banks in the area. Our bank's standing is not on par with Shin-Nippon Airlines, so it's a miracle we have a deal with them. However, none of this matters if we're operating in the red. Next month, the board will review this matter at the head office–I'll do my best to explain the situation to the executives'. Ogi and I were delighted to be able to work under Ishikawa as newbies. You were hired mid-career and had little bank experience, but neither did we at that time. Sometimes less experience means fresher eyes that can see the essence of problems others overlooked. A newer employee like you could explain the essence of this problem to the executives in charge."

Terada was silent for a few moments. "OK, I'll try again."

# Chapter 1  Two Imperial Councils

The Board Meeting to review the organizational reform of the branch offices began at 2 o'clock on April 25, 2016 at the head office. The attendees were President Hirata, Vice President Koyama, Managing Directors Yamada, Wada, Yabushita, and Nakata, Planning Department General Manager Ishida, HR Department General Manager Arai, Business Planning Department General Manager Nagata, and ten managers from the Otani branch. There were five people in charge: Deputy Managers of the Planning Department, Human Resources Department, Business Planning Department, and Branch Offices, and Takeshi Terada of the Planning Department.

First, the Otani branch manager reported on the progress of their organizational reform. "The reform has been about 80 percent completed, with 102 of the 125 target stores done. The remaining 23 stores should be completed by the end of June. We're aiming to improve the efficiency of all branch office operations by separating individual transactions from the corporate transactions, and then concentrating on about 60 smaller stores that specialize in new individual transactions. When I investigated one of the reformed branch offices, I got the impression that everything was more efficient."

Next, Mr. Arai, General Manager of the Human Resources Department, gave his supplementary explanation. "This establishment of new branch offices will create 60 more branch manager positions, a great win for our personnel policy. With the merger, our number of executives has increased beyond the capacity of positions. But more offices allows us to find a place for all of the former branch managers, subsequently allowing the deputy and section managers who are working hard in the Sales Department to receive promotions as well. There's no doubt that this will incentivize everyone's work efforts. This kills two birds with one stone."

Vice President Koyama had a bitter smile. "Both of you are singing your own praises. Today's meeting is being held with the intention to evaluate whether the reform is. The planning department must review this reform. I'd like the Planning Department to explain why in a little more detail."

Mr. Ishida, General Manager of the Planning Department, tried to explain. "At the last board meeting, the branch manager reported that the cost of this organizational reform would only be the capital investment for the new stores, expected to be about 10,000,000,000 yen. However, the other day, when the Planning Department interviewed all of the targeted branches, it became clear that more than half of the 700 independently-owned businesses we previously did business with were poached by other banks. When we calculated the amount these sole proprietors had contributed to the bank's profits, it came out to more than 10,000,000,000 yen annually. This is expected to have a significant impact on the bank's profits this fiscal year, so the Planning Department, which is in charge of the bank's overall profits, believes it's necessary to rethink this reform."

The Otani manager seemed surprised by these facts and immediately started making excuses. "This measure was implemented at the request of the HR Department. It would be a problem if our HR Department had to take responsibility for recovering this drop in profits."

Arai, Director of Human Resources, argued against this. "No, this measure is all about improving the efficiency of the branch operations, so of course the Branch Department should be held responsible."

The tension was heavy in the air. Vice President Koyama addressed them in a disappointed tone, "This is not about who is responsible. First, I'd like the branch manager to reiterate the purpose of the branch organization reform."

The branch manager had a troubled expression. "As I said earlier, the main goal is to improve the efficiency of the branch offices' operations. We've already heard good feedback about this in the branches we already rolled out the change in."

"Then, how much will the bank's profits increase with this improved efficiency?"

Otani answered with a troubled face. "It's difficult to gauge since the impact varies from branch to branch, so we haven't made a preliminary calculation yet."

Hirata smacked a hand down on the table and scolded the branch manager in front of everyone. "It cost us 10 billion yen to open the new stores, and you haven't even calculated the expected return on investment? Since when have we been so flagrant with our profits? This needs to be investigated immediately. Also, how did no one predict that we'd lose so many customers to other banks with this? All of this is inconveniencing small business partners we've had for years, they're going to feel neglected. It's only natural for them to switch banks. Were there any measures taken to prevent this?"

The branch manager kept his gaze down. "I'm afraid that we didn't."

The president asked the HR Director, "If this measure will supposedly increase the work output of the Sales Department's deputy and section managers, how much profit would we actually see from it?"

Director Arai replied, "We can't put that into exact numbers–it depends on the individual."

The president frowned deeper. "Then, how is this measure so wonderful?"

"You're right. I'm sorry," the director replied.

Finally, the president turned to Mr. Ishida, General

Manager of the Planning Department. "It was reported earlier that over 350 independent business owners were stolen by other banks, losing us over 10 billion yen a year. How was this amount calculated?"

Upon hearing the president's question, the manager of the Otani branch's face lit up with vindication. "Yes, my thoughts exactly. Isn't the amount you calculated simply the income of the businesses we lost? That number wouldn't reflect the money we'll be saving on payroll and such. It might as well be a blind guess."

"I'm asking the Planning manager, not you!" the president snapped at the branch manager.

"Then," the Planning manager told the president, "let's allow Terada of the Planning Department to explain, since he was the one who actually calculated this."


Terada had been on the phone with Naoto the day before the board meeting and his mentor had advised him to be ready for this kind of question from the president.

"President Hirata used to be the deputy director of the Planning Department when he was younger, back when I was in charge of cost accounting," Naoto began to explain. "One day he asked me, 'How accurate is the cost accounting the bank uses?' In other words, he was wondering if it could be used for management. So I answered him, 'Deputy Director Hirata, that's not the case. Unlike industrial companies, banks can't calculate manufacturing costs, but we can view employees as material costs. In other words, if the employee works well, then the manufacturing cost will be kept low and the profit margin high. On the contrary, if the materials are flawed, then the manufacturing cost will be high and the profit margin low. So if you can accurately estimate the amount of work needed for your customers, you can calculate the cost'."

In the board meeting, Terada turned to explain this in turn to the president. "As we established, a bank can't quite calculate manufacturing costs. However, it is possible to view our employees as our material costs. We know all of the transaction data with our customers from the bank's customer information system, so we can calculate how much work is needed. Prior to today's meeting, I interviewed all the targeted branches on how much time they spent doing business with sole proprietors. Specifically, the time spent on the preparation of loan approval documents, loan management, deposit transactions, foreign exchange transactions, and external business. By doing so, we could calculate the standard labor cost according to the pay-level of the employee and multiply it by the time spent. As a result, it turned out that our transactions with these sole proprietors were more than twice as profitable as larger corporations. In short, our calculation of 100 billion yen is by no means a random estimate."

"Branch managers, improving the efficiency of branch office operations is indeed an important measure," the president nodded. "But the whole point of improving efficiency is to reduce costs and increase profits. If the cost of creating this efficiency is higher than the profits it brings in, of course we should reevaluate it. It sounds like many basic steps were skipped over for this branch organization reform, in the rush to open up more management positions. It's not too late yet, so please urgently review this. Next, with the fierce competition for executive posts, I understand the desire to increase incentives for the lower-level managers, but we can't tangibly calculate the impact that would make. All of this needs to be examined again."

The president finally turned to Terada. "I used to be a researcher in the Planning Department, and a coworker named Takemi Ishikawa brought me an approval letter to cancel the Shin-Nippon Airlines account from the Fukuoka branch. I can still vividly remember that I said, 'Two newbies think New Japan Aviation's account hasn't actually contributed to the bank's profits?' Their analysis had found that it was putting us in the red, and that we should cancel their collection business. I majored in cost accounting at university too, so I understood some of it, but their analysis went into such high-leveled detail. I couldn't believe it was only their first year. It was a big deal, but what really impressed me was how they turned this complicated method into a simple equation that could help measure our profitability–I even tried using their worksheet myself. Their argument was so solid that no one could disagree. After reading the approval letter, we held a board meeting, much like today. There were ten attendees, including President Kishimoto, Managing Director Seriyama, Goshima, Yamano, and Itsuki, General Manager of the Sales Division, Head of Sales Tanaka, General Manager of the Planning Department, General Manager of the Business Planning Department, General Manager of the Fukuoka Branch, and myself, in charge of the minutes."

The president continued on, making eye contact with everyone at the table. "At that time, the manager of the Fukuoka branch was Yasuto Yamanouchi, a member of the University of Tokyo's Faculty of Law who lived by a strict moral code, like the samurai of old. I'll never forget the intimidating presence he gave off. He was outnumbered, but he still told Kishimoto, 'I know that their analysis isn't wrong. Please read it carefully until the last page.' Then he walked out. That certainly got Kishimoto's attention. He scanned the documents and said, 'We'll cancel the collection business for Shin-Nippon Airlines. If there's any problem, I'll take full responsibility.'

On the last page of the approval form, Ogi and Yamamoto

wrote that they believed in the future of Marunouchi Bank. And next to that, Yamanouchi wrote in red pen, 'There's no future for business that won't listen to the voices of their young employees'."

The president smiled at Terada. "At the end of your analysis report from today, there was something similar written, wasn't there? 'Here's to giving back one hundred times to Tokyo Marunouchi Mitsuwa Bank'."

As President Hirata stood up to leave the room, Terada told him, "I know one of the newbies you were talking about earlier was Naoto Yamamoto, my mentor who had been in the Planning Department for many years. He's already retired, but he still gives me advice all the time."

"He's helped me as well back at our American headquarters," the president told Terada. "By the way, Takemi Ishikawa, the man who sent in their approval letter, was my coworker. If he were still alive, he might be the president instead of me–he was a well-loved guy. I owe a lot to my own seniors, but now I'm leaving it to you."

The following week, Naoto received a call from President Sugawara. "Mr. Yamamoto," he started, "the branch manager came and apologized, and asked me to continue doing business at the Motosumiyoshi branch. Was this you're doing again?"

"I haven't done anything. This just means that our bank has a decent manager again. Thank you for your continued support."

Sadly, President Sugayama died of a cerebral hemorrhage five years later. It was when Naoto had returned to Nagasaki with Yoko. President Arizumi, who is in the same industry as Sugayama, gave him a call. "How is your wife, Mr. Yamamoto? I'm sorry I'm calling with some sad news today–President Sugayama collapsed the other day and died from a cerebral hemorrhage last night. He was 89 years old. The funeral service will be held at Daitokuji Temple. I know it would be difficult for you to come in person, but I wanted to let you know any way."

"I'm really sorry to hear that," Naoto lamented. "I wanted to hear President Sugayama say 'What, this guy!' one more time. I actually got a call from him last month, and he was feeling sentimental. He said, 'Mr. Yamamoto, I have no regrets in my life, I've lived the way I wanted to. But I have one thing I'd like to ask you. I know you're already taking care of your wife, but if I die before my wife, I want both of you to be there for her. I've put her through so much.' At that time, I said, 'President, don't say something so ominous. Where did your upbeat attitude go, that's unlike you? I'd be lost without my mentor.' I wonder if he could hear the concern in my voice, because he immediately followed with, 'I'm just kidding.' But

I could hear his voice cracking too."

When Naoto was working at the Motosumiyoshi branch, President Sugayama brought him to a club of fellow businessmen he had started called 'Kappa Kai'. President Sugayama was nicknamed 'Popeye' in this group, and he introduced Naoto to all of them. "This is Mr. Naoto Yamamoto from the Motosumiyoshi branch, I owe him a lot. He'll be a great person to know in the future, so keep in touch with him!"

'Kappa-kai' was held every month with about 20 participants, who all paid 50,000 yen each time as a membership fee. Naoto's job was to deposit this membership fee into the Kappa-kai account the next day.

President Sugayama would use that money to support any member who was struggling. More than 500 mourners attended his funeral, including all of the Kappa-kai members. A star of the industry had fallen that day, and a tremendous hole was left in Naoto's heart.

In August 1979, he met President Sugawara who helped him develop the 'on-site first principle'. Since then, the man has helped him in various situations for more than 40 years. There was no meaningful encounter without a parting. Through the death of President Sugayama, he realized that all the joy he's lived through so far would eventually lead to sadness. He hoped that when it came, it would have been worth it.

# Chapter 2 Working on Holidays

When Naoto was at the Fukuoka branch, Takemi Ishikawa of the Business Planning Department implemented 'profitability management', the method that Ogi and Yamamoto created to calculate standard labor costs. Soon, the equation was upgraded to the new 'Transaction Profitability Management Table', a document still used at the bank today.

Ishikawa was in the Business Planning Department for over 10 years and was one of the few other people that worked at the office on national holidays. At that time, Japanese banks were cutting back on the amount of money they lent out, but the liberalization of deposit interest rates was about to begin. It started in 1985, with the liberalization of large-scale fixed deposits beginning in 1987 and the liberalization of small-sized deposits starting in 1988. Marunouchi Bank was acting chairman of the Kanto Bankers Association (KBA) that year.

In order to minimize the drop in bank profits due to this liberalization of interest rates, the Bank of Japan's Credit Organization Bureau (now the Bank of Japan) was instructed to change the short-term prime rate for lending to a rate system that was linked to all procurement costs, including market financing and expenses. So, Takemi Ishikawa of the Business

Planning Department was put in charge of revising the bank industry's lending interest rate system. This would turn into the new 'short-term prime rate' (best lending rate). Marunouchi Bank's contribution greatly helped in the recovery of profits from the liberalization.

However, at this time, Ishikawa was worried because he could not overcome the last hurdle–the question of what to do with the expenses to be factored into the new short-term prime rate. He went to work every week on holidays to solve this problem.

One day, he popped into Naoto's office next door, "Hey Yamamoto, since you're in charge of cost accounting, do you know what the bank's expense ratio is? The Kanto Bankers Association is considering a new rate system for lending rates in an attempt to manage the drop in profits from the liberalization of deposit rates. I'm wondering how to factor in the expense ratio, do you have any ideas?"

"So you need an expense ratio everyone can agree on? All you need is a ratio based on the costs of deposits and loans."

"That much is obvious," Ishikawa laughed. "What I'm worried about is how to calculate those costs."

Naoto jumped right in. "You need to factor in the personnel expenses involved in any lending and deposits and then expenses like depreciation. I calculated the profitability of the lending and deposit business–the annual personnel expenses of the bank were about 53.5 billion yen and about 71.5 billion yen in property expenses. If you use those expenses as the numerator and the deposit total as the denominator, it would be about 0.4%."

"Yes!" Ishikawa exclaimed. "That's around where I estimated. Yamamoto, send me that data, so I can convince everyone else."

Naoto wrote down in detail how he calculated the expense ratio of 0.4%:

First, the lending expenses included the labor costs for negotiation and visiting with business partners, lending approval, execution, collection, and repayment and such, collateral management work for commercial bills, securities, and real estate, and any examination work, etc.

Similarly, the deposit expenses included the labor costs for the various deposit counter operations, cash management operations, utility bills and tax payment operations, account transfers, fixed-amount automatic remittances, and other operations in the Deposit Division.

Most of the property costs are depreciation costs related to lending and deposits, as well as expenses for any employees involved in those systems, and outsourcing costs, etc., totaling 71.5 billion yen annually.

The annual labor cost for lending and deposits is about

53.5 billion yen, the property cost about 71.5 billion yen, and the numerator is 125 billion yen. The total domestic deposit, which is the denominator, is 31.25 trillion yen, making the expense ratio 0.4%.


"Perfect!" Ishikawa shouted after reading through Naoto's notes. "Thank you, Yamamoto, that was really helpful."

That was the moment the new 'short-term prime rate' was born.

Many of the bank's operations couldn't be canceled, even if the individual cost was unprofitable. Even if the physical deposit boxes were costing the bank more money than they brought in, the bank still had to offer that service.

"Yamamoto, why don't you come over for a drink? To celebrate the birth of the 'short-term prime rate'."

When they got to Ishikawa's house, his wife had already laid out plates and plates of food.

"I'm Yamamoto from the Planning Department, I'm sorry to come over unannounced like this."

"I'm Sayoko, thank you for putting up with my husband at work. It's rare for him to bring someone home, so when he called, I knew something big must have happened."

"Then, let's celebrate with some beer first," Ishikawa proposed, looking between the two of them. "Honey, bring a few bottles of beer."

Their 'banquet' lasted for over two hours and Naoto got a little tipsy and talkative. "By the way, Ishikawa, I'm actually a little worried. Chief Osaki from the Ministry of Finance keeps sending me ridiculous busy work. Compared to Western banks, Japan is selling loans at low profits. We're being laughed at in Europe and the United States. Osaki says that in order to avoid that kind of external pressure, Japan needs to properly manage its lending practices. So the Kanto Bankers Association was asked to consider the rules for calculating the ratio that were set by the 'International Capital Ratio Regulations' at the Basel Conference in Switzerland."

Ishikawa listened and nodded along. "You've got it rough. I was asked by the Bank of Japan to come up with a new lending rate system, and you were instructed by the Ministry of Finance to come up with a way to put Japanese banking on par with the rest of the world. They're really throwing us some curveballs. So what exactly are you worried about?"

"As you know, the Banking Bureau is trying to avoid further criticism from Western financial supervisors, and has already set a bunch of regulations to curb lending all over the country. All banks are being forced to operate within that framework. But that's difficult to do realistically, so it's implied that they'll need to use 'unrealized lending' (loans that are temporarily repaid at the end of the month or at the end of the term in order to clear the total amount of lending regulations).

Major banks have unrealized loans of more than 3 trillion yen." Naoto hiccuped. "Since the unrealized loan was repaid at the end of the term, it wasn't included in the denominator when calculating the international capital adequacy ratio. If it was included in the denominator, the capital adequacy ratio of every bank would drop by more than a whole percent. What should we do about it? If the foreign bankers found out about this, they would boast about how Japanese banks are selling at low profits."

"That isn't something you can handle alone." Ishikawa shook his head. "That's something that the Bank of Japan has to solve."

Naoto doubted that the Bank of Japan would take this issue seriously, so he asked for Ishikawa's advice, since he had many acquaintances in the Bank of Japan. Ishikawa was close with the chief investigator of the Bank of Japan's Credit Information Reference Center, and suggested that Naoto consult him.

Naoto had a few contacts in the BOJ, but none in the Japan Credit Information Reference Center. So the next day, he made an appointment with Mr. Nagaishi, the senior examiner of the Credit Information Reference Center Corp.

"My name is Yamamoto from the Planning Department of Marunouchi Bank. Is there a senior examiner Nagaishi here?"

"That would be me, Mr. Ishikawa contacted me earlier.

What can I do for you?"

Ishikawa had told him, "Senior Examiner Nagaishi is a reliable person so you can speak frankly. We were in the same class at the Faculty of Economics at Nagasaki University."

"Nice to meet you. I'd like to ask you not to use it, but are you from Nagasaki?"

"That's right, I went to Nagasaki University's Faculty of Economics."

"Really? I was in the 24th class of the Faculty of Economics there."

"I was in the 21st year! What a coincidence."

"I'm sorry for the sudden consultation, but one of the officers at the Ministry of Finance has given me a daunting task. In order to avoid overloans due to the low profits and high sales of Japanese bank loans, we need to make sure that Japanese banks are operating strictly by recently-established international capital requirements. Therefore, Marunouchi Bank has been designated by Chief Osaki to review the calculation rules. However, as you know, many Japanese banks repay their loans at the end of the term using checks from other banks to clear their total amount of loans. Each of the top banks then operate as if there were no repayments at the end of the fiscal year, even though they have 3 trillion yen or more of 'unrealized loans'. They aren't included in the published loans, so if you expose them, the international capital adequacy ratio would drop by over one percent and be unable to clear the regulation value of 8 percent. However, I think exposing these unrealized loans to calculate the capital adequacy ratio is the only way to stop further damaging the credit of Japanese banks. What do you think?"

"I understand your concerns—I've also been afraid for the future of Japanese banking if this problem isn't fixed soon. I'll try to appeal to the director right away."

The Bank of Japan lifted the regulation on the total amount of lending allowed after that.

Fortunately, it was around this time that the economic bubble burst, and the actual demand for lending decreased, avoiding a credit loss for the entire country.

The international capital ratio regulation was based on the lessons learned from the financial crisis in Europe and the United States. It was introduced in 1989 after the final agreement from the financial supervisory authorities of each country. The two years from 1991 to 1992 were positioned as a transitional period, and this international capital requirement ratio regulation was officially introduced from the fiscal year ending in March 1993.

However, at this time, Japanese financial institutions were unfamiliar with the concept. Against the background of high stock prices, Japan was still cutting back on the volume competition for lending. While Western financial institutions were about to turn to fee business, Japanese financial institutions were still competing for quantity rather than quality. Under these circumstances, a major incident occurred in the announcement of financial results at the Bank of Japan Press Club in May 1992.

During this period, Marunouchi Bank was the acting chairman of the Kanto Bankers Association, and in the financial results announcements of major city banks, they acted as the overall coordinator of the financial results announcements. During the introduction period of the international capital adequacy ratio, the Banking Bureau of the Ministry of Finance was in a delicate stage, since it was in strict negotiations with each country on how much unrealized gains on stocks could be included in capital adequacy of Japanese financial institutions.

Mr. Osaki, the chief of the Banking Bureau of the Ministry of Finance, called Naoto and said, "Currently, the financial supervisors of each country are making a decision on how much their capital will reflect their own circumstances when calculating the international capital adequacy ratio. But Japanese banks need to realize that this regulation can't be easily cleared by including the unrealized gain of stocks in the capital. Therefore, please refrain from disclosing the estimated international capital adequacy ratio figures in this announcement of financial results. Thank you for your cooperation."

In other words, the Ministry of Finance was asking major city banks behind the scenes to refrain from disclosing the international capital adequacy ratio in their financial results. If Japanese banks could include 45% of their unrealized gains on stocks (the ratio after considering tax effects) in their equity capital, they could easily clear eight percent. This would stimulate financial supervisors in Europe and the United States, and make it difficult to include unrealized gains on Japanese bank stocks.

The announcement of the financial results at the Bank of Japan Press Club began with Fuyo Bank. Reporters were most interested in what the international capital adequacy ratios of all the major city banks were, and focused all of their questions around this.

Meanwhile, Fuyo Bank, which was said to have the highest ratio, had their number leaked at 9.09 percent. All of the major banks listed off theirs: Daiichi Bank at 8.76 percent, Igashi Bank at 8.87 percent, and Mitsuwa Bank at 8.5 percent.

Mr. Seriyama, Managing Director of Marunouchi Bank, stood up for their turn. "At this point, the international capital ratio regulation is in a transitional period, and the ratio of how much unrealized gains on stocks can be included in equity capital has not yet been decided. Therefore, it's not possible to announce the ratio yet, it would only mislead the actual situation."

The reporters gathered for this remark. "The rest of the numbers are useless if the KBA's Chairman won't announce theirs."

So the Ministry of Finance's proposal, which was trying to include 45% of the unrealized gains on Japanese banks' stocks in equity capital, made it through the transitional period without stimulating Western financial supervisors and led to the official introduction. Marunouchi Bank had made great strides as the chairman of the KBA. At a later date, Osaki thanked Naoto for his bank standing firm. "You guys are certainly different from other banks that only think about themselves, without considering national interests. Thanks to that, the entire Japanese banking industry was saved, and by extension, so were all Japanese companies."

As a result, major banks were able to clear this regulation gracefully, but due to the subsequent disposal of non-performing loans from the bursting of the bubble economy and the sharp drop in stock prices, they had to rely on subordinated bonds and public funds, which were expensive to issue.

# Chapter 3  Chief Osaki of the Inspection Bureau

Chief Osaki had been transferred from the MOF's Banking Bureau to the chief of their Inspection Bureau. His first act was to issue a notification to all financial institutions, stating that since 'wash sales' weren't recognized as realized profit in the United States, a fact revealed when the Marunouchi Bank listed on the New York Stock Exchange, they wouldn't be accepted in Japan either.

Forced to no longer rely on 'wash sales' on their balance sheets, all of the financial institutions made various efforts to avoid the risk of price fluctuations. It was Osaki's job to find any transactions that violated this new rule.

In May 1993, Osaki led the inspection at Marunouchi Banks, combing through all of their documents for days. The Inspection Bureau had temporarily hired an experienced certified accountant who specialized in auditing.

Osaki called Naoto to the special examination room. "It's been a while, Deputy Director Yamamoto. I haven't seen you since New York. Your bank was rough around the edges back then, but it's really shaped up now. The 'wash sales' were a problem at that time too, so I'm keeping an eye on the Planning

Department."

"And of course the Planning Department continues to make every effort to maintain our financial discipline."

"Yes, that's good. By the way, I brought five certified accountants who used to be in charge of auditing banks and securities companies. One of them reported something interesting. Do you want to hear it?" Osaki prodded.

"No, because there's nothing bad that needs to be pointed out."

"Alright, alright, that's fine. Since it involved my old friend Deputy Director Yamamoto, I thought I should tell you as soon as possible. But I don't need to talk about it. By the way, regarding your stock investment group, I wonder if Deputy Director Sugita can really be trusted."

Naoto shook his head. "He may be ten years younger than me, but he's a good, trustworthy guy."

Osaki raised a brow. "I'm supposed to have an interview with Director Tsukada and Deputy Director Sugita at 8 o'clock tonight, will you be there as well?"

"Yes, the Planning Department is in charge of the entire inspection, so you'll see me there."

So later in the evening, they gathered–Chief Osaki, Hiroshi Yamashita, a certified accountant from a major audit corporation, and Takafumi Kawakami on one side, and Deputy General Manager of the Securities Department Shigeru

Tsukada, Tadashi Sugita, and Naoto on the other.

First, Mr. Yamashita explained. "Your bank frequently buys and sells shares held with their trading partners with the intimate securities company Gekko Securities. There is indeed a week between selling and buying, to factor in the risk of price fluctuations. But recently, there have been huge losses to Gekko Securities with such trading transactions. Strange, since last month, there was a slight loss on the bank's side. How do you ultimately adjust for these losses?"

"We haven't made any adjustments," Deputy Director Sugita replied. "If we did, it would be considered 'compensation for losses' and violate Article 42 of the Securities and Exchange Act (currently Article 39 of the Financial Instruments and Exchange Act). As with any transaction, both parties bear the losses incurred."

Inspector Yamashita confirmed. "Deputy Director Sugita, if the risk of price fluctuations becomes apparent, is it true that the loss incurred would affect both parties?"

"That's right."

"Understood. So you claim that the trading of this stock with Gekko Securities is a regular transaction. Therefore, each side bears the loss caused by any price fluctuations."

Osaki confirmed with Director Tsukada again. "If you want to correct anything, this would be your last chance."

"As Sugita said, there's no mistakes," Tsukada answered

immediately.

"That's great, let's hope there's no regrets later."

Osaki was watching the frightening eye movements of Director Tsukada. It was impossible to miss his eyes darting about to avoid Osaki's gaze.

"Then we'll have a rematch starting at 10 o'clock, so be sure to tell whatever officers are in charge."

Osaki stood up, immediately giving Naoto a bad feeling. Familiar with Osaki's tactics, he knew that the man was grasping at something different from the usual bluff.

The rematch rang in at exactly 10 o'clock. Jiro Watanabe, the officer in charge of the Securities Department, arrived in a hurry.

This time, Osaki made a statement at the beginning. "It looks like we're all here, so I'll ask the same question again. The losses incurred in the stock trading with Gekko Securities are to be borne by each party, and you haven't adjusted any losses. That is correct?"

All three of the officers nodded in agreement.

With that, Osaki's expression changed. "Even if you say that, you must be feigning ignorance. Take a look at this fax. What in the world is this?"

Sugita paled when he saw it, but he quivered as he pretended to be calm. "Well, it's just a memorandum of what you've done so far. It's not unusual at all."

"This was obtained from an inspection by Gekko Securities," Osaki continued. "The manager in charge there confessed, 'This fax is a confirmation letter that we exchanged to confirm each other's losses so far and adjust accordingly'."

"That's right. It's just written confirmation, no more, no less," Director Tsukada stammered.

"Really? It's just a confirmation letter, Managing Director Watanabe? Director Tsukada?"

"Exactly," they responded in unison.

Osaki finally came in with the clincher. "Alright, but if that ends up untrue, I'll have to ask you to retire from the bank. I hope you're prepared for the worst, ruining your careers would be a simple task for me."

Managing Director Watanabe clasped his hands down on the table, and Osaki gave the three of them an ultimatum. "The person in charge of Gekko Securities said, 'This fax is a confirmation letter for loss adjustment.' Should I call said person here to talk?"

Upon hearing that, the three stood up and formally knelt down all at once to apologize. "You're right, forgive us."

However, Osaki did not allow it. "And this is why I gave you so many chances to confess. Just a memorandum? It's too late now," he finished the last part in English, smirking to himself.

Seeing the three of them prostrated on the ground, it felt

like his allies had been shot from behind. They couldn't fall apart like this in front of Osaki.

"Mr. Osaki," Naoto offered, "since Yamaichi Securities went bankrupt, there are only three major companies in the buying and selling of large numbers of stocks, and the trading environment has become quite severe. Could you consider the actual circumstances a little more?"

Osaki argued head-on with Naoto's claim. "Deputy Director Yamamoto, I was hoping they would answer honestly, precisely because I know that the environment for stock trading is getting tougher. Do you think I like to get angry or make threats? Either way, these three people feigned ignorance until the very end and I can't forgive that. Marunouchi Bank, Japan's leading bank, shouldn't be setting that example. If this isn't done right, it will be regarded as 'loss compensation' and may violate Article 42 of the Loss Compensation Prohibition Clause of the Securities and Exchange Act (currently Article 39 of the Financial Instruments and Exchange Act). It's not something that begging on your knees can make go away. At the very least, you would need to get a written pledge from the president.

Naoto dragged Osaki to another room and locked the door to keep out any distractions. Then he pulled out the last ace up his sleeve he had against Osaki–a last resort aimed at the 'competition'.

"Mr. Osaki, do you understand why people generate a 'profit' by buying and selling stocks they already own? Due to the recent plunge in stock prices, a large amount of stock amortization occurred and people are trying to make up for that profit loss. We're the only bank in Japan that still has a strict 'low price method'. The Ministry of Finance had previously mandated this low-price method to maintain the stability of banks, but now the standard has been relaxed and people can selectively apply the cost method. As a result, stock prices have plummeted even further. However, our bank is one of the few that still adheres to the low price method. Since we're so transparent in our operations, we have no way to make up for losses. While many Japanese banks have been criticized by foreigners as 'confusing' or 'suspicious', we applied the US GAAP, the strictest accounting standard in the world. Plus, we were listed on the New York Stock Exchange, the first in Japan. Is it okay for the Ministry of Finance to simply point out this matter and then hand over the responsibility to keep the rest of the Japanese banks in line? With this plunge in stock prices, few stocks have unrealized gains anymore. Even if you try to sell them, there are no more stock holdings that can turn a profit. This trading practice of lending and borrowing losses will disappear in the near future anyway."

Osaki abruptly stood up with a scowl. "Fine, Deputy Director Yamamoto. If you're so prepared, you better straighten up. Maybe you're right. But the Ministry of Finance's job is to protect Japanese banks, and since you insist there's no compensation for a loss involved here, I'll take my leave." With that, he stormed out.

The time was around one in the middle of the night, and Naoto still had one last important job left–punishing the three people responsible.

Naoto entered the room and glared at the group of men huddled in silence.

"Come on, everyone, it's time to fess up. Otherwise Mr. Osaki will accuse Marunouchi Bank of violating Article 42 of the Securities and Exchange Law. If that happens, you'll be subject to a much harsher criminal charge. Get ready for the worst."

Lying and betrayal had been embedded into Naoto's mind as one of the worst things a person could do since he was a small child. It was truly unforgivable.

# Chapter 4  Ministry of Finance

The bad debt problem had rapidly affected every financial institution. The Japanese government received severe criticism from overseas financial supervisors and requested that the Kanto Bankers Association (KBA) solve this problem at once.

At that time, it was Marunouchi Bank's turn to act as the chair for the KBA and the president moved to establish a company to buy non-performing loans.

Under the direction of President Wakata, Marunouchi Bank was ahead of other banks in not only the disposal of their own non-performing loans, but also the disposal of the non-performing loans of their subsidiaries and other companies. In order to continue this, it was absolutely necessary to proceed with using a non-performing loan purchasing company at once.

Thus, in January 1993, the 'Cooperative Credit Purchasing Company (CCPC)' was established, with 162 private financial institutions jointly invested to purchase non-performing loans with real estate as collateral.

The financial institution would sell the non-performing loans with real estate as collateral to the CCPC according to the judgment of the 'Price Evaluation Committee' composed of real estate appraisers and such. Marunouchi Bank was trying to strive forward with the support of the Banking Bureau of the Ministry of Finance, so that the difference between the price and the book value could be deducted.

However, the NTA (National Tax Agency) had been waiting for this.

President Wakata had called Naoto to his office one day. The man had a deep knowledge of tax affairs, so Naoto headed to the 8th floor thinking that Wakata's query was probably tax-related.

Wakata got right into it as soon as Naoto opened the door. "Mr. Yamamoto, the fact is that last fall, there was a big request from a big politician in the Liberal People's Party to the Kanto Banking Association. They wanted a company created to buy bad debts and solve Japan's problem all at once. The chairman had been considering this solution, but we just can't overcome this last hurdle–the stubbornness of the NTA. The Banking Bureau is backing us up, but the NTA under the same Ministry of Finance umbrella, won't allow the deduction of sales losses associated with the sale of non-performing loans. The tax representative of the Thomas auditing company has also been working on it, but the opponent is pretty tough. I thought I'd ask you for some good ideas to win against the NTA."

Naoto was not surprised by Wakata's question. However, even with his wide breadth of tax-related knowledge, Naoto couldn't think of any easy solutions. However, Naoto remembered that the NTA Commissioner had repeatedly said, 'We cannot give preferential treatment to a specific industry. Taxes are national."

Naoto answered the president. "There's only one way to go after the NTA–to win over the taxpayers first. The NTA has to ultimately answer to the people. Could you give me a little more time to flesh out this idea?"

"Next weekend," Wakata told Naoto, "said big politician will invite the NTA Commissioner and the Banking Bureau Commissioner to have dinner with four people, including myself. We need to decide on a tactic by then."

Naoto immediately went to the Kanto Bankers Association's library, around four in the afternoon. From that point on, there was only one hour until the building closed. He ran to the reception, thinking that he had to hurry.

At that time, he happened to meet Mr. Tsuji, the director of the KBA's Planning Department. This was a heaven-sent opportunity, and he figured it couldn't hurt asking Tsujimoto. "There are some materials that I need to find by the end of the day to help a problem in the KBA, so could you please extend the library hours a little?"

"No problem, I have something I need to look up too, so take your time."

"Thank you so much. I'll repay one-hundred fold

someday," Naoto replied.

"A hundred times better huh? Then please get me a full course of French cuisine and fine wine."

"I could make that happen," Naoto laughed. "Thank you."

"No, no, I'm just joking."

With this, he desperately began to search for a certain book–it would be the secret weapon to cut down the NTA.

The time was a little past 7 o'clock in the evening. Naoto rented a library ladder and searched every corner of the bookshelf. Hours later, he went down the ladder in defeat, only to slip.

He landed on his bottom with a grunt of pain. As he rubbed his sore head, an old book caught his eye on the bottom shelf. The one he was looking for, 'How to Determine the Crude Oil Purchase Price'. Naoto instinctively shouted in victory, sending Director Tsuji rushing over.

"Mr. Yamamoto, are you alright? Did you find it?"

"I'm fine." Naoto waved off his concern. "I finally found the book I was looking for, you really saved me here."

"I'm glad. What book was it anyway?"

"You'll have to wait and see."

"Don't be putting on airs now."

"The only thing I can say now is that this book might prove a point for a joint debt purchasing company that even the NTA can't argue with."

The book described in detail how a shipping company that transported crude oil from the Middle East to Japan determined the purchase price of the oil through an exchange with an oil distributor. In other words, since it took a long time to transport oil from the Middle East to Japan, there were detailed rules on how to incorporate the risk of fluctuations in crude oil prices into the contract. Said contract was endorsed by the NTA. The NTA had approved the 'provisional price' estimated between the shipping company and the oil wholesale company at the time of the initial contract when the crude oil was purchased. Furthermore, it was decided in detail how the two companies would adjust the risk of subsequent price fluctuations.

Naoto uses this precedent to record the first loss (primary loss) at the 'provisional price' when the financial institution would sell the non-performing loan to the purchasing organization, and then allow the National Taxation Agency to record the final loss (secondary loss) at the 'fixed price' at the time of sale to the third party.

Naoto was convinced that the NTA would have to accept a decision they had previously made. He explained it all to President Wakata, along with Mr. Yawata.

Wakata told them, "Alright, this might have saved the Japanese banking industry. Thank you for all your hard work."

Wakata confidently attended the dinner meeting that

weekend. The attendees were Toshihiro Sankai, a major politician of the Liberal People's Party, Ichiro Katsui, Director General of the National Tax Agency, Mitsusaku Kanai, Director of the Banking Bureau, and Tsuneo Wakata, Chairman of the Kanto Banking Association.

The NTA Commissioner apparently opposed Wakata and Naoto's proposal, stubborn as usual. "It's not possible to certify a loss on sale (primary loss) due to a purchase at a provisional price as tax-free. If we allow such deductions, they would be considered preferential treatment to the banking industry, which goes against our fair policy."

Wakata argued back, "Director, you're saying that in the crude oil purchase contract between the shipping and the oil wholesale company, the NTA had already approved the 'provisional price'. Nevertheless, I think it would be unfair to not allow the banking industry to buy non-performing loans at a 'provisional price'."

The Commissioner of the NTA was at a loss for words.

The Director of the Banking Bureau also spoke in support of Wakata, "Japan needs to deal with its bad debts problem as soon as possible, so that our economy can recover. Shouldn't we allow the banks tax-free treatment here to keep Japan from sinking any further in debt? Taxes can't be collected if all of the taxpayers are bankrupt."

The politician gave the concluding remarks. "President

Wakata, please establish the Joint Debt Purchasing Organization as soon as possible to start the non-performing loan purchasing business. I will take responsibility for clearing up any tax issues with the Minister of Finance."

From April 1994 to March 2001, the Joint Debt Purchasing Organization had purchased and brought in about 15.4 trillion yen of non-performing loans for just 5.8 trillion yen. The company was able to receive tax-free treatment for the loss of 9.6 trillion yen. The amount of non-performing loans successfully decreased by 15.4 trillion yen.

This killed two birds with one stone for financial institutions: Reducing the non-performing loans and reducing the burden of loss.

However, the non-performing loans purchased by the Joint Debt Purchasing Organization from various financial institutions continued to decline with the price of the collateralized real estate. This led to the market price falling significantly below the provisional price from the initial purchase. This was the so-called 'secondary loss'.

Naoto told Osaki, who had then been transferred to the Ministry of Finance's Banking Bureau, about the 'secondary loss' so provisions could be made right away.

At that time, the Banking Bureau of the Ministry of Finance had the authority to decide on the establishment of new reserves, so banks were not allowed to make reserves on their own.

"Chief Osaki, due to the recent decline in land prices, the price of non-performing loans has fallen accordingly, causing a large amount of secondary loss. If it's not dealt with now, it will be even more difficult later."

"Deputy Director Yamamoto, what are you talking about?" Osaki shook his head. "I don't understand anything about these new provisions. The bank sold the bad debts to the Joint Debt Purchasing Organization. Why should we make reserves for somebody else's debt?"

"Please go and read the contract from when the non-performing loans were sold to the Joint Debt Purchasing Organization. Until the Joint Debt Purchasing Organization sells this non-performing loan to a third party and finally disposes of it, the bank that brought it in will bear the subsequent loss. Therefore, it's the banks that brought in the non-performing loans that have to make provisions for secondary losses."

Osaki was astonished. "That's ridiculous. Why doesn't the current KBA chairman, the Fuyo Bank president, come to explain this himself?"

"It'll be a problem no matter who explains it. Anyway, the secondary loss is so large that the accounting audit will not pass unless we make a provision for the expected loss. We'll now make a provision for secondary losses from the settlement of accounts."

The position of the financial inspection was completely reversed. Banks were reluctant to make provisions, even though they knew they needed it to pass.

After thinking it over for a while, Osaki came back with some conditions. "Fine, it's okay for your bank to make a reserve, but there are three conditions. First, decide on the name of the reserve right now. Second, the reserve should be set up at all banks nationwide under the leadership of the KBA. Third, get the consent of the National Tax Agency. Got it?"

"How about 'Reserve for the loss on sale of receivables' for the name? Tell the KBA's chairman that all banks that sold non-performing loans to the Joint Debt Purchasing Organization will get this allowance." Naoto replied. "But I can't do the third condition. Why do we need to get the tax authorities to agree on an accounting allowance that can't be deducted?"

"Like you said," Chief Osaki explained, "we don't need the NTA's consent, but it was the NTA that handled the loss at the provisional price for Japanese financial institutions when the Joint Debt Purchasing Organization was established. So if the provisional price has dropped so significantly, it's only right to explain it to the NTA properly. When this secondary loss gets big, the public will accuse the NTA of allowing it to happen, so they'll need to be able to defend themselves."

He hated to say it, but Osaki was right. The two departments had been in conflict for so long that he forgot they all had the same ultimate goal. Osaki had a unique sense of justice, one that must have made the Ministry of Finance proud.

# Chapter 5  A Merger of Equals

One day, Naoto was called by Managing Director Yamano, the man in charge of the merger negotiations with Tokyo Nihonbashi Bank.

"Deputy Director Yamamoto, the director of the International Planning Department is still in their meeting. Could you wait in the drawing room for a little?"

"That's no problem." Though Naoto was surprised to hear about the International Planning Director's involvement.

The secretary popped their head out after a few minutes. "Actually, Director Teranishi wants you to join in on their meeting."

"Pardon the intrusion…" Naoto said hesitantly, still confused on what this meeting would be about.

"Mr. Yamamoto, come right in, we don't want to take up too much of your time."

Naoto sat next to the director of the International Planning Department, Mr. Teranishi.

Teranishi grinning at him. "You look well as usual! With the bad debt problem, the regulation of international capital adequacy ratios, and the introduction of market value accounting for Japan's Big Bang (financial deregulation), you're going to be busy every day."

"It'll be nothing compared to all of the work you're going through, Director Teranishi."

"Mr. Yamamoto," Managing Director Yamano started, "this is just a general question, but what do you think the best date for the merger would be?"

Naoto was caught off-guard.

Teranishi must have noticed the surprise on his face. "It's time to prepare for the absorption-type merger of the New Japan Trust. It looks like it's going to be difficult to deal with their bad debts, and we have a responsibility as the parent company."

Teranishi was in charge of rebuilding the New Japan Trust before he became the director of the International Planning Department, so of course he was the best person to consult.

New Japan Trust was a subsidiary of Marunouchi Bank, so even with a merger, it was unlikely to impose a heavy administrative burden and the merger date wouldn't matter much.

"Generally speaking," Naoto replied, "since both companies need to settle their assets and liabilities by the merger date, April 1st would have the least administrative burden as the end of the fiscal year."

The managing director nodded. "That's right. On any other day, you'd need to settle again."

"Unlike the merger partner having many overseas bases, like Tokyo Nihonbashi Bank, New Japan Trust has no overseas bases and only a few branches in Japan, so I don't think it will cause much trouble," Naoto said, baiting the hook.

The two heard 'Tokyo Nihonbashi Bank' and looked at each other. The managing director nodded to the other man, "You should ask him."

"Overseas, merger dates are based on local standards, so you can use normal settlement procedures," said Teranishi. He then paused and his face fell.

"I've heard that before, but it's not relevant here since there are no overseas branches in New Japan Trust, there shouldn't be a problem…" But Teranishi clearly wasn't asking for his opinion on the New Japan Trust merger. No, they were preparing for another one with Tokyo Nihonbashi Bank.

After that, Naoto was asked a series of questions in quick succession, all of which the two men should have already known from any basic merger treatise.

Once they wrapped up the conversation, Naoto added, "Oh, I forgot to say one important thing. If the bank being absorbed specializes in trusts, it would no longer be able to carry out trust business after the merger. Also, if the other party specializes in foreign exchange, the approval will be lost. So I think it's a good idea to close the transactions before the merger, before those transactions become self-dealing when merged."

From down the hall, Naoto could still hear the two men snickering, the director saying, "He got me there."

About a month after that, the morning edition of the Nihon Keizai Shimbun published an article entitled, 'Marunouchi Bank and Tokyo Nihonbashi Bank merged on an equal footing'.

Marunouchi Bank's president Wakata was particular about this merger being known as an 'equal merger' from the beginning. It was designed to keep the morale of the employees of the Tokyo Nihonbashi Bank, the extinct bank, but there was another big reason as well.

Actually, President Wakata had called him about a month prior and asked a similar question. "Mr. Yamamoto, is there any difference between Japan and the United States in terms of taxation regarding the merger?"

Naoto jumped right into detail, knowing the president had to be familiar with tax affairs. "First of all, there's no provision in the tax law regarding the tax affairs of mergers in Japan. However, Article 285 of the Commercial Code (currently the Companies Act) stipulates the 'below market value principle' and assets accepted from companies extinguished due a merger must be accepted below the market value. Therefore, the tax law is based on this concept, so if you accept the merged assets at a price below the market price, there should be no problem. On the other hand, in the US merger tax system, mergers are organized as an organizational restructuring tax system according to Article 368 of the Internal Revenue Code (IRC), so it differs depending on the reorganization form. In other words, if it's considered to be due to an acquisition, all assets received would be valued at market price and the difference (unrealized gain) between the market value and the book value would be taxed. But if it's considered due to equity pooling (pooling the shares of both companies into one), then the assets of the extinguished company could be accepted as they are at book value and no tax will be levied. The idea behind Japanese commercial law is rather close to this idea of equity pooling."

"So you think that the merger in Japan won't be a problem as long as they accept assets below the market price," Wakata summarized.

"That's right. However, it's important to note that in the United States, size can be a criterion for an acquisition. A merger with a smaller company is likely to be considered an acquisition."

"Well, in that case, tax is levied on the unrealized gains of the other company. Is that all? Are there any other potential problems?"

"If it's certified as an acquisition in the United States, there's a big problem–you'd have to mark all of the assets you accept at market value. In the first place, mark-to-market accounting hasn't been introduced in Japan yet (later introduced in 2000), so there's a fatal issue of how to do this. The merger is time-sensitive, so the only realistic response would be to pay a high fee to a US investment bank and ask for a market value of the asset."

"Alright, when we merge, we'll have to be careful not to have it labeled as an acquisition in both Japan and the United States."

However, after hearing about the merger of Marunouchi Bank and Tokyo Nihonbashi Bank in Japan, the US Securities and Exchange Commission (SEC) asked, "The merger ratio of Marunouchi Bank and Tokyo Nihonbashi Bank is reported to be 1 to 0.8. Could you explain how this was calculated? When deciding the merger ratio in the United States, the stock price is the most important factor. According to a survey by the Committee, the ratio of the three-month average, six-month average, and one-year average immediately before the announcement of the merger was around 1 to 0.6."

In response to these concerns from the SEC, President Wakata, Vice President Kishimoto, Managing Director Yamano, General Manager of the Planning Department Amino, and Chairman Nagai of the Merger Preparation Committee gathered right away.

Wakata, who understood this problem best, cut to the chase. "Everyone, the SEC has requested that we show the reasoning for the 1 to 0.8 merger ratio. The real purpose of this question was based on the underlying suspicion that we are deliberately trying to adjust the merger ratio to apply the equity pooling method. The SEC is on the lookout to prevent US-listed companies from abusing this equity pooling law. Therefore, we need to respond carefully."

Vice President Kishimoto responded, "In Japan, it's the view of commercial law scholars and audit corporations that there's no problem as long as the assets of the Tokyo Nihonbashi Bank are accepted at the 'market price' or less as stipulated in the Commercial Code. So this is only a problem for the United States, but we still must avoid Japan's equity pooling law and the U.S. acquisition law."

Managing Director Yamano spoke up next, "Can we convince the SEC that there are no problems with commercial law, tax law, and accounting in Japan?"

"The other day," Planning Department Manager Amino replied, "when I talked to Davis, a former SEC chief inspector for the Thomas auditing company, he said, 'Currently, there are more and more people trying to evade taxes through equity pooling, so the SEC is really cracking down.' So, I don't think the SEC will take that well."

Finally, Nagai, the chairman of the Merger Preparation Committee, said, "I heard Mr. Yamamoto's thoughts on this issue yesterday, so I'll call him and talk to him directly."

So, Naoto was called into the meeting room and Nagai prompted him to repeat what he said yesterday. "The aim of the SEC is to find any equity pooling that's being abused in the United States. I think it was the difference in size between Marunouchi Bank and Tokyo Nihonbashi Bank that caught their attention from the beginning. In the United States, corporate value is all about stock prices so the merger ratio is also determined by the stock price. As they pointed out, the ratio of stock prices immediately before the announcement of the merger was between 1 to 0.63 and 1 to 0.66 for the three-month average, six-month average, and one-year average. So I think that the 1 to 0.8 ratio is proof that the acquisition was feigning equity pooling. As you all know, the stock price is the value of the company per share. So either we reduce the number of shares issued by Tokyo Nihonbashi Bank or increase the number of shares issued by Marunouchi Bank. The former would be a reverse stock split (multiple shares made into one share), and the latter would be a stock split (one share split into multiple shares)."

Naoto continued, "Both have their advantages and disadvantages. For example, when a reverse stock split is implemented, the stock price will likely decline and anger the Tokyo Nihonbashi Bank shareholders. So it seems like a good idea to split the issued shares of Marunouchi Bank instead, considering that the 1 to 0.8 merger ratio caused considerable criticism from the Marunouchi Bank shareholders. If we calculate back how much we should increase the shares held by our shareholders, or conversely, if we dilute the corporate value per share, it will approach 1 the 0.8 ratio. With this method, the SEC should be convinced."

"This option not only convinces SEC," Nagai concluded, "but will also convince our shareholders, two birds with one stone."

"Aren't you forgetting another important effect, Mr. Nagai?" President Wakata added. "By adopting this option, you will succeed in this merger. So to speak, 'three birds with one stone'."

Thus, the merger agreement between the two banks was signed the following week. In the 'merger conditions' column of the agreement, it was written as follows:

· Merger method: Equal merger by equity pooling
· Merger ratio: 1 to 0.8
· New name: Tokyo Marunouchi Bank, Ltd.
· Number of issued shares increased from 4 billion shares to 8 billion shares
· Stock split: Free delivery to shareholders of Marunouchi Bank
· Issuance of 2 billion dollars of convertible bonds

# Chapter 6  US Securities and Exchange Commission

The Cooperative Credit Purchasing Co., established in 1993, completed the purchases of non-performing loans in March 2001 as originally planned. The Resolution and Collection Corporation (RCC), which is based on the Deposit Insurance Corporation of Japan, was established in April 1999 to take over this business.

Tokyo Marunouchi Bank, as a company listed on the New York Stock Exchange, annually reported to the US Securities and Exchange Commission (SEC) and received a review back from the SEC once every three years.

This review was conducted by answering questions from the SEC, but the hundreds of questions were often convoluted. Meanwhile, the Planning Department received a question from the SEC covering 127 items regarding the annual report ending on March 31, 2003. "Tokyo Marunouchi Bank has sold over 650 billion yen worth of non-performing loans to the Resolution and Collection Corporation as part of the disposal of non-performing loans, but at that time, a loss of 4.2 billion yen was incurred. This is clearly evidence that the allowance for doubtful accounts was in short supply. Therefore, the previous fiscal year's financial results need to be adjusted."

This threw the bank into chaos. Managing Director Wada, who had taken over Managing Director Yamano's responsibilities, immediately called Naoto, "Yamamoto, what does this all mean? It's impossible for us to revise the previous term's financial results. I'm going to be demoted. Do something!"

Naoto suspected that there might have been a misunderstanding, so he called Chief Inspector Moore, who had helped him with the New York Stock Exchange listing, to clear it up. "This is Yamamoto from Tokyo Marunouchi Bank. Is Chief Inspector Moore there?"

"Hi, Yamamoto," Inspector Moore answered in Japanese. "This is Moore, it's been a long time. How are you? Do you need something?"

"Mr. Moore, your Japanese has improved! Where did you study?"

"You told me to study Japanese more, so I studied on my own. What can I do for you today?"

"The other day, we received a concern from the SEC, and I think it might have been a misunderstanding due to a shortage of allowance for doubtful accounts from the large loss on sale back when we sold non-performing loans to the RCC. I'd like to explain it all in detail, if that's okay?"

"Oh, that's all?" Moore sounded relieved. "Even in the

United States, bad debts are sometimes bought and sold in the market, but there's no large loss on sale like in Japan. Why is there such a loss? I assume that the allowance for doubtful accounts was insufficient in the previous fiscal year's financial results. It's far beyond the standard five percent of the final profit."

"Mr. Moore, that's not the case. Most of the loss on sale was actually a secondary loss. The allowance for doubtful accounts was a reserve for the primary loss, and said loss was properly offset so there was almost no additional loss. The secondary loss was collateralized after selling the non-performing loans with real estate collateral to the consolidation and collection agency. The loss was actually caused by a further drop in real estate prices."

Moore was just as surprised to hear this as the chief of the Osaki Bank had been. "What? You sold the non-performing loans to the Resolution and Collection Corporation? Why does Tokyo Marunouchi Bank need to make a provision for the secondary loss of the non-performing loans? It is not a genuine sale of non-performing loans. Isn't that a 'wash sale'? That's a big problem."

He had accidentally raised Moore's suspicion. At that time, Naoto remembered that when he had established the Joint Debt Purchasing Organization, a similar scheme was explained in the US bank's annual report. It used the 'Other

Real Estate Owned (OREO)' account to transfer bad debts to another account.

"This situation is the same as the U.S. OREO account," Naoto said. "The US bank probably also made a reserve for secondary losses after transferring bad debts to that account."

Moore seemed to finally understand after that comparison. The problem was settled. However, he was still concerned about the insufficient provisions for secondary losses. "Then, you didn't have enough reserves for secondary losses? What account did you use for the reserves?"

"It's an account called, 'Reserve for loss on sale of receivables'."

"Then, the allowance for loss on sale of receivables wasn't properly estimated."

Naoto rebutted Moore's claim again. "Mr. Moore, that's not it either. In Japan, existing non-performing loans will be newly generated within two years based on the 'Financial Revitalization Program' under the guidance of the Financial Services Agency since 2002. We're obliged to sell any existing bad debts within three years and separate them from the balance sheet. So financial institutions were actually forced into this situation, they had no choice but to bulk sell bad loans. In other words, each financial institution sold at a discount from the original non-performing loan price, so the difference inevitably occurred as a loss on sale."

Moore was silent for a few moments. "Although there are bulk sales in the United States, there's never such a large loss on sale. This is because the loss is estimated before the sale contract is concluded, and the allowance is recorded immediately after. In Japan, isn't it possible to estimate the loss on sale before concluding the bulk sale contract and record the allowance for that expected loss?"

Moore's question pointed out a fatal flaw in the sale procedure, which was the late provision for loss on sale associated with bulk sales in Japan. It was all a problem with their timing.

Naoto honestly admitted, "You're right. That was our problem."

"So if you change the board's decision-making process for bulk sales in the future, we won't request a restate of the previous term's financial results."

"I'll make sure it's done, thank you."

Naoto reported to Managing Director Wada in detail about this interaction.

"That's a relief, I won't have to be demoted." Wakata sighed. "That's good, that's good."

"No, Chief Inspector Moore says, 'In the future, changing the institutional decision process of the board of directors is a condition that we do not have to revise the financial results this time'."

"I don't care about any of that. I just need to report to the SEC that it was changed."

"That would be a direct breach of promise. I'll contact Moore back to tell him the director in charge isn't willing to change the board's procedures."

"Wait, wait, I understand, I understand, Yamamoto. I'll do it, I'll do it properly."

Thus, the SEC chief inspector's point changed the institutional decision process of the Japanese board of directors. Rather than waiting for the purchase price to be calculated by the Price Judgment Committee of the Consolidation and Recovery Organization, each financial institution estimates the loss on sale at the time of the bulk sale at the internal board of directors meeting at the end of the fiscal year, and sells the receivables. The audit companies also greatly welcomed this new process.

# Chapter 7  The End of the Seven Banks Association

The 'Seven Banks Association (Financial Friendship Association)' was a system of accounting and taxation by the top seven banks of major city banks (Daiichi Bank, Fuyo Bank, Igashi Bank, Mitsuwa Bank, Marunouchi Bank, Mitsukoshi Bank, Toyo Bank). After discussing how to respond to various changes in accounting and taxation systems, the overall direction was decided, but due to the agitation of the Ministry of Finance entertainment corruption case, this meeting was also certified as equivalent to a dispute. The meeting closed in March 2000.

Deputy Director Obayashi of Daiichi Bank, who was the secretary of the last 'Seven Banks', gave a greeting. "I'm really sorry, but with today's meeting, the traditional 'Seven Bankers Association' is being put to an end after seventy years. I'd like to express my sincere gratitude to the Chief Osaki of the Ministry of Finance for coming to this event even with his busy schedule. From now on, our role will be taken over by the Planning Department of the Kanto Bankers Association, and we appreciate your continued cooperation."

The curtain would close on the end of the 'Seven Banks'

in a harmonious atmosphere.

At that time, Deputy Director Ota of Mitsuwa Bank, the first Kansai bank to be the chairman of the KBA, said, "The banking industry is about to enter its most difficult period yet, due to the bad debts problem and the plunge in stock prices. How many of these seven banks will survive the next five or ten years?"

Every time Naoto attended these meetings, it reminded him of his college years.

Naoto majored in commercial law at Nagasaki University, one of their most popular programs.

Professor Shizutani looked like a stereotypical scholar at first glance, but he gave strict guidance to the students. A total of twelve fourth graders were enrolled in the Commercial Code Seminar. In 1976, when his class graduated, the economy fell into a depression from the effects of the second oil crisis, so job hunting was completely a 'buyer market' for companies. A total of 216 seniors from the Economics Department at Nagasaki University were desperately flocking to interviews

Only a handful of these graduates managed to find jobs they wanted, mostly at financial institutions, but some at local government offices.

At that time the Seven Banks Association was made up of Yoshida of Daiichi Bank, Yamakawa of Fuyo Bank, Mita of Igashi Bank, Kawahara of Mitsuwa Bank, Naoto of Marunouchi

Bank, Mizutani of Mitsukoshi Bank, and Moriyama of Toyo Bank.

However, 20 years later, these seven banks would be consolidated into three groups: Daiichi Bank and Fuyo Bank were merged into the Inaho Bank Group, Igashi Bank and Mitsukoshi Bank formed the Mitsukoshi Igashi Bank Group, and Mitsuwa Bank, Marunouchi Bank, and Toyo Bank into the Tokyo Marunouchi Mitsuwa Bank Group. Of the seven banks, Marunouchi Bank was the only bank that wasn't 'extinct' in a merger.

Naoto still vividly remembered Yoshida, who had a job offer from Daiichi Bank, saying this after their last seminar, "Let's all get together again in five years. I'm looking forward to seeing how successful everyone gets."

Yet, they never did get together again. Yoshida retired from Daiichi Bank early at the age of 45.

In addition, Mita, who went to Igashi Bank, couldn't handle the strict quotas and quit to return to Nagasaki, and later opened a tax accounting office. When Naoto returned to Nagasaki for the holiday, he happened to bump into him while visiting a grave, and Mita was surprised by how successful Igashi Bank had become. Naoto didn't mention to his old classmate that he had gotten a job offer from Igashi Bank that he had declined for Marunouchi Bank instead. A decision he was glad he made.

Speaking of Igashi Bank, Naoto had once visited their Tokyo headquarters in Otemachi when he was in charge of budget management for Marunouchi Bank and wanted to learn from the best.

The first thing he noticed was the speed of the elevator–he arrived at the Financial Planning Department on the 12th floor in no time. Naoto asked the person in charge, "Mr. Okada, how is your elevator so fast?"

Okada laughed and replied, "Mr. Yamamoto, the elevators aren't particularly fast, but if you look at the ceilings on each floor, you'll notice that they're a little low. This cuts down on time in the elevator, plus voices can reach farther down the hall. Two birds with one stone."

Naoto had to admire the thorough rationalism of Igashi Bank. Yet, he had another concern in the elevator. He continued to ask Okada this question. "Why does the 'close' button have 'out of order' put on top? I saw that in the other one too. Is it the same for all of them?"

"Yes, I put it on all the elevators, to save on electricity bills. Each press of the 'close' button costs 10 yen. Besides, isn't it dangerous to close the door in such a rush?"

Naoto marveled again at their cost efficiency. However, the greatest thing about Igashi Bank wasn't just that. The domestic loans in the securities report for the 2011 fiscal year for small and medium-sized enterprises were about the same amount as Mitsukoshi Igashi Bank and Tokyo Marunouchi Mitsuwa Bank–about 36 trillion yen. In terms of interest rates, Mitsukoshi Igashi Bank was 1.24 percent and Tokyo Marunouchi Mitsuwa Bank was 0.92 percent. As a result, the difference in annual interest income on loans would be more than 100 billion yen. Mitsukoshi Igashi Bank's interest rate was comparable to those of Shin-Yokohama Bank and Shin-Shizuoka Bank, the top banks in the region.

When Naoto started his career at Marunouchi Bank, it seemed like they would never catch up to Igashi Bank in terms of rankings. However, Igashi Bank took a huge hit from the bursting of the bubble economy. During that period, all banks, except Tokyo Marunouchi Bank, changed their stock evaluations from the 'low price method' (the lower of the market value and the book value, so a depreciation burden is incurred if the market value falls) to the 'cost method' (valuation by the book value without a depreciation burden). Stock prices continued to plummet after that, and the unrealized loss of Igashi Bank exceeded 3 trillion yen. Yet, the highly profitable Igashi Bank successfully eliminated this with an upside-down merger (a merger in which a small company swallows a large company). Everyone considered it 'accounting magic'.

Fifteen years later, Mitsukoshi Igashi Bank was listed on the New York Stock Exchange. The chief inspector of the SEC asked, "Why does the Igashi name remain even though Igashi Bank was the absorbed bank in the merger?"

Igarashi Bank had disappeared once, changing the new bank's bank code, which indicates the order of a bank's establishment, from 0003 to 0009, which was the last bank code amongst the city banks. To keep the higher, older bank code, the newly merged bank kept the Igashi Bank name instead.

In the end, almost all of his college classmates had left the banking industry early on in their careers. In that respect, Naoto was fortunate. The name 'Marunouchi' was able to survive through multiple mergers. He often wondered why some banks survived and others didn't. The only real difference would be the management. There were two types of managers–those who listened to the opinions of their subordinates and the ones who ignored them. History would prove which type of management was right

# Chapter 8  The Bank Tax in Tokyo

On February 7, 2000, the Governor Iwahara of Tokyo announced at a regularly-scheduled press conference that he would introduce a bank tax to major financial institutions in Tokyo for a limited period of five years. This would ideally collect taxes from banks that were forced to settle in the red due to the disposal of non-performing loans at that time.

Akihito Kishimoto of Tokyo Marunouchi Bank, the acting chairman of the Kanto Banking Association, had visited the Tokyo Metropolitan Government Office to meet with Governor Iwahara three days before this press conference. It snowed the entire day, so Naoto accompanied Kishimoto.

The interview started at 10 o'clock, right on schedule, and Governor Iwahara severely criticized the bank in the usual way. "The banks continue to settle in the red due to the disposal of non-performing loans, and haven't paid their corporate business taxes for five years. Yet the 'net business profits' (bank's own profit index close to the operating profit of general corporations) were the highest they've been. Chairman Kishimoto, isn't that wrong? After all, the taxation method is wrong. Therefore, we've decided to tax the 'net business profit'. It'll be announced the day after tomorrow."

Kishimoto was surprised and argued, "Governor, the banking industry is having a difficult enough time dealing with bad debts. How could you add on to this? Let alone, applying this tax only to major banks goes against the 'principle of fairness'."

Governor Iwahara wouldn't listen. "Then when will banks start paying taxes? The whole city is in trouble due to financial difficulties, and the banking industry has already had so many bailouts. How is that fair?"

Naoto listened to both sides and thought, 'This isn't a problem that can be solved through discussions, but maybe it could be in court.'

Governor Iwahara's new policy was nothing more than a strategy to improve his popularity, with no regard to how it would work in the real world.

How could Naoto persuade the governor without offending him?

"Your concern is justified, but there are a few misunderstandings concerning the bank's 'net business profit' index. The 'net business profit' actually doesn't include the 'credit cost', which is the main business risk for banks. It's not included because we don't know when a bad debt will occur. That's why banks evaluate the performance of each branch using the performance management index called 'net operating profit', which is the operating profit minus this bad debt cost.

Originally, the bad debt cost would gradually be incurred over time, and would be reduced from this 'net business profit' every fiscal year. Therefore, the 'bad debt costs' associated with the deterioration of credit risk included in the non-operating profit are managed separately. As you said, I also think it's a good idea for the banks to bear some kind of tax burden even if they are in the red. However, an 'external standard taxation' method might be the most suitable, where a wide and shallow net is applied according to the scale of capital and such."

He continued, "Therefore, I'd like to propose to the Governor of Tokyo, that instead of imposing a tax unique to the bank's 'net business profit', the government could impose a percentage of the 'external standard tax'. That method of distribution as a local tax would be better understood by the citizens of Tokyo."

Governor Iwahara occasionally took notes and nodded while listening to Naoto's story, unusual for him. At the end of his speech, the governor of Tokyo applauded Naoto and said he'd take it into consideration.

Ten years ago when the banking industry was really booming, this idea might have been successful with the support of the citizens of Tokyo. Yet not many citizens of Tokyo agreed with the introduction of this 'bank tax', which would give the final guidance to the dying banking industry due to the disposal of non-performing loans.

In the end, the Kanto Bankers Association decided to dispute this issue in a legal setting. The Tokyo District Court ruled that it was illegal for the Tokyo Metropolitan Government to independently introduce external taxation into corporate enterprise tax for major financial institutions. The Tokyo Metropolitan Government appealed this, but the Tokyo High Court rejected their complaint at the appeal hearing, and returned the 'bank tax' of more than 162.8 billion yen that had already been paid by the bank.

The tax rate of the refund surcharge was 4.5 percent at that time, and the total annual amount reached 7.3 billion yen. Governor Iwahara was unable to lower his raised fist. It was an extremely large amount of money paid from the taxes of the citizens of Tokyo.

# Chapter 9  9/11

On the morning of September 11, 2001, terrorists of the radical group Al Qaeda hijacked a United Airlines passenger plane and plunged into the Twin Towers building on the 110th floor above the World Trade Center, at a height of 417 meters. With nearly 3,000 victims, it was the worst terrorist attack in history.

There were several New York branches of major Japanese banks in the Twin Towers. At that time, twelve employees of the Fuyo Bank New York branch, who had moved from the 79th floor to the 82nd floor, were killed in the terrorist attack. Two United Airlines passenger planes plunged directly into the 82nd floor.

Until three years prior, Marunouchi Bank had also had offices from the 84th to the 86th floor of the World Trade Center.

Naoto visited their New York branch in the Twin Towers of the World Trade Center the day after Marunouchi Bank was listed on the New York Stock Exchange on September 19, 1989. At that time, two of his coworkers had transferred to the New York branch. One was Toru Matsuda, who would later become the general manager of the Human Resources Department, and the other was Kenji Tajima, who would become the general manager of the International Planning Department. The two were elites from the Faculty of Law at the University of Tokyo, and were among the top of their class. They held a welcome party for Naoto that night and invited him to the Japanese restaurant 'Kyoto'.

Naoto asked them why they picked Japanese food. They claimed it was because Japanese food was considered high-class in New York at the time, too expensive for the local Japanese population and they didn't want to miss the chance.

The next morning, they said, 'Let's talk souvenirs,' and guided Naoto to the rooftop of the Twin Towers. The elevator was fast and they arrived at the roof in no time. When Naoto looked down from the rooftop, three large military helicopters were flying side by side, and far away he could see planes flying at the same height.

"The view from here is enough of a souvenir," he thought and asked his friends to take a picture of him with the city in the background. As Naoto gazed down from the Twin Towers, a cold chill ran up his spine–a strange and eerie feeling he had never experienced before.

The 9/11 terrorist attacks happened twelve years later. He had completely forgotten about that moment until he saw the news on TV.

Back in Japan, seven years later, on April 1, 1996,

Marunouchi Bank merged with Tokyo Nihonbashi Bank. Naoto was devoted to the integration work as the Deputy Manager of the Planning Department.

He was toiling away one day when he received a call from Matsuda, who had been promoted to deputy manager at the New York branch. "Yamamoto, it's been a while! At least seven years we listed on the New York Stock Exchange. I'm finally returning to Japan to the HR department next month. But I have one more problem before I leave. We're also integrating offices with Tokyo Nihonbashi over here, and no one can decide whether to move to Marunouchi Bank's offices at the World Trade Center, or to the Tokyo Nihonbashi offices that are right by Rockefeller Center in Midtown. Naturally, I prefer the Rockefeller Center since the rent is cheaper. But our employees are insisting that everyone should move to the Marunouchi offices, since we're the ones absorbing them. Give me some advice on how to convince them."

Naoto's answer poured out before he could think about it. "While Marunouchi Bank is the surviving bank, I also personally think it'd be better to integrate into the Rockefeller Center Building offices. I can't think of a particular reason at the moment, but that's what my gut is telling me. I didn't get a good vibe at the Twin Towers when I visited before."

"What do you mean by bad vibes?" Matsuda asked. "No one's going to be convinced by your little sixth sense."

"Let me think about it for a day, I'll call you back tomorrow." Naoto hung up and rubbed the bridge of his nose.

Naoto was tossing and turning until around four in the morning. He had an odd dream at that time–the same one he always had when he was young and had a fever. The one where his mother stood on the cliffs above the Suwa Shrine in Nagasaki while holding a baby.

But this time, his mother was alone. Looking closer, it wasn't his mother's face, but the face of his father's birth-mother, Tsuki, staring off to the east. It was the direction of the Pacific Ocean, to the Americas, and to New York.

Waking up in a cold sweat, Naoto suddenly had an idea on how to convince Matsuda's coworkers. Consolidating to the Rockefeller Center would save them from some US tax issues.

In the US tax affairs, a merger wasn't seen as a business combination, but rather an acquisition. Therefore, the branch that was integrated would be acquired at the current market price, and the US tax authorities would tax this as an 'unrealized gain', the difference between the market value and the book value. So, the smaller the market value of the offices acquired, the lower the taxes would be.

Naoto contacted Matsuda the next day and told him that it would be better for Marunouchi Bank to integrate to the Rockefeller Center Building because of this tax loss. As expected, nobody could argue with economic rationality and a difference of billions of yen.

Thus, in September 1998, the New York branch of Marunouchi Bank moved from the World Trade Center to Rockefeller Center, just three years before the 9/11 terrorist attacks.

In fact, Tadashi Nagashima, who was previously the matchmaker for Naoto and Yoko's wedding ceremony, was transferred to the New York branch in September 1999, narrowly avoiding disaster.

There are no 'if's in history, but if there hadn't been a merger between Marunouchi Bank and Tokyo Nihonbashi Bank, or if they had decided to integrate to the World Trade Center offices, many of their employees would have been victims. Anyone's actions could change the fate of so many people around them. Twenty years have passed since then, but the sadness of the bereaved families still lingers. Cowardly act of terrorism could never be tolerated.

# Chapter 10  The 2008 Financial Crisis

In September 2008, the Lehman Brothers, one of the three major investment banks in the United States, collapsed, causing a global economic turmoil–the so-called 'Lehman shock'. There were whispers on Wall Street that the next bankruptcy would be Morgan Stanley.

The reason for this was that the price of securitized products called 'subprime' had plummeted due to the sharp increase in mortgage arrears.

Most investment banks sold securitized products incorporating this subprime mortgage all over the world. Investment banks went bankrupt one after another from 2006 due to the combination of the collapse of house prices and stock prices. These investment banks were raising funds by selling off their assets, but eventually they ran out. This time, a crisis similar to the one in which Japanese banks went bankrupt due to the problem of bad debts caused by the bursting of the Japanese bubble occurred in the United States.

Morgan Stanley asked Tokyo Marunouchi Bank to undertake a capital increase, and others asked Mitsukoshi Igashi Bank for capital support as well. At the request of

Morgan Stanley, Tokyo Marunouchi Bank had entered into discussions to establish a joint venture in Japan. The plan was nicknamed 'Blue Red'–blue stood for Morgan Stanley and red for Tokyo Marunouchi Bank. The two companies met every Friday in Ebisu.

Naoto was in charge of finance and taxes at these meetings. In addition to this, Koichi Tazawa of the Planning Department, who later became the president, and Shigeru Tsukada, the General Manager of Marunouchi Securities, were involved as well. From the other side was Max, the director of finance and taxation, and Sebastian, the director of securities.

At the meeting, they discussed whether Marunouchi Bank could consider and agree on the joint venture establishment plan submitted by Morgan Stanley.

The idea was that Marunouchi would invest 300 billion yen in cash in the new company and provide Morgan Stanley with a Marunouchi Securities store in Japan as a joint store. Meanwhile, Morgan Stanley would dispatch 200 experienced personnel with investment banking know-how to the new company. As a result of calculating these business values, the investment ratio would be 51 percent on Morgan Stanley's side (which could be made a subsidiary) and 49% on the Marunouchi side.

The total investment amount from Marunouchi was estimated to be 392 billion yen, through providing cash and stores, while the total investment amount from Morgan Stanley was 408 billion yen calculated based on the comparison of peers of the same scale.

But Naoto just couldn't agree with this estimate, thinking, 'Our investment value is 300 billion yen in cash and half the market value of capital investment is 920 billion yen, for a total of 392 billion yen. On the other hand, the investment value on your side is 200 employees estimated at 408 billion yen, but something doesn't feel right.'

So Naoto asked Mr. Akagi how they calculated the worth of the employees.

Akagi replied with confidence, "At an investment bank of the same size in the United States with the same know-how as these 200 people earns about 25 billion yen a year on average. If you think about 20 years of work, they would earn 500 billion yen in total. If you convert this to the current value (discount calculation), it would be 408 billion yen."

Mr. Tsukada, General Manager of Marunouchi Securities, nodded along to this explanation, but Naoto was not convinced by any means. Certainly, there was a method of calculating business value as a 'comparative law of the same trade'.

Naoto thought back to the starting point, 'What was the purpose of this meeting in the first place?' Then, Naoto gradually caught on to the other party's trick.

In other words, Morgan Stanley was in need of funds to

pay the salaries and bonuses for future employees, all in cash. The cash aspect was something they should try to avoid.

However, they had to prove that these 200 people could really earn 480 billion yen in the future. In other words, they needed to use the 'comparative law of the same trade', a method based on the past average hours, under emergency situations, such as the stock price plunge. Their ultimate goal was to raise cash, make it a subsidiary by investing 51%, and get the dividend in cash. And the biggest purpose was to get the customer base of Marunouchi Securities, which would generate future cash.

Naoto asked Akagi again, "In the first place, the 'comparative law of the same trade' is premised on average factors, not on the abnormal situations of the investment bank's management crisis like now."

Akagi's face fell. "Of course, the numbers are based on the past normal averages, not these most recent abnormal times, but this situation won't continue on forever, right?"

Naoto did not let up. "Could you recalculate how much the business value will be based on the current abnormal situation?"

"I can by the next meeting, I'll calculate the business value of dispatched labor on the premise of an abnormal situation for reference."

Mr. Tsukada, who was listening to this exchange, looked

at Yamamoto with an expression that said, 'I'm worried you're leading Akagi around by the nose'.

Naoto postponed the final agreement, so that they could avoid any 'traps'. The initiative was reversed and the next meeting was postponed.

However, Morgan Stanley no longer had the time to set up a joint venture with Marunouchi. They were struggling to pay their monthly salaries and had no idea how to raise bonus funds.

At that point, Naoto was called by Chairman Kishimoto. "Is the 'Blue Red Project' going well?"

Naoto answered honestly, "Chairman, it's not going as of now. Perhaps they don't have the time to set up a new joint venture anymore. Funding for their next payroll and year-end bonuses seems to be their number one concern right now."

"That's a shame."

After this, Morgan Stanley finally fell into their reality of a shortage of funds at the end of the year. Meanwhile Marunouchi's top executives have begun to enthusiastically realize their long-held dream of having one of the three largest investment banks in the United States under their umbrella.

# Chapter 11  A 9 Billion Dollar Check

Even though the 'Blue Red Project' fell apart, the fire was still smoldering. Naoto had begun preparing to hand over the work he had been in charge of in the Planning Department for over 20 years to four deputy directors in preparation for his retirement.

However, Morgan Stanley's cash flow had become even tighter, and the 'Blue Red Project' was revived to give direct capital support.

In September 2008, the Morgan Stanley CEO requested that Nobuo Kuroyama, President of Marunouchi Tokyo Mitsuwa Financial Group, for a 9 billion dollar capital increase.

This amount was 21 percent of the total number of issued shares of Morgan Stanley, which was the amount that Marunouchi Tokyo Mitsuwa Financial Group could make as an affiliated company (more than 20 percent). At that time, the president of Tokyo Marunouchi Mitsuwa Bank was Katsunori Nagai. His predecessor, Shigeru Itsuki, had also served as the president of the holding company for four years.

The purpose of this was to transform the bank-led management system to a two-headed management system consisting of a bank and a holding company. Seven years had passed since the holding company was established, and it was finally time for the holding company to function as its original parent company.

Naoto had been a member of the establishment preparation committee back when the holding company was newly established in 2001, and he hoped that the holding company's original subsidiary management function could be established as soon as possible. Otherwise they could be suspected of conflicting interests in terms of consolidated governance. The deal of about 900 billion yen was the highest investment amount ever, but nevertheless, this investment decision was required in a very short period of only two weeks.

Furthermore, the reconstruction of Morgan Stanley involved the US Treasury, the Japanese government, and the Chinese government, creating a tense situation that was extremely influenced by political speculation. Morgan Stanley's stock price on September 2, 2008 was  41.30 dollars per share, and on the 29th when the basic investment agreement was signed, it was 29.99 dollars per share. It had plummeted to half the price, which indicated the danger of bankruptcy, and dipped below 10 dollars per share the next month.

"Yamamoto," President Nagai started, "I think you know the current situation– it's extremely urgent, but we can't do this deal unless it clears various conditions. It's likely that the investment stock would have to be amortized soon, and there's a big risk that this investment could fail. First of all, there's the issue of investment form. Investing in common stock is not a risk that can be taken as a management under the situation where the stock price of the other party is plummeting. Therefore, since the investment form depends on common stock, I think we have to make it a preferred stock instead of an investment. If it's an unlisted stock, the risk of amortization is extremely low. The second point is the question of who the investor is. Originally, it was Marunouchi Securities, since they could enjoy the most benefits from becoming an affiliated company, but Marunouchi Securities no longer has the liquid funds. It's also a difficult time for Tokyo Marunouchi Mitsuwa Bank to make an external investment. So, the last option would be to have the holding company become the investment entity–but it's tricky for the holding company to raise investment funds. They could borrow it, and then use the dividends collected from the subsidiary to pay it back. There's a risk that after investing, the other party's management would get even worse and public funds would be injected by the US government, diluting the voting rights of this investment stock. Should the 21 percent stake fall below 20 percent, it'll be impossible to become an affiliated company. I think it will be possible if we assume the approval of the Japanese and US governments. Yamamoto, can you think of any other possible risks?"

Naoto had been thinking about this since the very first

draft of the plan, so he was able to immediately answer the question. "One risk is compliance with international capital ratio regulations–for investments in overseas financial institutions, the same amount (about 900 billion yen) as the investment amount must be deducted from the capital adequacy when calculating the international capital adequacy ratio. The investment amount will also be tripled and added to the risk assets, so it'll hit us twice. The risk of falling below 8 percent of the international capital adequacy ratio is the most important risk factor for management. In the unlikely event that it does, we'll receive a business improvement order from the Financial Services Agency. To that end, I think it's necessary to prepare for a domestic capital increase at an early stage (after that, a public offering of 900 billion yen was announced in Japan).

Naoto looked up to make sure the president was still following. "If the investment entity was the holding company, there'd be problems under Article 52-23 of the Banking Act. It's stipulated that 'a bank holding company must not have a foreign company that operates a banking or a securities business as a subsidiary.' This investment involves both the Japanese and US governments, so it's a good idea to check everything with the Minister of Finance of Japan and the United States. Also, as a tax concern, the investment yield is apparently 10 percent, but dividends from US companies are subject to foreign tax withholding, so it would actually be just 8 percent. This can be recovered by the foreign tax credit system (a system that allows tax collected in foreign countries to be deducted from taxes paid in Japan), but since there's almost no profit or domestic tax payment, the holding company alone couldn't take advantage of this. But by reviving the consolidated tax payment that was once canceled to take over the loss of Mitsuwa Bank, they can recover using the profits of the subsidiaries of the entire group. But nothing is possible unless we can borrow the money necessary in this economy."

President Nagai closed his eyes while listening and sat very still. When Naoto finished, he opened his eyes and said, "That's a lot for me to think over, thank you."


On September 29, 2008, a basic investment contract between the two companies was signed. After that, the stock price continued to fall, and on October 10th, it fell below ten dollars a share. But with the approval of the US-Japan financial supervisory authorities, the price bounced back to 18.10 on October 13. On the payment date of the investment, the bank was closed for Columbus Day in the United States, so the bank transfer was not possible. Instead, Marunouchi went to Morgan Stanley's law office with an 100 dollar million check and handed it to the Vice President directly.

In this way, the 'long two weeks' for both companies was officially over. Since this investment, the Marunouchi

Tokyo Mitsuwa Financial Group had completely changed the management style of the financial industry. They made repeated investment in subsidiaries, such as the US TOB subsidiary and a consumer finance subsidiary. The top management of the financial industry challenged themselves more and more to grow their investment strategies.

# Chapter 12  Eight Presidents

In November 2009, when Naoto returned from Nagasaki to Kawasaki with Yoko and started home care, Akihito Kishimoto died at the age of 89. Naoto has served for more than 15 years while Kishimoto was active at the bank, either as managing director, vice president, president, or chairman of the board.

Later in February 2011, former president Tsuneo Wakata passed away at the age of 94. The grim news continued in May of that same year, with Katsunori Nagai's sudden death at the age of 74.

Only two years after Naoto started Yoko's home care, three presidents he had served under died in quick succession–he prayed for all of them.

Hajime Yamanaka, the first president Naoto served at Marunouchi Bank, died in 2004, and Kazuo Yabuki, the following president, died in 2009. Ichiro Takayama, the first president of the newly merged Tokyo Marunouchi Bank, also died in the same year.

Therefore, of the eight presidents Naoto served in the Planning Department, only two were still alive, Shigeru Itsuki and Nobuo Kuroyama. Naoto looked back on his memories of the eight presidents he served.

## <No. 1, Hajime Yamanaka>

He never got to talk to President Yamanaka, the president when Naoto first transferred to the Planning Department, but he walked around with the dignified air of an international banker.

## <No. 2, Kazuo Yabuki>

Under President Yabuki, Naoto was in charge of shorthand notes at board meetings, such as the policy review meeting sponsored by the Planning Department, so he often had to ask him to repeat things many times. He was a fairly heavy smoker and often smoked during meetings.

Once during the meeting, Naoto went to clean out the man's full ashtray. At that time, he jokingly said to Naoto, "Thank you, I accidentally smoked another box. Mr. Yamamoto, now you can get out of note-taking duty."

Naoto felt a sense of intimacy with the president and his good sense of humor. One time after Yabuki had long retired, Naoto bumped into him in the corridor leading to the parking lot on the third basement floor.

"Yamamoto,  you're getting a little chubby. You have to go on a diet."

Naoto was surprised that Chairman Yabuki had remembered his name and face after all that time. However, it was not Naoto, but Chairman Yabuki who really had to go on a diet–he also hadn't recognized the man. Most of the managers had big appetites, otherwise they wouldn't have the energy for so much work.

### <No. 3, Tsuneo Wakata>

Naoto was often consulted by the next president, Wakata. He had a deep knowledge of tax affairs, and most of the questions were about high-level tax affairs. He was particularly impressed by a question he received from the man a few days ago at the board meeting held on September 25, 1990, when the signs of the Japanese economic bubble bursting were beginning to appear.

During this period, non-performing loans began to increase gradually at each bank. Meanwhile, the secretary of President Wakata called Naoto, "The president is calling, are you available?"

The chairman was the only one who could say, "I'm a little busy at the moment," to the president.

So, he hurried right up to the president's office on the eighth floor.

The president started talking as soon as he got to his desk. "We're a listed company on the New York Stock Exchange, so when we make financial statements, we use US GAAP to certify non-performing loans. This certification standard is different in Japan and the United States. Which one can be said to be more representative?"

Naoto was surprised by the cutting question. Of course, the president knew such a detailed specialty. Even though the president was busy, he often studied US GAAP.

"There's no big difference between Japan and the United States' way of thinking about the recognition of non-performing loans. In both cases, loans with delinquent payments on the principal and interest are non-performing loans. However, Japan views non-performing loans as loans that are overdue for a year or more that haven't had the principal and interest paid after the second year. So in the year before it becomes a delinquent loan, the interest is taxed as a normal loan." Naoto walked to the other side of the desk. "But in the United States, if a loan payment is  overdue even once, it's immediately considered a non-performing loan. So when the economy is good, there's no difference between Japan and the United States. But when the economy deteriorates, the US will have a higher number of non-performing loans since the US GAAP recognizes them earlier. I think their system is more realistic."

The president continued to fire off questions. "Why do we use tax standards to identify non-performing loans in Japan? Why would the tax authorities want to delay the recognition of non-performing loans as long as possible?"

Naoto was once again surprised by the president's

intuition regarding tax affairs. "You're right. When trying to set a new rule, there are almost always a hundred opinions. The tax law is based on fairness for all citizens, so most people were alright with that as the basis. Didn't the managers at that time think that it was preferable?"

Upon hearing that, the president said to Naoto, "As a manager, is that kind of situation really ideal? I wonder if those managers really wanted to know the actual risk of their company. In other words, when the economy turns sour, the number of non-performing loans in the US will seem to increase at a quicker pace than in Japan. However, the reality is that Japan will be in the same amount of trouble."

"That's right, we need to report bad information accurately to management as soon as possible."

Naoto looked at the monthly delinquency status report from the branch office (a report required for tax filing), and worried that the non-performing loans seemed to have been gradually increasing. The signs of the bursting Japanese economic bubble had already appeared. The US GAAP non-performing loans had already surged more than twice as fast as Japan.

When the president heard this information, he immediately gave instructions to Naoto. "Mr. Yamamoto, this could be a big problem. Hold a policy review meeting on 'the future management policy of lending' right away for all of the relevant officers."

This meeting was held on September 25, 1990 to sound off a warning to management and to discuss whether they should continue to push forward with new lending or put a brake on it.

The attendees of the policy review meeting were President Wakata, Vice President Takahashi, Managing Directors Kishimoto, Seriyama, Goshima, Itsuki, Okamoto, and Wada, the General Manager of Business Planning Department, the General Manager of Branch Office, the General Manager of Planning Department, and the General Manager of Loan Department. Naoto was in charge of making the materials and taking the minutes.

First, the general manager of the Business Planning Department and the general manager of Branch Offices explained the lending trends of other banks in detail and the lending demand trends for each of their branches.

President Wakata listened to all the officers before speaking his own thoughts at the end, as usual. Wakata was often referred to as the "balance-adjustable president" by his employees.

Naoto initially thought that the president did not have any firm opinions of his own, but when he observed his reactions, he realized Wakata was afraid that his own opinion would affect everyone else's if he spoke first. He was a sincere gentleman that always started the meetings by saying, "Everyone, please give me your frank opinions."

The first person to speak was Managing Director Goto. "The demand for lending at the branch offices is still strong. We believe it's our duty to our business partners to meet this demand."

The manager of the business planning department also made a statement in line with that. "As for the trends of other banks, there are some areas where we are struggling due to the offensive of Kansai banks, but we are fighting almost evenly with Tokyo banks. I don't think it's a good idea."

Most officers insisted that lending should be increased in order to recover from the inferiority of other banks.

However, there was only one officer who disagreed with this. It was Managing Director Kishimoto, the director in charge of planning. "The Japanese economy has been showing signs of yen depreciation and stock depreciation in recent years, as it has been steadily rising. In addition, the authorities have regulated the total amount of loans to real estate agents. And the price of real estate is gradually declining. According to the report from the Planning Department, monthly delinquent loans are gradually increasing. It is not time to put a brake on the promotion of lending."

Most banks were in charge of managing overdue loans, but only Marunouchi Bank compiled and managed the lending delinquency reports from the branches. This was because the

Planning Department was organizing non-performing loans based on US standards.

In addition, most banks had an independent accounting department in charge of settlement of accounts, but Marunouchi Bank does not have an independent department called the accounting department, and it is under the direct control of management as a group (main accounting group) in the planning department. Therefore, it was able to flexibly sound a warning to management. Because of these differences between the two banks, the Marunouchi Bank was able to grasp the actual situation of non-performing loans earlier than other banks, so it warned the management. It was no exaggeration to say that this was the result of listing on the New York Stock Exchange.

Managing Director Wada, who was in charge of the sales floor in the Kansai area, snapped at Kishimoto "We can't just put the brakes on the other banks. Especially in the Kansai area, our inferiority continues."

Furthermore, the loan manager defended Managing Director Wada. "For now, even if we say that delinquency is increasing, it is still within the range of cruising speed. There is no clear sign that it is increasing. I think that the depreciation of the yen and stock prices are also temporary."

At the meeting, most of the officers commented, "Given the severe situation of inferiority to other banks, it is too early to put a brake on the promotion of lending."

After seeing the exhaustion of opinions, Mr. Wakata asked Mr. Komori, the director of the planning department, as he had planned. "Mr. Komori, what is the status of recent US GAAP delinquent lending?"

Komori reported the US GAAP recent overdue lending figures he had received from Naoto before the meeting began. "I would like to say that US GAAP delinquent loans have more than doubled to about 730 billion yen, an increase of about 400 billion yen in the five months from the end of the previous fiscal year to about 333 billion yen to the end of last month. Is increasing, and the situation is extremely terrible."

Upon hearing that, Managing Director Wada immediately argued, "The US GAAP delinquent loan figures are not always real. Under US GAAP, once the principal and interest payments stop, they quickly become delinquent loans. This is too extreme. It's a standard, and I don't think it fits the reality of Japanese lending practices."

Therefore, Wakata asked the loan manager about the status of overdue loans based on Japanese standards.

"Japanese standard delinquent loans were 270 billion yen at the end of the previous fiscal year and 280 billion yen at the end of August last month," the loan manager answered, "so the increase was only a slight increase of 100 billion yen in five months, and it was almost flat. It is changing."

Wakata nodded to the numbers he expected. From here, Wakata began to take the initiative in this conference. Wakata finally started talking about his thoughts here. "I think that US GAAP non-performing loans during the recession are mirrors of what will happen in Japan. In the meantime, Japanese-standard non-performing loans will not double, but will triple or quadruple. There is no doubt that it will be done. Managing Director Kishimoto expressed concern that it was time to put the brakes on, but I personally agree with him. However, it is certain that there is a reason for Mr. Wada's opinion that 'US GAAP is a little too strict from the viewpoint of lending practice'. I think it's a little premature to put a brake on lending right now. However, it is impossible to make a management decision to continue to step on the accelerator for lending promotion. Therefore, I would like to propose to you. How about taking your foot off the accelerator you are currently stepping on and applying the engine brake?"

The officers of the lending promotion group nodded to this proposal that emphasized Wakata's balance and became silent.

Actually, Mr. Wakata's remarks at this meeting triggered the subsequent policy to curb new lending by Marunouchi Bank. At this time, a stepping stone was laid to dispose of non-performing loans ahead of other banks. The fact that this management decision was correct shows that it is different from other banks in the total amount of loss disposal of non-performing loans thereafter.

The total amount of non-performing loans lost in the 'lost decade' of the securities report from 1992 to 2001 was about 8.7 trillion yen at Tokyo Marunouchi Bank. Inaho Bank is about 16 trillion yen, Mitsukoshi Girder Bank is about 12 trillion 200 billion yen, and Mitsuwa Bank is about 9.800 trillion yen. It can be seen how quickly the leading Tokyo Marunouchi Bank started to deal with the loss of non-performing loans.

It is often said that Wakata's achievement was the merger with Tokyo Nihonbashi Bank, but in fact it was the first to start the disposal of non-performing loans that contributed to the subsequent performance of Tokyo Marunouchi Bank.

Moreover, the target is not limited to the bank itself, but also extends to subsidiaries and related non-banks (financial institutions other than banks that do not accept deposits), and is ahead of other banks in the disposal of non-performing loans held by the entire group.

According to the securities report, most major banks started full-scale disposal of non-performing loan losses at subsidiaries and related non-banks from the fiscal year 1995, but Marunouchi Bank started from the fiscal year 1993, two years earlier. However, at the time of the merger with Tokyo Nihonbashi Bank in 1996, these processes had already been completed.

**<No. 4, Ichiro Takayama>**

Marunouchi Bank and Tokyo Nihonbashi Bank merged on April 1, 1996 to form Tokyo Marunouchi Bank. Ichiro Takayama of Tokyo Nihonbashi Bank was appointed as the first president. However, the Japanese government appointed economist Heizo Takeda as the Minister of State for Financial Services in an attempt to solve the long-standing problem of bad debts of Japanese banks at an early stage. It was decided to introduce an 'early corrective action system'.

This system was extremely strict, as the Ministry of Finance could issue business improvement orders and business suspension orders to banks according to the degree of capital adequacy using the international capital adequacy ratio agreed in each country. The Ministry of Finance has established a 'Financial Inspection Manual' to determine the soundness of the assets of banks, which are the denominator, when calculating the international capital adequacy ratio, and strict financial inspections were conducted based on this. All banks needed to establish a system for self-assessment of assets by the end of March 1998.

As an aside, if this 'early corrective action system' had been introduced a year earlier, it was possible that the birth of the Tokyo Marunouchi Bank was postponed or did not come true. This system had such a great impact on bank management, and some banks were forced into bankruptcy.

Under these circumstances, at the Tokyo Marunouchi Bank, which was the first to establish this asset assessment system, the board of directors was confused as to whether or not to apply this system ahead of schedule in the September 1997 interim settlement of accounts. That should be because it was expected that if this was applied, it would result in a huge deficit of over 1 trillion yen.

Most officers insisted that it should be applied from next year's final settlement, as stipulated in the Ministry of Finance's notification. Perhaps most banks were expected to apply from the final settlement.

Shinto Takayama summoned Naoto before the board meeting. "Mr. Yamamoto, if the new bank's new asset assessment rules are applied, it will result in a deficit of over 1 trillion yen. Should I apply this from the final settlement of the next year according to the notification of the Ministry of Finance? I'm wondering if it should be applied. What do you think of this?"

"I think other banks will probably apply from next year's final financial results, but I personally think that it is better to apply it earlier, because in the economic downturn, the disposal of non-performing loans will be delayed," Naoto answered honestly. "However, I think that we should grasp the actual situation as soon as half a year and take the next measures as soon as possible. I don't think you'll agree with the huge deficit settlement that could be watering."

President Takayama nodded. "You're right. I think the bad debt problem is just the beginning. Therefore, the next step should be taken early, but to do so, there is only one big problem: what the Ministry of Finance thinks, so I want you to check it."

"Understood, I'll check it as soon as possible."

Naoto made an appointment with Mr. Osaki and searched for the intention of the Ministry of Finance.

"Deputy Director Yamamoto, Tokyo Marunouchi Bank is completely different from other banks. I received an inquiry from an officer of a major bank earlier. This is the third bank. Do you know what kind of inquiry it is?"

"Isn't it the same inquiry as ours?"

Osaki ridiculed and replied, "It's the opposite question to your bank. They asked, 'This notification will be applied from the final settlement of accounts at the end of March next year. It doesn't matter if you don't apply it from this interim settlement of accounts, isn't it?'"

"So how did the section chief answer?"

"I replied, 'As notified, it will be applied from next year's final settlement, so there is no need to apply it from this interim settlement.' They agreed, so finally I told them, 'However, if you have a system that can be applied in this interim settlement, you may apply it from the interim settlement. That's what it means to be early in the early corrective action system'."

Thus, only the Tokyo Marunouchi Bank applied this system from the interim settlement of accounts, and although it was less than 1 trillion yen, it still resulted in a huge deficit of 941.3 billion yen. The Tokyo Marunouchi Bank became the world's number one bank in terms of total assets due to the merger, but in this interim settlement, it fell into the world's number one deficit settlement bank.

Normally, it was common sense to carry out deficit settlement in the final settlement, and it was said that it was 'forbidden' to carry out in the interim settlement. This is because if a large deficit settlement is carried out in the interim settlement of accounts, the settlement of accounts will be in the red for the second consecutive term, the interim settlement of accounts and the final settlement of accounts.

By the way, the reason for the huge deficit was stated in the 1997 half-year report (half-year version of the securities report) of the Tokyo Marunouchi Bank. "This is mainly because we completed the establishment of internal controls such as the self-assessment system for assets in the current interim period and recorded an allowance for doubtful accounts in response to early corrective measures."

## <No. 5, Akira Kishimoto>

Kishimoto was Wakata's right-hand man. Of the eight presidents, Naoto served the longest in Kishimoto. He was said to be the 'prince' of Marunouchi Bank from early on. Yet, due to the merger with the Tokyo Nihonbashi Bank, the president was delayed by two years from the schedule, and the term of office of the president was transferred to the next Itsuki in the previous four to two years.

However, it is not well known that the last two years have triggered the subsequent push of the Tokyo Marunouchi Bank to the top bank, probably because of his short tenure. It was a turbulent two years.

Among them, Naoto was most impressed by the event in March 2000, when Kishimoto was the chairman of the Kanto Bankers Association.

As an aside, the chairman of the Kanto Bankers Association that year was Mitsuwa Bank. Since the Kansai-affiliated Igashi Bank merged with Mitsukoshi Bank, which will be the next chairman's bank, Kansai-affiliated banks will also join this chairman's bank's rotation system.

However, Mitsuwa Bank, which became the chairman of the Kanto Bankers Association for the first time, took responsibility for avoiding financial inspections and dropped out of the chairman's bank, so the next Tokyo Marunouchi Bank took over the chairman's bank two months earlier.

Therefore, Kishimoto would be in charge of the chairman of the Kanto Bankers Association for one year and two months instead of one year.

At this time, the problem of non-performing loans was all over, and the Japanese banking industry was criticized by the domestic media and overseas financial supervisors for the criteria for recognizing non-performing loans, and the entire Japanese bank was pushed to the point of sinking. Japanese banks were forced to drastically review the criteria for certifying non-performing loans in order to restore trust.

The Japanese banks were no longer allowed to continue to recognize non-performing loans based on tax law standards, and were in an imminent situation.

Naoto was called by President Kishimoto and asked about the options for how the Kanto Bankers Association should deal with this difficult situation. "Mr. Yamamoto, if you come this far, I don't think there will be anything you can do without reviewing the criteria for certifying non-performing loans, but halfway reviews are no longer allowed during this period. I think a bold review is essential, so I want to hear your thoughts."

Naoto was thinking that such a situation would come sooner or later and that he would suit a new standard for certifying non-performing loans. He proposed to Kishimoto, "Chairman, there is only one option that everyone at home and abroad can convince. It is to change the recognition of non-performing loans from Japanese tax standards to US standards. However, if this is adopted, it will be able to withstand the loan amortization burden. Not a few banks will be sacrificed, and we must be prepared for it."

"After all, is it a change to US GAAP as I expected? The only option is to go through this difficult situation. I think there will be some sacrifice, but if you keep doing it, the Japanese banks may be wiped out."

As the chairman's bank, Kishimoto changed the non-performing loans that had been certified by tax law standards to the US standards, which were said to be the strictest in the world at that time. Kishimoto, who was strongly opposed by regional banks and other major banks nationwide, while being forced to make a bold review by the Financial Services Agency, was not frightened by the dissenting opinions and did not take a step here with a strong determination and conviction.

However, Kishimoto had only one big concern. It was that the US GAAP non-performing loans were not always correctly recognized in Japan, including the media. The media was too specialized to explain to the readers, so I didn't dare to pick up the chestnuts in the fire.

One day, Naoto was called by Kishimoto and asked how to deal with this problem. "Mr. Yamamoto, the Japanese media has announced that even restructured loans that are not included in non-performing loans (delinquent loans) under the US GAAP are included in non-performing loans. Then, Japan's bad debts are steadily expanding, which may lead to further misunderstandings from financial supervisors in other countries. Therefore, in order to resolve such misunderstandings, it is necessary to clearly distinguish between non-performing loans and non-performing loans and explain them in an easy-to-understand manner. To that end, a new name is needed to collectively refer to these entire claims. Is there any good naming?"

Naoto immediately got a name mixed with English and proposed it to Kishimoto. "Chairman, there is no generic name for these in the United States, but if you mix English, it can be perceived by readers as if it really exists in the US GAAP. So, how about using this as a 'risk management claim'?"

Kishimoto was overjoyed and agreed with the naming. "It's a risk management loan. It's a pretty good name. English is also included, so let's go with this."

In this way, the naming that Naoto came up with was adopted, and after that, this term was adopted in the Banking Act created by the Financial Services Agency.

Before this, Naoto had proposed two new legal and accounting terms. One was the 'net operating profit' (corresponding to the operating profit of general companies), which was said to represent the ability of banks in 1984 when banks became able to handle the sale and purchase of government bonds. It was later renamed to 'net business profit' to include the gain and loss on sales of receivables.

As an aside, Naoto insisted that the cost of the main business such as loan amortization should be included in the "net business profit" at the time of this change, but there is a history that it was postponed due to the opposition of each bank. It is well known that this has been used as a good material for the introduction of bank tax (external standard taxation) by the later governor of Tokyo, Iwahara. At this time, Governor Iwahara appealed to the citizens of Tokyo.

"While the bank says that it is in the red due to the disposal of non-performing loans, it has the highest profit ever in the" net business profit "that represents the profit of its main business. However, it has not paid a single yen of tax.

The second was 'provision for loss on sale of receivables'. This was a provision for the subsequent secondary loss (loss due to the decline of mortgage real estate) for the non-performing loans with real estate mortgages sold to the Joint Claims Purchase Organization. This was another digression, but at this time Naoto requested the chief of Osaki Bank to make a new allowance for this secondary loss.

Therefore, 'risk management claims' was the third name that Naoto came up with. President Kishimoto was often referred to as 'the president who refused public funds' or 'the president who sold the head office for restructuring'. However, as the chairman of the Kanto Banking Association, Kishimoto carried out bold, elaborate and well-thought-out reforms to change the criteria for recognizing non-performing loans from tax law standards to US standards in order to avoid criticism from domestic and foreign banks. He was the president who made a big difference in solving the debt problem.


Naoto went to say hello to Kishimoto when he retired from the bank. At that time, Kishimoto came to the bank every day as a 'special adviser', so Naoto assumed that he could drop in on the man.

"Mr. Yamamoto, could you wait a moment while I check if he can see anyone?"

The odd wording concerned him–was the man sick?

He went to his office on the ninth floor at the appointed time, and Kishimoto came out in a wheelchair pushed by his wife. "Yamamoto-kun, it's been a long time. I heard all about your endeavors since I left. Is it time to retire already? Where are you going next?"

Kishimoto's cheerful voice dragged an honest answer from Naoto. "No, I haven't decided yet. I'm going to spend a little time thinking it over."

"If it's you, you could find a job anywhere. I can call in a favor to anyone in the Marunouchi Group."

"Thank you for your concern, but I think I need to recharge a bit and find a new purpose on my own."

"Yes. I don't know what to charge, but feel free to tell me if anything happens. I have this mild stroke and my left half is a little crippled, but I'm still as young as I am. I'm just fine."

"Well, I'm relieved to hear that. I'll report back when I've decided on something."

Yet, he never visited Kishimoto after that. Eight years later, Kishimoto died at the age of 89.


### \<No. 6, Shigeru Itsuki\>

It was Shigeru Itsuki, President Kishimoto's successor, who closed the chapter of the bank's crisis. Itsuki had become the most unlucky president of the eight. Not once during his four years in office did he see a financial statement in the black.

After the 'bad debt problem', he went from the frying pan into the fire with the 'stock price plunge' and the 'deferred tax asset problem'. The bad debt problem had changed its shape and became even more serious, the final touch of the Big Bang. The finished 'market value accounting' was highlighted as another problem, all while Itsuki was in charge of steering the management through this sea of issues.

President Itsuki was later asked at a press conference to announce the financial results about how to deal with this quadruple suffering, and said, "The Bank was listed on the

US Stock Exchange in 1989 and has been actively promoting global standardization. The introduction of market value accounting ahead of schedule was also decided for the purpose of management transparency. It took a lot of effort, but thanks to that, our management system has evolved."

President Itsuki was said to be the 'unlucky president', but in fact, he was familiar enough with accounting and tax affairs to boldly challenge various institutional reforms, and laid the groundwork for Tokyo Marunouchi Bank to rise to the top ranking. He was a truly meritorious person.

The major reforms he undertook were:

Low-value method of assets (comparing the year-end valuation of assets to the lower one by comparing the market value and the book value and amortizing the difference), market value accounting (accounting that was mainstream in the United States where everything is evaluated by market value), introduction of deferred tax assets ahead of schedule, Solving the deferred tax assets problem, Application of the first consolidated tax payments for financial institutions, advance application of impairment accounting for fixed assets, and even more. He completed all of these during his term.

As a result, he never experienced a surplus in his four years in office. However, in the era of both presidents Kuroyama and Nagai, who received the baton after this decision, a top bank that was neither pushed nor pushed was born.

Of these, Itsuki's management decision, which Naoto remembers most clearly, was 'low-price stock protection'.

Japan's stock price peaked in December 1899 when the Nikkei Stock Average exceeded 40,000 yen, and then continued to plummet, and in 2004, the last year of the four-year term of President Itsuki. At the end of March, it fell below 10,000 yen and reached the lowest price in history at 676 yen.

Under these circumstances, the Financial Services Agency has abolished the accounting standards (mandatory regulations required by banks) that were as strict as US GAAP, which had been required of all banks to maintain the financial soundness of banks. Changed to accounting standards that were applied to general companies.

Meanwhile, Naoto was called by the chief of the Osaki Bank of the Financial Services Agency. "Deputy Director Yamamoto, in fact, a big politician of the Liberal People's Party should take all possible measures to avoid the collapse of Japanese banks, loosening the standard of end-of-term stock valuation from the low price method to the cost method, and holding it. He is telling us to allow the market value of real estate in order to realize the unrealized gains of real estate. Personally, the change to the cost method in such a plunge in stock prices is strange, and the contradictory measures of market valuation of real estate, which is the opposite of that, are not ridiculed by Western financial supervisors. I'm worried about it. However, since our upper management is vulnerable to politicians, there is a high possibility that they will accept them. Deputy Director Yamamoto does not mind pretending to be like this, what do you think of the response to anything?"

"I agree with Mr. Osaki. If you do that, you will be accused by overseas financial supervisors that Japan's accounting methods are a mystery. However, a major Japanese audit company would not admit that."

"That's right. The audit corporation can't admit it. Now that Deputy Director Yamamoto, the banking industry's decency office, has the same idea as me, I'll stick to the sense of justice, albeit with a little effort."

However, the pressure of politicians was tremendous, and the FSA's settlement accounting standards were abolished the following month. Banks, like general companies, have adopted a system of selective application of the low price method and the cost method for the year-end valuation of stocks. Furthermore, the introduction of market value valuation of owned real estate has been approved as it will contribute to the capital enhancement of general companies.

Nevertheless, Osaki and Naoto had a faint expectation that the audit companies would take the last stand. However, when looking back at the results, banks all over the country had surged ahead and changed to the cost method to avoid any depreciation burden and also conducted market value evaluations of any real estate owned.

Nevertheless, only one bank in the whole country continued the low price method. That was the Tokyo Marunouchi Bank.

President Itsuki made the following statement at the board meeting that decided this. When he talked about difficult accounting and tax issues at board meetings, he always said to Naoto, who was sitting there, before he got into the main subject. "Mr. Yamamoto, if you make a mistake in what I'm going to talk about, feel free to say it's wrong."

By saying this, if Naoto didn't say it was incorrect, it was proved correct to everyone. He always had a good point.

"Now, I would like to suggest to you about the year-end valuation of stocks. The Financial Services Agency has so far required all banks on the settlement accounting standard to save banks that cannot tolerate the amortization burden of stocks in the wake of the recent stock price plunge. We have relaxed the criteria that we may change the low-value method to the cost method. We expect most banks to change to the cost method. However, we would like to continue to adhere to the strict low price method for the following three reasons. First, there is no good reason to change from the low price method to the cost method when the stock price plummets. Second, in Japan, the introduction of the market value method has already been decided two years later due to the accounting big bang. Third, as Tokyo Marunouchi Bank is a US-listed company, the market value method is required for stock valuation under the US GAAP, and there is no choice in the cost method. In other words, the same manager cannot explain to the audit corporation with a double-edged statement that there is a possibility of recovery under Japanese GAAP, while judging that there is no possibility of recovery of stock prices under the US GAAP."

The remarks made by Mr. Itsuki, including Managing Director Wada, did not give any room for refutation to the officers who insisted that the cost method should be changed in line with other banks.

Naoto witnessed the tremendous determination of President Itsuki, who looked to the future as a manager.

"The top management is what we want to be," he said.

As an aside, the chief of the Osaki Bank later told Naoto about the management decision of the Tokyo Marunouchi Bank at that time. "Thanks to the Japanese banks for continuing the low-price law. To overseas banking supervisors, 'Tokyo Marunouchi Bank continues to use a separate low-price method (a valuation method that does not restore the book value like the market value method even if the market value recovers), which is stricter than the market value method in the United States.' They would say they didn't understand the Japanese standard financial statements. But when I showed and explained the US GAAP financial statements from Tokyo Marunouchi Bank, they understood it right away. Thanks to you, I was saved."

Although President Itsuki carried out various reforms, the Tokyo Marunouchi Bank still has about 15,000 yen in 'consolidated surplus', which represents the true strength of the company in the published securities report. It can be seen that it was by far the best at 100 million yen, compared to Inaho Bank's about 460 billion yen, Mitsukoshi Igashi Bank's about 610 billion yen, and Mitsuwa Bank's about 760 billion yen. In other words, the Tokyo Marunouchi Bank had already maintained the financial position of the top banks even after achieving such severe reforms.

### \<No. 7, Nobuo Kuroyama\>

Nobuo Kuroyama followed Itsuki to work on the rescue merger of Mitsuwa Bank, making him the first president of Tokyo Marunouchi Mitsuwa Bank in 2006.

Kuroyama was a sportsman and was active in banks as a soccer player. Naoto remembers receiving a certificate of commendation for 20 years of service when Kuroyama was the director of the personnel department. He has a long experience in system fields, and in the merger with Tokyo Nihonbashi Bank, he was in charge of systems and directed system integration.

Naoto was asked a question by President Kuroyama at the time of the rescue merger of Mitsuwa Bank. It was a question about the acceptance of Mitsuwa Bank's assets in connection with the merger. "Mr. Yamamoto, Mitsuwa Bank has a loss of about 2 trillion yen due to repeated deficit settlement. According to Mitsuwa Bank's future profit plan, this loss of 2 trillion yen can be offset against profits in five years. It cannot be resolved, and most of it cannot be used and is truncated. However, it turned out that this deficit will be completely eliminated in five years because our profits will be added by this bailout merger. According to accounting standards, a tax saving effect of 800 billion yen, which is about 40% (tax rate) of 2 trillion yen, is expected, so this will be capitalized as a deferred tax asset and the same amount of profit will increase. In anticipation of this, bank analysts wrote a forecast article stating, 'Tokyo Marunouchi Mitsuwa Bank is expected to have an upward revision of its business performance,' and as a result, our stock price has skyrocketed. However, I'm worried that if the profit increases by 800 billion yen at a stretch, the employees will misunderstand that "this is the power of the new bank" and feel relaxed. Therefore, I would like to ask you if there is a way to avoid recording this profit of 800 billion yen in the income statement for the current period. I don't think this 800 billion yen profit is the true power of the new bank."

Naoto couldn't help but worry about the man's sincerity. Where was such a fair and gentleman-like top management? If you're a business owner, you shouldn't be unhappy about increased profits. Even so, the profit that will increase this time is an extraordinary profit of 800 billion yen. However, he should not record more profit than he can. His heart is afraid of the pride of the employees. After all, Kuroyama president is like a sports player, and he is a manager who is devoted to fair play.

"Okay, I understand," Naoto replied. "There's only one way. If you accept the tax effect of this deficit as an asset in the merger without going through the income statement, record it as profit in the income statement for the current period. You don't have to. However, this requires the consent of the audit corporation. This is because deferred tax assets are not a 'selection rule' that they may be capitalized if the tax effect is recognized, but a 'compulsory rule' that they must be capitalized. Therefore, the audit corporation should insist that it must be capitalized and the same amount of profit should be recorded in the income statement. The only way to counter this is to go back and insist that the loss was accepted due to the merger. Whether or not the audit corporation approves it."

Listening to this, Kuroyama gave an instruction to Naoto with a relieved face. "That's it. I will explain to the audit corporation. By the way, if the audit corporation approves it, how will we announce this externally? We anticipate an upward revision of business results. Will the analysts understand it?"

At this time, Naoto already had a public scenario in mind. So he explained to him how the analysts were convinced. "The tax effect of tax deficit (deferred tax assets) was originally taken over as the acceptance of assets at the time of the merger, but at the time of the merger, the profit plan of the new bank has not yet been formulated. However, it was not known how much this deficit could be used. However, when the new bank's profit plan was formulated this time, it was found that the entire deficit could be used, so the entire amount was taken over retroactively to the time of the merger. Therefore, it is an accounting process that increases the surplus on the balance sheet by the same amount as a merger acceptance process, rather than passing through the income statement for the current period."

The next day, Naoto had the BOJ press club gather with media companies and analysts to carefully explain the merger acceptance process using specific figures and charts. The media and analysts showed their understanding through the sincere and sincere response of the Tokyo Marunouchi Mitsuwa Bank. In addition, this didn't cause the stock price of Tokyo Marunouchi Mitsuwa Bank to fall.

### <No. 8, Katsunori Nagai>

The last person Naoto served while in the Planning Department was Katsunori Nagai.

Nagai was a shy person. Naoto first talked to him when he was the manager of the office next to theirs. President Yabuki and Nagai had been conversing in a conference room between the two offices, and Naoto had accidentally walked in on them.

"Do you need something, Mr. Yamamoto?" Yabuki had asked.

Naoto guided the chairman to the related business office next door. Nagai was there, and the chairman spoke to Nagai.

When Naoto was about to return to his seat, he overheard some surprising news from the president. "How are you preparing for the merger with the bank in Nihonbashi? Is it going well?"

Nagai also seemed to be surprised. Seeing Nagai's surprised expression, the chairman hurried back to the boardroom on the ninth floor, wondering if he had said something unpleasant. According to Nagai later on, Chairman Yabuki believed that Nagai was the chairman of the merger preparation committee with the Tokyo Nihonbashi Bank, which was being held underwater. Since the chairman revealed the story of the merger to Nagai, Nagai was secretly announced as the chairman of the merger preparation committee.

Nagai then acted secretly, but one day he seemed to have a change of heart and barged into the planning manager's office. Naoto was called in soon after, and Nagai locked the door to begin to explain. "Mr. Yamamoto, I'm going to talk about top secrets, so please don't say anything else. Actually, we are currently talking about a merger with Tokyo Nihonbashi

Bank under the hood. However, I received a phone call from a reporter from the Nihon Keizai Shimbun earlier and requested an interview to confirm whether the merger with Tokyo Nihonbashi Bank was true. I didn't say 'Don't make a joke', but when I searched for what kind of information the other party had, I found that it had fairly accurate information. The reporter said, 'If you can't be interviewed, I'll post the merger article in tomorrow's morning edition.' So, just in case, I had to prepare for what to do if it was released in the morning edition of tomorrow. I would like to ask Mr. Yamamoto to deal with the Bank of Japan and the Tokyo Stock Exchange. I managed to get the article before the morning edition of tomorrow was distributed, and if the story of the merger was posted, I would prepare for the extraordinary executive committee and respond to the Ministry of Finance."

Nagai rushed to the Nihonbashi printing shop of the Nihon Keizai Shimbun in the morning and got a freshly printed morning edition. The story of the merger was really scooped at the top of the page. This was reported to Chairman Yabuki, President Wakata, and Deputy President Kishimoto, and future measures were discussed.

Nagai moved to arrange an extraordinary executive meeting. Naoto told Nagai what to do when the TSE confirmed the authenticity of the merged article in the morning edition, and agreed.

Perhaps before the market opens, the TSE's listing control office should confirm that today's morning edition is true, and trading of shares in both banks will be suspended until the truth is known. If we didn't decide what to do in the morning, it was expected that the transaction would remain suspended and a great deal of confusion would occur.

Nagai set up an extraordinary executive committee and wrote down the text of how to announce the merger externally. "Marunouchi Bank and Tokyo Nihonbashi Bank have decided at today's extraordinary executive meeting of both banks to start considering a merger."

At 11 am when the extraordinary executive meetings of both banks were over, an external announcement was made in this text.

Naoto contacted the listing management office of the Tokyo Stock Exchange and informed the Executive Committee's decision. He also threw a press release to the Bank of Japan's press club. This was the end of the hectic 'long half day'.

For the first time, Naoto knew the speed of rotation of Nagai's head and his skillful work, and realized that Nagai was not just a person.

One year later, this merger was realized, but just before the merger conditions were decided, Nagai rushed into the general manager's office of the planning department again. "Mr.

Director, the US SEC (Securities and Exchange Commission) has just contacted me to show the grounds for the merger ratio of 1:0.8 with Tokyo Nihonbashi Bank. How should I answer?"

At that time, the merger ratio was decided by agreement between top management, and there was no ratio that was calculated clearly numerically. Of course, there was no fairness opinion (a written opinion by a third party investigating and announcing the validity of the merger ratio) as it is today. The figures reported to the management were calculated using four factors: stock price transition, average profit for the last five years, unrealized gain and net assets of their latest stock, and profit projections for the next three years. With all of these, the merger ratio came out around 1 to 0.6.

Nagai also called Naoto to the manager's office at this time. When Naoto heard the story so far from Nagai, he quickly calculated something and talked to the director and Nagai.

"President Nagai, it's 1 to 0.6 when calculated with the basic indicators, but it is good to make it to 1 to 8 by the agreement between the management of equal merger, but that will cause complaints from the shareholders of Marunouchi Bank. It is difficult to explain to the US Securities and Exchange Commission and the Ministry of Finance. Therefore, it is a proposal, but couldn't it be possible to add to the merger conditions that the shareholders of Marunouchi Bank will be provided with a five-minute free of charge? Then, it will be as close to one to eight as possible."

Nagai was in a science class when he was in high school, and he was good at mathematics. He would then take into account the shareholder ratio (the number of shareholders at Marunouchi Bank is one to three times that of Tokyo Nihonbashi Bank), and as Naoto said, when the merger ratio approaches 1: 0.8, he said. I was able to calculate quickly in my head.

Nagai told the planning manager. "Let's implement a five-minute free capital increase to the shareholders of Marunouchi Bank, the manager. Then, the merger ratio will be as close as possible to 1: 0.8, and external explanations will be possible. Would you like to go with this?"

Thus, this proposal was reported to the top management meeting the next day. The merger ratio of the two banks was settled at 1: 0.8 just before the conclusion of the merger agreement.

Nagai has a good reputation for writing skills, and he often revisits the documents written by his subordinates. Nagai's clich? at that time was, "This memo has not reached the level of the planning department. Try again!"

Nagai was transferred to Marunouchi Trust Bank as a managing director in 1999. This seems to have been caused by his refusal to transfer abroad. He had experience in rebuilding the subsidiary New Japan Trust Bank, and was also a leading person who knew all about the trust business. Everyone thought that Nagai would never return to Marunouchi Bank, but he was involved in the business integration with Marunouchi Trust Bank in 2001 and returned to Marunouchi Bank as a director and loan manager. It may have been decided at this point that Nagai would replace his predecessor, Kuroyama.

One day, Naoto was called by the FSA chief Osaki on the phone. "Deputy Director Yamamoto. I have something to talk about, so please come right away."

Naoto hurried to the Financial Services Agency.

"Deputy Director Yamamoto, you are also the deputy director of the holding company and the bank. The holding company's main business is to manage the business of its subsidiaries. Thank you for your help so far. I'll tell you one good thing. We have been conducting financial inspections of trust banks since last week, but most trust banks have been in the red for the last three years. It is also in the red for tax purposes, and there is no taxable income (profit that becomes the taxable standard for tax purposes) and it is in a state of deficit (accounting loss). Deputy Director Yamamoto, under these circumstances, the provisions of Audit Committee Report No. 66 do not allow deferred tax assets to be recorded for five years. The upper limit is one year at most. Audits by audit corporations have also become stricter these days, and most trust banks are only allowed one year's worth, which may result in the withdrawal of four years' worth of deferred tax assets. Then, wouldn't there be a trust bank that would be insolvent (debt exceeds assets)? I wonder if the Marunouchi Trust Bank is okay."

Naoto immediately told Nagai–he had never seen the man so surprised. In a hurry for the third time since the scoop of the merger with Tokyo Nihonbashi Bank and the question of the merger ratio from SEC.

"Yamamoto, that's going to be a big deal. If you're insolvent, the management will be totally retired and become the management bank of the Financial Services Agency. The holding company that manages the subsidiaries will not be free. In the first place, if the management integration with the Marunouchi Trust Bank was unsuccessful, even its management responsibility could be questioned. This is a story that will affect the entire group if not managed. Yamamoto, are there any good measures?"

Naoto fully talked to Nagai about the idea he had been thinking about for a long time. "There is a way to introduce consolidated tax payments that were lifted this year. If consolidated tax payments are applied, the standard for recording deferred tax assets will also be considered on a consolidated basis, and only one year's worth of deferred tax assets can be recorded for four years. Marunouchi Trust and Banking, which will have to withdraw its shares, will be able to use the five-year deferred tax standard approved by Tokyo Marunouchi Bank, which will allow Marunouchi Trust and Banking to avoid excess debt."

In this way, Marunouchi Trust Bank escaped the insolvency crisis. Nagai often said, "The people in the Planning Department should know as much about accounting as the Accounting Department." The heart of this was that if you do not have more specialized knowledge and information than the other party, you cannot win a discussion against them. To put it the other way around, it also means that 'accountants should study more planning work'.


Marunouchi Bank had since become known as the top bank due to these eight presidents' actions. During this time, Marunouchi Bank was never the extinct bank in a merger, and the name 'Marunouchi' was kept in the name until the very end.

Naoto often asked himself, "Why do some banks fail and others prosper?" And every time, the answer came down to a difference in management.

The winning banks had managers who listened to their subordinate's opinions, while the failed 'one-man' managers continued to trust only their own opinions.

Marunouchi Bank's many successes proved that its unwritten rule, that each president only serve four years, was the most efficient at creating positive change.

# Epilogue  The Challenges of the Top Bank

Naoto has recently often seen weekly magazines and magazines that featured funny articles about the top affairs of his bank. He's often stunned in the article, and often unbelievable if this is true. However, it was like the saying, 'if there's smoke, there's a fire'.

At least, he had never read such an article about the presidents of the past eight people who Naoto served in the planning department.

Naoto thought of the president after Nagai. After Nagai, there were three people: Nobuyuki Hirata, Kei Koyama, and Kanetsu Miyake. Then, in April 2021, Atsushi Tazawa was appointed as the president without 13 people.

Naoto investigated the 'state of officers' in the securities report, wondering if the unwritten rule of four years, which was stubbornly followed by successive presidents, was inherited properly after that.

President Hirata was appointed president of the bank in April 2012 and chairman in April 2016. Therefore, the term as president was four years, the same as the previous presidents. However, he retired as chairman in April 2021, making his term as chairman five years. In addition, he became president of the holding company in April 2013 and chairman in April 2009.

Therefore, the term of office of the president of the holding company was six years, and the term of office of the chairman was two years.

The next president, Koyama, was rumored to be the prince of the Marunouchi Bank, like his predecessor Kishimoto, and was fully appointed as president in April 2016. But due to health reasons, he had to retire in May 2017, his term of office the shortest in the bank's recent history.

The third president, Miyake, was in sync with Koyama, but was appointed president in June 2017 and chairman in April 2012. Miyake's term of office is also four years. In addition, the president of the holding company was appointed in April 2009, and the chairman was appointed in April 2012, so the term of office of the president is two years.

By the way, President Nagai, who was the last to serve Naoto, was appointed president in April 2008 and chairman in April 2012. The term of office is also four years. He took office as the president of the holding company in April 2010, and retired in April 2013, so the term of office of the president is three years. He has not been appointed chairman of the holding company.

In short, it can be seen that the unwritten rule of the president's term of four years has been properly followed.

However, the chairman of the bank is Nagai for four years, Hirata for five years, and Miyake for the third year.

Examining the term of office of the chairman in the past, it can be seen that the term of office of the chairman has recently increased since Kishimoto, Itsuki, and Kuroyama are all two years.

The chairman was positioned to assist the new president for two years, but the term of office of the three most recent presidents completely overlaps with the term of office of the new president, and the role of the chairman is from the 'assistant role' of the new president to 'jointly'. It seems that the position has changed to 'manager'. Naoto suddenly wondered, "Why is the term of office of the chairman longer without being followed even though the term of office of the president is four years? Are completely overlapped. In other words, Nagai has jointly managed Hirata, the new president, rather than assisting him for four years."

Naoto shared a liquor table with Nagai and remembered the story he was telling. The story must have been his true intention, as he was a drinker, not a young man with no alcohol tolerance. "Yamamoto, my role is to connect until the birth of 'Oyama President of a Bank'."

From this, it seems that Nagai wanted to maintain the right to nominate the next president of Hirata for the purpose of continuing to cast the chairman for four years. In short, it seems that he wanted Koyama to be the president while his eyes were black.

As a result, Nagai will continue to be the top management for eight years (four years of president and four years of chairman), and Koyama will be appointed as the next president of Hirata, as Nagai expected.

Koyama is from the University of Tokyo, and was said to be the Prince of Marunouchi Bank from early on because of his speed of rotation, low demeanor that does not make enemies, and excellent writing ability, and everyone around him believed it and did not doubt it.

Naoto remembers hearing from Managing Director Seriyama many times when Koyama entered the Marunouchi Bank. "Depending on where Yamamoto-kun and Koyama-kun are assigned, the research manager and the planning manager at that time fought a fierce battle. In the end, the battle between the two was first in the research department and then in the planning department. It was settled by putting it on."

However, it seems that the director of the investigation department was surprised at his extraordinary ability and did not let go of him even though the transfer deadline had come. In addition, the planning manager got angry. "You are thinking only about the Research Department, not the entire Bank. He is not the treasure of the Research Department, but the treasure of the entire bank. So please move to the Planning

Department as soon as possible." It seems that the director of the investigation department reluctantly transferred him to the planning department.

However, fate is ironic, and it so happened that the long-awaited President Koyama would drop out a year and a month later for health reasons.

From here, it seems that the gears of the top personnel of Tokyo Marunouchi Mitsuwa Bank have begun to go crazy. In a hurry, Miyake, who was recalled from a securities subsidiary as a substitute, was appointed as the president. Hirata followed the Nagai method and continued the joint management system with Miyake for four years.

As a result, it is true that Hirata's term of office as chairman was the longest, five years, including one year as an assistant to Koyama. In fact, Hirata is said to have effectively nominated President Tazawa, the next president of Miyake.

In this way, Hirata's term of office as the top management (4 years as the president and 5 years as the chairman) extended to 9 years.

After all, the chairman assisted the new president for two years, and after that, the conventional method of leaving it to the new president may have been the original method of training the younger generation of top management, which Marunouchi Bank was aiming for.

Further complicating top management personnel is the

system in which the president of a subsidiary bank has also served as the president of the parent holding company since the establishment of the financial holding company in 2001.

By the way, the term of office of the president of the holding company is three years for Nagai, six years for Hirata, and two years for Miyake, and the term of office of the chairman is zero for Nagai, two years for Hirata, and one year for Miyake.


Kishimoto called him in April 2001, when he had retired as president and became a special management advisor instead.

Naoto asked him, "What do you think of your tenure as a top management, which was as short as two years for the president, two years for the chairman, and four years in total?"

Kishimoto answered immediately, "I don't think the two years as president were short. As you know, those two years were as rich as four years for me, and they were terrible two years. So I have nothing to regret. Due to the merger with Tokyo Nihonbashi Bank, the rails I am in charge of may have become a little shorter, but thanks to everyone's support, I was able to lay a solid and sturdy rail. Rather, I think I was able to concentrate and throw as much as I could because my tenure was short. If the term of office is extended, it will be humanity that I still want to do this for myself. In that case, as a result, we will close the path of the younger generation who have been working hard toward the next. That's why the unwritten rule that the term of office of the president is two terms and four years has been passed down to Marunouchi Bank for generations. I think that management must keep this unwritten rule in the future."

Naoto was keenly aware at this time that Kishimoto's way of thinking was the original DNA of the Marunouchi Bank, and this was the royal road for the management of the Marunouchi Bank.

Naoto got to his feet. "What do you think about the future division of roles between the newly established holding company and the bank? The holding company is technically the parent company, but I feel like it's really just a subsidiary of the bank. I shouldn't do that. Unfortunately, I don't feel that it's far from the 'original consolidated management' that the adviser should aim for when the holding company was newly established."

Kishimoto said to Naoto with a bitter smile. "What you want to say is that the lack of understanding of the consolidated management of the executives when the consolidated tax payment was introduced recently is far from the original consolidated management."

It was a story that originated from information from the Chief of the Financial Services Agency, Osaki Bank. "Deferred tax assets of Marunouchi Trust Bank under Otaku will not be allowed to be recorded for five years from this settlement of accounts," he said, which triggered the introduction of consolidated tax payment.

Naoto immediately reported this information to Managing Director Nagai, who was in charge of planning at the time, and suggested that consolidated tax payment should be introduced as a countermeasure. Nagai, who has a quick mind, immediately gave a go-ahead, and Naoto hurriedly convened a board meeting.

As an aside, this actually became a bottleneck, and when Mitsuwa Bank merged for relief, it was forced into a situation where it could not take over the company's 2 trillion yen deficit. Indeed, the "things that I think I've done later" that Itsuki was concerned about have actually happened.

However, in the consolidated tax payment, the profit (taxable income for taxation) of the affiliated subsidiary is applied from the old deficit and the tax of the entire group is calculated, and the Marunouchi Trust Bank holds a lot of the old deficit. As a result, the profits of the Tokyo Marunouchi Bank became as if they were taken to the Marunouchi Trust Bank in calculating taxes.

The officers of Tokyo Marunouchi Bank all said, "It's strange," and began to pursue the responsibility for introducing consolidated tax payment.

At the forefront of this sentiment was Managing Director Wada, who thoroughly criticized Naoto. "Yamamoto, you said at the board meeting that decided to introduce a consolidated tax system, that the introduction would not affect the interests of the Bank at all. However, in this settlement of accounts, it is one of the interests of the Bank. The department has been taken to the Marunouchi Trust Bank. What does this mean? Explain!"

Naoto looked at the officers. "As I explained at the recent board meeting, the consolidated tax payment system would add up the profits of the entire group and calculate the tax amount of each subsidiary. Therefore, profits from the profits of the subsidiaries and the difference in tax position. It is quite possible that the amount of tax and tax will fluctuate a little.

However, tax savings can be achieved for the entire group, and profits for the entire group will increase compared to when individual tax payment is selected. Isn't this the original consolidated management? If you say that there is a lot of profit or a little profit between the subsidiaries under the umbrella, there is no way that you can do the original consolidated management."

President Itsuki also piped in, "Marunouchi Trust Bank alone has poor profitability, and deferred tax assets cannot be capitalized for five years, but if consolidated tax payment is introduced, profits will be considered on a consolidated basis, so it will be the same as before. You can now capitalize for five years and avoid insolvency. As a result, even if our profits seem to decrease a little, the profits of the entire group are higher than those of individual tax payments. In this way, the holding company, which is the parent company, needs to always consider the overall optimization of the group. Isn't this the 'original consolidated management' we should be aiming for?"

The opponents of Managing Director Wada, who had criticized the consolidated tax payment, were silent in the remarks of President Itsuki.

Naoto believes that what is required of the top banks in the future is the original consolidated management centered on the holding company, which is the parent company.

Twenty years had passed since the Tokyo Marunouchi Bank established a holding company as a parent company in the Yurakucho Building in 2001. It was time to start consolidated management for the entire holding group.

In a system in which the holding company (the parent company) and the bank (aka the largest subsidiary) concurrently serve as officers, conflicts of interest can become a fatal obstacle, and there is no way that consolidated management can be carried out in which the fairness of the subsidiary is questioned.

The holding company in the future will invite third-party management professionals who have no stake in the subsidiary, formulate rules common to the group to evaluate the performance of the subsidiary, and then group according to the performance. We should aim for the original consolidated management (consolidated governance) by appropriately allocating the limited management resources of people, goods, and money as a whole from the viewpoint of overall optimization. That is an important issue that will be required of top banks in the future.

# Part 2
# Education Volume
## (The Education Foundation)

# Prologue  The Secretary-General Selection

The search for Naoto's successor was led by the Association and conducted through a dispatching company called 'Senior Partner'. More than 100 applications flooded in less than a week after the job ad was posted. Naoto was amazed at how much the Foundation's name recognition has risen compared to five years ago.

Senior Partner sent Naoto a list of the 32 people they had narrowed down to after reviewing their applications. It was an intimidating group–almost all of them were from prestigious universities, and had worked in government offices or famous companies. Naoto couldn't help thinking that if he applied now, he wouldn't even make it to the interview round.

At that time, a phone call came to the Foundation. Megumi Hosokawa, who is in charge of accounting, received the call and called out to Naoto, "Mr. Osaki of the Financial Services Agency is on the phone for you."

"What is it this time?" Naoto asked, suspicion thick in his tone.

A familiar voice responded, "Yamamoto, how are you? It's me, Osaki from the Financial Services Agency Certified

Accountant Audit and Review Board. I'm sorry. The Foundation is really expanding its business. There are finally 10 companies that have adopted international accounting standards. We have exceeded the number of companies. Thanks to you, the Financial Services Agency is also helping. Thank you very much."

"You didn't have to call me just for that. What's really the matter? I'm leaving the Foundation at the end of this month."

"What are you saying? I could sense in the air that you would be leaving soon. You've had a lot of trouble for five years, I don't understand why you're going to retire at this time."

"You know everything well. That's right. Thank you very much for your help. By the way, let's ask you what you really need today. It's not like you're coming to the inspection again."

Osaki had cut to the chase. "Secretary-General Yamamoto, in fact, two former subordinates of mine are applying for your successor. That's why today's phone call is to say hello to them. Is a great person to bring to the Foundation. I'll give you a taiko, so hire one."

"Unfortunately," Naoto explained, "I don't have the authority to pick my successor. It's the great man of the association who makes the final decision. I'm sorry. I can't help."

"It may be the association that will ultimately decide on

a successor secretary, but it's still your job to narrow down the applicants by document screening. I know you hate bureaucrats, but these two I really want people to pass the document screening. If I remain as the final candidate, I will do something about it. First of all, it is important whether or not I can be included in the final candidate."

Naoto answered Osaki honestly. "When asked by the chairman of the association about the conditions for the successor secretary-general, I answered, 'Not from government offices or large companies, but a person who is well-versed in small and medium-sized enterprises and who is well-versed in business is suitable'. So I think it'll probably be difficult for them."

"Maybe. Either way, please keep an eye out for them at the interviews!"

"I don't think it will meet your expectations."

Naoto checked the two's resumes, out of curiosity.

Takashi Ogiuchi (60 years old) Assistant Manager, Supervisory Bureau, Financial Services Agency.
Graduated from Faculty of Economics, University of Tokyo, Certified Accountant.
Hobbies include reading.

Goro Yada (60 years old) Assistant Manager, Research

Division, National Tax Agency

Graduated from Faculty of Law, Kyoto University, Tax Accountant

Hobbies include golf.


Naoto passed them through to the interview stage, simply to see what kind of people they were.

The first interviews started the next day, conducted by five people: the managing director of the association, the manager of the personnel department, the manager of the dispatching company, the section manager, and the secretary-general. It started with a schedule of five people in the morning and six people in the afternoon, and the interviews for all of them were completed in three days.

Naoto thought that it was almost impossible to judge whether the person was suitable for the secretary-general of the Foundation in an interview of about 30 minutes per person.

In particular, this interview is also a senior interview that decides the second and third workplaces, and almost all applicants are musicians of Kuchihaccho Tehaccho, and it is a difficult task to find out the aptitude in 30 minutes.

So, Naoto didn't ask any questions about his career or work history like other interviewers. No, Naoto asked the same questions he always asked the students in his evening lectures. "What would you do first if you became the Executive

Secretary of this Foundation?"

The first applicant answered this question as follows, "I would use my past experience to completely review the organizational management first."

The next applicant said, "I've had a lot of experience in internal control work at my previous job, so the first thing I'd do is verify that the Foundation's internal controls are working well. Then, I would re-establish the optimal internal control system for the Foundation."

And third, Takashi Ogiuchi, one of the applicants from the Financial Services Agency, answered, "I'd observe the work of the staff for a week. After that, I'd go over my thoughts, and if there was any room for improvement, I'd work on reforms with everyone's consent."

Ogiuchi's answer piqued his interest. Because, first of all, his story was exactly the same as Naoto thought when he first came to the Foundation. Next, the casual humility with the staff was exuding. Finally, it was because they had a sincere idea that 'after mutual consent'. Naoto was impressed that there was something that Osaki could be proud of.

The last interview of the day was Goro Yada from the National Tax Agency. He answered the same question, "I'd first think about what I could do with the work of this Foundation, and then ask each and every one of the staff in charge of that work what they are aware of. If we think we can solve it, we will work together with the staff to solve it."

He was envious that Osaki had such put together subordinates.

The 32 people's primary interview ended in 3 days as scheduled, and the 5 interviewers entered into a meeting to select 5 of them. The interviewers selected the top five, and gave them 10 points for the 1st place, 8 points for the 2nd place, 5 points for the 3rd place, 3 points for the 4th place, and 1 point for the 5th place, and scored the interview results of all the interviewers.

As a result, the following five candidates for the second interview were decided.

1st: Akira Konishi (59) General Manager of Marunouchi Commercial Law Department
Graduated from Faculty of Law, University of Tokyo, Lawyer

2nd: Takashi Ogiuchi (60) Assistant Manager, Supervisory Bureau and FSA
Graduated from Faculty of Economics, University of Tokyo, Certified Accountant

3rd: Goro Yada (60) Assistant Manager, Research

Division, National Tax Agency,

Graduated from Faculty of Law, Kyoto University, Tax Accountant

4th: Kenji Ishihara (58) Deputy Director of Aozora Shinkin Bank

Graduated from Waseda University Faculty of Law, Registered Management Consultant

5th: Shuji Morikawa (57) Deputy Director of Internal Audit of Ichigashi Chemical

Graduated from Faculty of Economics, Hosei University Internal Auditor

However, the managing director of the association suggested that another substitute should be selected in case one of these five people declines the second interview.

In that case, there was an opinion that it would be better to select from the remaining four people, but the managing director inevitably stuck to the selection of substitutes and let everyone approve of his proposal.

In response to that, another person from the Kanto Bankers Association called Yokoyari Taro recommended by the managing director was added. The number of points earned by Yokoyari was ten, and only the managing director was in first place, but no other interviewer recommended it. The horizontal spear was in the lower rank in the whole.

> Alternate: Taro Yokoyari (62) Deputy Director of the Japanese Bankers Association
> Graduated from Economics Department, Keio U., Registered Management Consultant

In this way, six people proceeded to the officer interview a week later. Naoto had taken his leave before the results came out, so the Foundation's chief Morita called him when the decision was made. "We decided on Mr. Taro Yokoyari as your successor."

At that time, Naoto wondered why Yokoyari had been selected as a substitute candidate, but he was no longer in a position to question their choice. However, Naoto remembered having a bad impression of the man at the first interview. He had answered Naoto's question, "I'm confident in any work of the Foundation, just as I'm confident that I can use my many years of experience to further develop this Foundation."

He was too confident in everything and likely wouldn't listen to others' opinions.

However, when Naoto later visited Osaki of the Financial Services Agency, he asked a strange question. "Yamamoto, thank you for your hard work for five years. After all, you were the secretary-general as I expected. It was Yamamoto-chan who rebuilt the Foundation in just five years and made it so good. It's a credit. By the way, Yamamoto-chan, the president of the association, do you know where he retired and re-employed next?"

"I have no clue."

"Don't you really know? It's a lie, didn't you know? Actually, his second workplace is Yamamoto-chan's old nest banking industry. It's also an officer of the Kanto Bankers Association. It's like a managing director."

Naoto was surprised to hear that, but he wasn't sure why Osaki suspected that Naoto knew this.

"Yamamoto, I was disappointed with you at the very end. You eliminated my subordinates to make the chairman of the association the managing director of the Kanto Bankers Association, and replaced him with someone from the Kanto Bankers Association, Yokoyari Taro. I didn't make a barter deal. I can't forgive that. Then, the selection of the secretary-general wasn't a race that pretended to be a public offering."

Naoto finally understood what Osaki meant, but it was a big misunderstanding on the other man's part. Naoto confided honestly to Osaki, "You can't tell anyone else, but I put your two subordinates as first and second in the first interview. Yet, the other day, Mr. Morita told me that Taro Yokoyari was selected, even though he had been an alternate."

Osaki's voice became incensed. "What, he was only an extra? That's even more strange. Who pushed him up on the list?"

"It was up to the executive director of the Association."

Osaki seemed convinced. "I see, so maybe the former chairman gave direct instructions to the managing director? Either way, I can't forgive these kinds of underhanded dealings. I feel sorry for my subordinates, I'll have to look into this further."

In this way, Osaki took an unexpected action in order to uncover the fraudulent public offering. He entered unannounced inspections of both the Foundation and the Society as a supervisory authority. So he investigated the Foundation's secretary-general's open recruitment process for fraud.

In other words, the purpose of this inspection was to verify the governance (internal control) of the organizational operations of the Foundation and the association. The selection of the secretary-general of the Foundation required the decision of the board of directors (corresponding to the board of directors of general companies) as an important matter for selecting employees, so the decision process was verified.

Osaki took the lead and called on the Foundation's chief Morita and the managing director of the association to submit all the documents related to the open recruitment procedure, and after grasping the evidence, asked the managing director,

"Senior Managing Director, you are the only one who rates Taro Yokoyari in the first place on a scale of ten, but none of the other four interviewers put him in the top five. Why did you put him as the first choice?"

"I valued Taro Yokoyari for his remarkable achievements as the Deputy Director of the Japanese Bankers Association. There were no personal feelings."

"That's right. Then why was Taro Yokoyari, who was evaluated lower in the first interview, selected as a substitute? You didn't set up a frame called a substitute to lift Taro Yokoyari."

"That's not the case. I consulted with the other four interviewers about the alternates and got everyone's consent, I didn't do it at just my own discretion."

Osaki pointed his last secret evidence to his managing director. "Then, why is the score of this document that describes the results of the primary interview distributed in the officer interview tampered with? Please answer clearly. In this document, the substitute Taro Yokoyari is the top score."

The managing director was in a hurry to pursue Osaki, and made an excuse in distress. "Mr. Osaki, that's just an excuse. I didn't tamper with the scores. It's a mistake in the secretariat's input. Don't blame me for your subordinates' fair loss."

The dispute between the two followed parallel lines, but Osaki concluded that the secretary-general's open recruitment procedure was not appropriate. He asked his managing director to consult the Foundation's board of directors and board of councilors (equivalent to a general meeting of shareholders of a general corporation) and report the details to the Financial Services Agency.

The managing director was pursued this responsibility by the board of directors and the board of councilors, and was demoted from managing director to director. The former chairman was punished with strict caution.

It was a few days later that Osaki called Naoto. "I recommended two of my subordinates for the future of the Foundation. However, the managing director and former president of the association ate the Foundation for their own benefit. There is no future for the Foundation if there are rotten officers. You have to do something urgently."

Five years had passed since then, but as Osaki predicted, the operations of the

Foundation had declined. Naoto regretted the whole process. Selecting the Secretary-General should have been more transparent, before he resigned. As Osaki said, "I can't forgive this kind of injustice," Naoto also thought that he had to put it somewhere before this drop.

In February 2021, the chairman of the Tokyo Organizing Committee of the Olympic and Paralympic Games resigned as the chairman, taking responsibility for the disdain for women. However, the chairman who resigned that day decided to replace him in a closed-door parley. It was unheard of for the chairman, who was forced to resign, to appoint his successor.

This is not allowed in the organizational management of a public interest incorporated Foundation. Eventually, in response to criticism from the public and the media, the nomination at this closed-door meeting was canceled the next day, and a selection committee was set up to decide on a candidate for succession.

However, the selection of candidates for this selection committee was also unclear, and it was difficult to say that it was appropriate as a process for selecting the chairman of a public interest incorporated Foundation.

Because, originally, the chairman of the public interest incorporated Foundation was stipulated to be decided by mutual election of directors, and in principle, someone from among the directors could run for mutual election to succeed. First, the directors should have held a board meeting to go through this process.

Therefore, if there was no candidacy from the director, a selection committee consisting of third parties should be held to openly solicit or recommend candidates.

In the end, the Olympic Minister, who was not a director, suddenly became a candidate, and after obtaining his consent, he was appointed as a director, which was an overwhelming process. It seems that the selection process was extremely politically powerful, but I had to wonder if this method was in the spirit of the Olympics and Paralympics.

Naoto saw this slapstick drama in the news and realized that it was necessary to formulate rules in advance for the process of selecting the next secretary-general of the Foundation. It is to formulate fair rules that some people cannot arbitrarily select, and to determine the transparent process. The point is to disclose information on the process of selecting open recruiters.

Disclosure is the only emergency stop button to prevent fraudulent officers. In addition, the disclosure needs accountability to explain why the Secretary-General decided.

Naoto contacted Osaki of the Financial Services Agency and tried to discuss this.

Osaki merely laughed and said, "I wanted you to make that rule before you had retired. It's too late now. The new secretary-general can rebuild the Foundation however they want. Maybe I'll apply next time."

"And I once again apologize for that."

# Chapter 1  Death of the Foundation Chief

Naoto had returned to Nagasaki with Yoko, and on December 10, 2017, while Yoko was hospitalized for medical treatment, Naoto got a call from Funada at the Foundation.

"Mr. Yamamoto, I'm sorry to say Chief Morita died yesterday due to cirrhosis of the liver. He was 63 years old. He had recently been hospitalized, but his condition changed suddenly last night. The funeral service will be held at Zojoji Temple at 11 in the morning tomorrow. I figured it would be difficult for you to attend because of your wife, but I wanted to let you know."

"Thank you, Mr. Funada. That's a shame, he was two years younger than me. Thank you for telling me, I'll send my condolences."

Although he had only been with Mr. Morita for five years, Naoto felt like he was a comrade who had fought with him for decades. Naoto had been born after WW2, but he wondered if losing comrades felt like this.

Actually, Naoto had received a phone call from Morita from the hospital last month. He hadn't expected any of this and ended up joking with him. He regretted not listening more carefully.

At that time, his only concern was that Mr. Morita had apologized too many times. "I'm sorry, the director. Actually, after that, the fellow staff members who were raised by the director said that he wanted to retire as a group. I was angry and detained as to why I was making such a joke. However, the new secretary-general did not stay at all when he heard the staff's offer to retire, and took the attitude that if he wanted to quit, he would do whatever he wanted."

"Mr. Morita, you're not bad. It's because I threw a job along the way. Had I been able to work with them a little more, this wouldn't have happened. I'm the one, so the chief doesn't blame me so much. Naoto continued, "What about your liver? Did you get a little better after being hospitalized? Of course, you're not drinking."

"Of course. However, I've been drinking a lot of alcohol for many years. I can't get rid of it by staying in the hospital for a month or two. I want to drink alcohol without it. Everyone was waiting for the director to come back."

"That's right. I'm sorry that I wasn't able to think about the Foundation because of my wife's long-term care, and I'm sorry that I was estranged from everyone. I'll be back in Otemachi. Please wait until then."

This was the last conversation he had with Mr. Morita.

He had a job at the association and experienced various

departments, and he was so familiar with the events of the past association and the problems of the current association that it was said to be the 'lifestyle of the association'. Naoto had been helped by him so much.

About two years after joining the Foundation, when Naoto was called by an officer of the association, Morita worried about something and said, "Shall I go with you?" There was a story from the officers that Morita was certainly worried about.

Mr. Yamashita said, "You have been asked by the Financial Services Agency to urge companies to introduce international accounting standards, but you haven't taken any concrete action yet. Are you all motivated?"

Naoto answered stunned, "I'm sorry. I'm currently in contact with key people from major companies and asking them to introduce international accounting standards individually for each company."

The managing director asked further questions, "So, as a result of your visit, have you come up with a concrete story for the introduction of international accounting standards?"

"We haven't talked about a concrete introduction yet."

"That kind of lenient thing could be embarrassing for the association at the FSA's interim report meeting next week. Please do something about it!"

At this time, Morita suddenly broke off, and the association rebelled against Managing Director Yamashita, who also reports to him.

"Speaking of the managing director, it was the All Japan Accountants Association, which represents the accounting audit industry, that was instructed by the Financial Services Agency regarding the introduction of international accounting standards. The Foundation was asked by the association to act as a flag singer. Isn't the association the ultimate responsible person?"

The managing director looked like he was hit by a painful part and asked Vice Chairman Omori for help. "Do you have any good ideas that you can justify to the Financial Services Agency that you are doing it properly?"

"It's a good idea that Secretary-General Yamamoto consults with major companies individually. It's Mr. Yamamoto, so it's not just about asking corporate officers. Probably after that. Are you listening to their needs from the practitioners of the company?"

Naoto waved his hand to Vice Chairman Omori and replied with a gesture that this was not the case.

"Director, why don't you talk about that?" Morita observed.

"What do you mean?" the managing director asked.

Naoto had been preparing the talk for a seminar on companies with international accounting standards under the surface from last month in the early morning hours. He told

Vice Chairman Omori, "Actually, I'm listening to the needs of the business people in charge of the company, but I'd like to compare the recent topics that the company is interested in with the accounting ideas of Japanese standards, US standards, and international standards. I'm also thinking about holding a seminar using the original English text."

This is the English original text of US GAAP when Naoto was in a bank and had a lot of discussions with the accountant in charge of accounting audit corporation Thomas about the idea of US GAAP.

Therefore, we could not win the discussion unless we read the original English text in advance. They often interpret the original English text for their own convenience, and it was essential to have a good understanding of the original English text in advance in order to seal it.

Vice Chairman Omori agreed with the idea. "Hey, that sounds interesting. I would love to participate. By the way, what is the theme of that?"

"The first theme is 'deferred tax assets', which has become a hot topic these days."

Chairman Yamane leaned forward. "That's the best. It's the most seasonal theme right now. And the comparison of the three accounting standards using the original text is also interesting for accountants. Mr. Yamamoto, that seminar is a good idea. Not only people but also certified accountants and practical assistants can be invited."

The story of Morita slipping brought unexpected results, and this meeting became bright like Morita's character at once. This was Morita's special skill to cheer up and brighten the surroundings.

The most memorable thing about the first work he did with him at the Foundation was that he faced the crisis of the Foundation's dissolution.

"I know some of the companies I've been acquainted with, so I'm going to recruit members from tomorrow."

He said that he took the initiative to solicit visits even though he had never done sales before. There weren't any results, but that vitality was certainly amazing.

It's been five years since then, but Naoto remembers it like yesterday. Even when Naoto resigned from the secretary-general, he took the initiative to hold a farewell party. Morita was a cheerful and friendly personality, and was the spirit of the Foundation that he could not hate even if something went wrong. He sincerely prays for his soul.

# Chapter 2  Mass Retirement of the Staff

Naoto retired from the Foundation on June 30, 2016. At the time, there were 15 Foundation staff and 3 more sent from the Association. There was also Takeshi Terada, who was a part-timer when he died on February 18, 2020.

Terada quit his part-time job right after Naoto retired from the Foundation and joined Tokyo Marunouchi Mitsuwa Bank instead. He had come to visit Yoko at the hospital in Nagasaki, and to introduce the Yamamotos to his new wife. That night, Naoto invited them to the famous Chinese restaurant 'Kouzanro'. Terada was a little tipsy and told him, "Mr. Yamamoto, in fact, a colleague I was with during the practical training period recently told me that the Foundation has not been operating well since Mr. Yamamoto retired. After all, the organization changes depending on the policy of the leader. The other day, I went to drink with Mr. Funada, and he seemed to be quite dissatisfied with the new secretary-general. The atmosphere of the Foundation seems to be much worse than when Mr. Yamamoto was there."

However, Naoto heard that Terada's story at that time was just a story of complaints and dissatisfaction within the organization that is common when the leader changes.

After that, a call came from Funada of the Foundation and it turned out that what Terada had been talking about was more serious than he expected. "Mr. Yamamoto, I'm thinking of leaving the Foundation. It no longer has a vision or dream for the future, nothing to aim for. I'm at my limit."

Yamamoto was surprised, "Hey, Funada, have you been talking to Terada? Cool your head a little and think it over again. When leadership changes hands, you only notice the bad points of the current leader, compared to the previous one. But any leader must have their good points, or else they wouldn't have made it that far."

Funada did not say, "I understand," until the end of Naoto's story.

Naoto regretted that Terada, who had come to visit Yoko at the roadside station hospital for the first time at this time, should have listened to him better when he talked to Naoto, but he devoted himself to helping Yoko in the hospital. Naoto, who is doing it, couldn't do anything about it.

Naoto took out the album he received from the staff when he retired from its cardboard box and opened it. There was a 'good luck flag' with comments from all of the staff:

· Secretary-General, we only worked together for a short time, but thank you very much for teaching me various things! I hope

I can use all of this valuable experience in my future. 'You can make your living anywhere in the world', right? I hope you do your best to care for your wife. –Takeshi Terada

· Secretary-General, thank you for your hard work. I'm glad I was able to work with you for a longtime. I will make full use of your teachings in my future work, I owe you a lot. –Yasuhiro Funada

· Mr. Yamamoto, two years went by in a flash, but thank you very much for all of the valuable experience. Your saying that 'the way you work depends on your boss' has stayed with me. Keeping this teaching in mind, I aim to be a person who can logically convey my thoughts to my coworkers. Thank you for your guidance. –Wataru Takiyama

· Mr. Yamamoto, I've been very grateful to you for a long time. Your attitude toward work and the importance of having life goals inspired me. Please take care of yourself and do your best. Please come to the Foundation from time to time. –Megumi Hosokawa

· Mr. Yamamoto, thank you for all your hard work. I can't imagine the director retiring and resting slowly. If I can come visit you, I'd like to have a meal with you. Please take care of yourself. – Ayaka Yamada

・Thank you very much for your kindness, Mr. Yamamoto. I feel that there are still many things I would like to know. I will do my best by making use of what I learned in our early morning study sessions every day. –Kayoko Matsuo

・Mr. Yamamoto, thank you very much. From now on, we will carefully protect what the secretary-general has built. I'm really thankful to you. –Mariko Fukuoka

・Mr. Yamamoto, two and a half years flew by, but I am very grateful to you. Thank you very much for your guidance during the study sessions and work every morning, even though I had no knowledge of accounting. Please continue to love yourself. –Kumiko Nakata

・Thank you for teaching me various things at the early morning study sessions every day. I was able to gain very valuable experience. I will continue to study every day. –Mari Nakano

・Mr. Yamamoto, I've been indebted to you for three years. Thank you for giving me the opportunity to work for the Foundation. Taking advantage of this experience, I would like to continue working toward a higher level. I'm really thankful to you. –Kyoko Motomura

・Thank you very much, Mr. Yamamoto. From the director, I learned the importance of working responsibly. I will do my best in my future work with this motto. Thank you very much. –Mitsuyasu Negishi

・Mr. Yamamoto, I am very grateful for your strict guidance for the three years since I joined the company. I will continue to devote myself to work every day without forgetting what I was taught. Thank you so much so far. –Kohei Yamashita

・Director, thank you very much for these past three years. We are very grateful to our newcomers for their guidance every morning through study sessions. I will do my best by making use of the teachings from the director in my future work. I'm really thankful to you. –Yamada Jiro

・Thank you very much, Mr. Yamamoto. We will build a magnificent skyscraper on the Foundation that the director has built. Banzai. –Yasuo Nagata

・Thank you very much from both the public and private sectors. Please continue to watch over the Foundation warmly.

Also, please come to the Foundation once in a while. I'll be waiting. –Atsushi Takeda

It seems that 10 of these 14 Foundation staff, excluding Terada, had retired as a group. Naoto tried to contact all ten of these people, and all of them had the same sentiment: "I just lost the motivation to work for the Foundation."

And what surprised Naoto was that the new secretary-general did not try to detain the staff who offered to retire at all. In the end, they seem to have decided to retire after concluding that they were not recognized or needed by management. Naoto had heard this same story from his seniors during his banking days: "Yamamoto, when a company goes bankrupt, executives change frequently, but it's still manageable. But when employees start to quit, it's over."

Therefore, Naoto thought that the veteran new secretary-general, who should be familiar with it, should not hold back the retirement of the staff, but in reality it seems that it was never the case.

Probably, there are two reasons why the secretary-general did not stay.

One was that the new secretary-general really hated the staff and wanted to replace them with new staff, and the other was that the new secretary-general easily thought that anyone could do the work of the staff.

Naoto listened to the story from ten people and found that it was the latter.

In other words, the new secretary-general thought, "It's a simple job that anyone can do, such as a Foundation job, so if you want to retire, please do it yourself. There are many alternatives. I will not stay."

Naoto asked the retired staff another question. "Did the new Secretary-General do the Foundation's work properly? No way, he was only managing your work, right?"

The answer returned from everyone is that the new secretary-general was the only job to manage everyone's work.

Many of these bosses are from large corporations who believe that managing the work of their subordinates is their job. In a large company, the organization is a pyramid type, and if the staff working at the bottom and the chief of the middle manager are solid, the section chief or department manager will turn around as an organization regardless of the person.

However, the Foundation is a micro-enterprise with 15 employees and 3 seconded employees. Naoto thought that in order to operate this Foundation, the secretary-general must first set an example.

In other words, what is the operation method of the organization? "If you have to show it, tell it, show it, and praise it, people will move." This was the saying of Isoroku Yamamoto, who was the Commander-in-Chief of the Allied

Fleet of the Imperial Japanese Navy during the Pacific War, to 'move his subordinates'.

Probably the reason why the organization of the Foundation is not operating well now is that the new secretary-general did not take this first action. However, it is also a fact that this cannot happen unless the person has practical experience.

When Naoto retired from the Foundation, he replied to the president of the association when asked about the qualities of his successor. "Chairman, the Foundation is a small organization, so I think it's better to have someone from a small business who has a great career and who has a great career, and who can take the lead."

The chairman argued against this. "Isn't that strange? You're from a great big company. I'm still thinking of asking someone who has experience with big companies."

"Chairman, I certainly came to the Foundation from Tokyo Marunouchi Mitsuwa Bank, which is now a big company, but that wasn't the case when I joined. My first store was the Fukuoka branch. At that time, even when I visited a company saying 'It's a Marunouchi bank on the outside', I was often asked "Where is such a bank?"

When he answered, "It's one of the four corners of the Tenjin intersection," he said. "The buildings at the four corners of the Tenjin intersection are the Fukuoka Bank Building, the

Iwataya Building, and the Mitsubishi Corporation Building. What is the other building?" When I said, 'The other is Tenjin Building', the other party said, 'Oh, that's Tenjin Building'. I told the other person, 'Yes, the Marunouchi Bank is on the first floor of the Tenjin Building'. Some people said that Marunouchi Bank was 'Oh, a company that makes electric fans'. In other words, Tokyo Marunouchi Mitsuwa Bank is now said to be the top bank, but at that time it was similar to the Industrial Bank of Korea. So I had no idea that I got a job at a big company. I've been thinking about becoming a top bank since then."

The chairman listened to this story and was convinced at that time, but Naoto forgot that the chairman was from a major audit company. After all, his successor has become a person from a large company.

# Epilogue  The Foundation's Mission

Naoto looked back on his five years at the Foundation. From the beginning, he always left home at five o'clock in the morning. It would still be pitch black at that time in the winter, but Yoko, who later hated the darkness, always got up with him and came to the front door to see him off. Time flew with this routine.

Even after the Foundation moved to Otemachi, the train that went to work was the first train departing from Miyazakidai Station at 5:30 in the morning. The Otemachi Financial Center Building, where the Foundation was located, was managed by the Marunouchi Estate.

The room was always pitch black, and turning on the lights was Naoto's first job in the morning.

After that, he prepared the materials for the early morning study session from 8 o'clock and waited for the staff to come to work. He always decided to have rice balls and egg sandwiches at the convenience store for breakfast.

Whenever Naoto had a problem with his work, he had a habit of reading Article 3 of the Foundation's Articles of Incorporation over and over again:

"Our corporation accurately grasps the needs for education and training of certified accountants, those who have passed the certified accountant examination, those who are engaged in accounting practices, and anyone interested in accounting and auditing, and seek to develop suitable teaching materials. The purpose is to improve the professional knowledge, professional skills and professional ethics of these persons regarding accounting and auditing, and to contribute to the development of human resources who can make accurate accounting and auditing decisions."

When Naoto read this article for the first time, he immediately realized in a lengthy sentence that 'this was created by the founders of the association', and felt something strange. Perhaps something strange was felt when read by someone with experience in a general company like Naoto.

Naoto thought that the order of the three parties at the beginning of this article was wrong. First, the 'certified accountant' comes, then the 'certified accountant exam passer', and finally the 'accounting practitioner', and the accounting practitioner of the company is the last. However, in the text that follows, 'a person who is widely interested in accounting and auditing' is mentioned first in accounting and then in auditing. He had to seem inconsistent.

Naoto thought that if he was the founder, he must have written this article briefly as follows:

By conducting education and training for those involved in accounting and auditing practices, we will enhance the specialized knowledge and skills of these persons and develop human resources who can make accurate accounting and auditing decisions. Naoto was always asking himself whether the Foundation was really working for this purpose. When he was absolutely unconvinced, he had confirmed it in the light of Article 3 of the Articles of Incorporation. While Naoto was repeating such things, he began to wonder if the Foundation was making a big mistake. In short, he realized that the purpose of establishing the lofty Foundation, which the founders set out, was far from what they were actually doing. The Foundation has three businesses: a practical training business for those who have passed the certified accountant examination, a continuous specialized training business for maintaining the qualification of a certified accountant, and an accounting practitioner training business for corporate accountants. Who is responsible for the people, goods, and money for these three businesses?

First of all, practical training is a junior development project conducted by the association, and it is natural that the association bears the entire burden. Continuous specialized training is also training to maintain the qualification of a certified accountant, and the association also takes full care of it. In order to secure such funds, the association collects membership fees from accountants and audit corporations.

However, only accounting practitioner training is built to be covered by the membership fee of corporate members. Companies join members and pay membership fees for the training.

Therefore, the reason why only accounting practitioner training is treated differently from the other two training businesses is that there was no investment on the part of the company at the time of establishment.

This would be the case for companies as well. In other words, companies are not in a position to take charge of education for practical assistants who are the trainees of certified accountants and training to maintain the qualifications of certified accountants. On the other hand, from the perspective of the association, the association is not in a position to educate corporate accountants.

Naoto wondered if this could be resolved somehow, and finally found a solution.

The idea was, 'By having a certified accountant, a practitioner, and a corporate accounting practitioner participate together in a seminar hosted by the Foundation, we will combine these three in the same training'. In other words, it is not the logic of the side that implements the training, but the 'trainee first' that puts the side receiving the training first.

By doing so, exchanges between these three parties should be possible, and the training should be extremely meaningful, and that is the method that is in line with the original purpose of establishment.

However, there was a big problem there. It was how to organize a training that all participants were interested in.

Naoto came up with a plan after thinking about it. It is 'a training in which oneself, who has experience in a company, plans this training, and the instructor of the training also serves as oneself'. Naoto, who had experience in the company, knew better than anyone else the needs common to all the participants.

Naoto used this method to gather about 30,000 training participants about 300 times in three years.

The contents of the training included:

- ❖ Corporate Accounting Practice
- ❖ Bank Accounting Practice
- ❖ International Accounting Standard Introduction Practice
- ❖ Tax Effect Accounting Practice
- ❖ Industry-Specific Accounting Practice
- ❖ Company and Audit Business Management, such as 'How to Deal with Corporations'
- ❖ Actual Conditions of Fraudulent Accounting
- ❖ The Significance of Listing on the US Stock Exchange

❖ Tax and Accounting: Tax strategy, Management and Taxes, Tax Barriers

❖ International Accounting Standards

The breakdown of the training participants was that the practitioners of the company, the practical trainees, and the certified accountants each participated in a well-balanced manner with about 10,000 people. For Naoto, this was considered the most realistic and effective method.

Originally, it seems that it was the intention of the founder to jointly manage the three businesses by jointly investing the future business operation funds between the company and the association at the time of establishment. In reality, that was never the case.

Furthermore, after Naoto retired, the Foundation's business seems to have centered on practical training and continuous specialized training.

Based on this reality, there is only one option left for the Foundation.

In short, the practical training business and the continuous specialized training business are essentially businesses that the Foundation undertakes from the association, and fall under the category of "contracting business" for tax purposes. Therefore, the accounting practitioner training business also undertakes accounting education and training on the company side, and receives membership fees from the company in return.

In other words, all three of the Foundation's businesses are positioned as "contractors" and their efficiencies are completed. Then, the management resources of the Foundation are appropriately allocated according to the result.

For that purpose, it is necessary to create a common performance management index that can judge efficiency. Three projects are evaluated based on the index. Therefore, it is not possible to make an appropriate evaluation if the councilor and directors on the evaluation side are 90% of the association and 10% of the company as they are now. First of all, the first decision is to make the same number of people involved in the association and those involved in the company 5 to 5.

Naoto persuaded the directors and councilors to make this happen before his retirement, but due to time constraints, he had to give up halfway through. Entrusting this to the next generation to take charge of the Foundation would be a "hundred times return" to the Foundation of Naoto who retired in the middle of the road.

Even if I make a mistake, I hope that the Foundation will not become a substantial subsidiary of the association and specialize in "practical training business" and "continuous specialized training business" and will not quit the training for accounting practitioners of companies.

In that case, the significance of the Foundation's existence would be completely lost, and the Foundation would become a mere branch office of the association, which was entrusted with the management of practical training and continuous specialized training by the association.

And another important thing that Naoto is thinking about is the exchange between the Foundation, the company, and the certified accountant.

The mission of a company's manager is how to manage the limited management resources of 'people, goods, and money' in an efficient and overall optimal manner, thereby maximizing the profits of the company.

On the other hand, the mission of a certified public accountant is as stated in Article 1 of the Certified Public Accountants Act.

"As a certified accountant, as an audit and accounting expert, by ensuring the reliability of financial documents and other financial information from an independent standpoint, fair business activities of companies, etc., protection of investors and creditors, etc. It is our mission to contribute to the sound development of the national economy."

At first glance, the missions of the two seem to be different, but the mission of the business owner is to maximize the profits of the company through efficient and overall optimal management, and on the extension of that, the certified accountant's ultimate goal is 'national people'. 'Contributing to the sound development of the economy' should be in line with the vector.

However, in reality, the company side insists that 'the accountant does not understand the actual state of the company's business', and the accountant side refutes each other, saying that 'the company does not understand the accounting standards correctly'.

Naoto thinks that it is necessary to unravel the good old days of the past in order to improve the situation where it is difficult to think that the relationship of trust between the two is always going in the right direction. That is, it is "warm old wisdom new".

In April 1976, when Naoto joined the Marunouchi Bank, accounting audits of companies by certified accountants were still limited to only a few large companies. The opportunity for this to become the current accounting audit system was the revision of the Commercial Code Audit Exceptions Act (Act on Special Exceptions to the Commercial Code Concerning Audits, etc. of Joint-stock Companies) in 1981.

With this amendment, the scope of mandatory accounting audits has expanded to companies with total liabilities of 200 billion yen or more, and the importance of accounting audits has increased at once.

Marunouchi Bank outsourced this accounting audit to the

'Toho Accounting Office', which was opened in Yaesu by the bank's OB.

This was a small accounting firm with a total of about 20 people, but all of them were burning with a sense of mission as an accountant. Partly because of this, the Touhou Accounting Office was able to take charge of two companies representing the Marunouchi Bank and the Marunouchi Corporate Group called 'Secon'.

At that time, accounting firms did not have an "accounting audit manual" like they do now, and accountants and corporate accounting staff are discussing daily with each other to find out what accounting audits should be. It was an era.

However, an event that suddenly changed such a relationship occurred in 1989. It is a big event that Marunouchi Bank will be listed on the New York Stock Exchange.

This ended the peaceful and peaceful relationship between the company and the accountant. The emergence of a ridiculously strong enemy, the US Securities and Exchange Commission (SEC), forced the two parties to shift from a distant relationship to a cooperative relationship at once.

Because, in order to confront the strong enemy of the SEC, we could not afford the time to let each other's opinions fight freely. There were a lot of important issues that had to be decided from now on.

One day, Naoto was surprised to receive such a question

from the SEC. "It's time to stop holding stocks with business partners in Japan. Compared to the net assets (total assets minus total liabilities) that show the strength of banks, the risk of a large drop in stock prices is too great. Isn't it?"

Of course, Japan also had a 'Corporate Finance Division, Securities Bureau, Ministry of Finance' equivalent to the SEC, but the difference in ability between the two was clear.

In the accounting world at that time, US GAAP was at the forefront, and Japanese GAAP was regarded as a completely local standard, and even the Corporate Finance Division was studying US GAAP all the time.

Naoto had attended several meetings that were regarded as 'study sessions' for US GAAP, but he did not have time to study for the exam when he was listed on the New York Stock Exchange, and he suddenly took the US GAAP exam.

The biggest difficulty was how to deal with the 'consolidated financial statements' that have not been introduced yet, and the 'market value accounting' that was introduced as a response in Japan 20 years later.

The accountant and the accountant in charge went to work every week on holidays, had a lot of discussions from early morning to late night, solved the problems one by one, and completed the 'US GAAP Manual'. At this time, both offices worked together so that the work could be done efficiently. This has dramatically increased mutual trust.

However, since such a response was allowed at that time, it may be pointed out that 'internal control related to financial reporting' would be inappropriate if such a thing was done now.

The listing on the New York Stock Exchange significantly changed the way Marunouchi Bank managers thought about accounting. The previous response, 'Don't give out any extra materials to the accountant', had changed to 'discuss all the details with the accountant well in advance', and this idea became the basic policy for all subsequent Marunouchi Bank's audit companies.

After that, Touhou Accounting Office was taken over by Thomas Audit Company, which occupied one of the current four major audit corporations, in the process of selection of audit corporations.

Also, at that time, the team listed on the New York Stock Exchange had an excellent accountant from 'Mita Accounting Co., Ltd.', which was also under the umbrella of Thomas, as the team head.


Naoto, remembering this past history, continued to ponder how to best restore the relationship of trust between the company and the certified accountants, and whether the Foundation could contribute to it.

And at one point, when Naoto was talking to the participants at one of his seminar lectures, the answer suddenly came to the light. The theme of the seminar was 'How to Face Companies and Certified Accountants', and it hinted at the direction the Foundation should aim for in the future. In other words, the Foundation would act as a conduit between companies and certified accountants.

Specifically, by temporarily pooling the audit fees paid by the company to the accounting audit corporation in the Foundation, and then establishing a new system in which the Foundation estimates and pays the appropriate accounting audit fees according to the accounting audit results.

This function must be a neutral institution that keeps a certain distance from the company and the accounting auditor. Therefore, the Japan Business Federation and the National Accountant Association cannot deal with the risk of conflict of interest.

It is a perfect role for a neutral Foundation that is in charge of training projects for corporate accounting practitioners, certified accountants, and practical trainees. For that purpose, it is indispensable to put excellent human resources on the company side into the councilors, directors, and secretariat of the Foundation, which are mainly the officers of the association.

If joint investment and joint human resources can be invested in the Foundation, this Foundation will have various functions such as training planning, teaching material development, book publishing, lecturer selection, cooperation with associations and universities, as well as assessment of audit fees. It will be possible to make it.

The ultimate purpose, which is an extension of that, is to "contribute to the development of the national economy."

The Foundation had reached its 10th anniversary and finally entered its second stage. That stage was likely the original purpose of the Foundation, the 'ideal way of accounting education and training in Japan', that the founders had been aiming for.

# Part 3
# Nursing Volume
## (At-Home Caregiving)

# Prologue  Death of a Peer

On March 22nd, 2020, Naoto got a call from a classmate from his time at Nagasaki Minami High School, to let him know that Yojiro Nakase had died of lung cancer.

Nakase had been a junior high and high school classmate, in all of the same classes when Naoto was in his third year of high school. He was a nice guy involved in volleyball and rugby and was smart, tall and handsome.

Naoto still remembers his remarks at the all-school student rally during his second year at Umechu (Umegasaki Junior High School was abbreviated as "Umechu").

At that time, long hair was beginning to become popular, especially among young people. Umechu is said to be a bad junior high school that is also famous in Nagasaki, and long hair has begun to increase, especially among problem students.

Principal Katsue Hagiwara came up with a secret plan to make all male students shave their heads by the school rules to prevent this. However, the boys strongly opposed this and pressured other students to oppose the shaved head.

Therefore, the school side held a school-wide student rally, and Principal Hagiwara who went up to the stage rolled up his left sleeve and complained to everyone that he was sick due to this problem and was dripping at the hospital today, and all the students. In the vote, he proposed to set the boy's shaved head in the school rules.

In response to this, the bad group stood up and gathered all the students from all the schools prior to voting, and the pros and cons each gave a cheering speech. In this cheering speech, the bad group was overwhelmingly dominant, and no one doubted the victory of the opposition. The bad group appealed that long hair like the Beatles would be at the forefront of the future, and everyone agreed.

Meanwhile, Yojiro Nakase, the captain of the volleyball club, who was also regarded as a bad group, raised his hand and asked if he could say something.

All the students quieted down for a moment and Nakase spoke. "What's wrong with the shaved head? The shaved head is clean and dries quickly after washing, and doesn't require a hair dryer. It's also economically rational. I'm a big fan of the shaved head."

With this one word from Nakase, the inferior supporters were able to turn around. Principal Hagiwara and the teachers applauded Nakase for this remark.

Naoto and Yoko participated in the alumni association of the 21st year of Umegasaki Junior High School held on November 17, 1991 for the first time. Until then, she had participated alone, but she thought that this would be Yoko's last reunion, so she participated together. The place of the alumni association was "Tokaen" in the Chinatown of Nagasaki Shinchi, and it was held from 6 pm.

Tokaen was close to his apartment, so Naoto walked to the venue with Yoko. It wasn't long enough to walk normally, but it took more than an hour as he walked slowly with Yoko, who closed her eyes and lost her balance.

Five or six female classmates were already sitting at the reception, waiting for everyone to get there. When they saw Yoko, they all seemed surprised at the stark difference from the last reunion.

"Yoko, are you okay? Open her eyes, look at her, Tsuyako."

"What's wrong? Can you see?"

"Are you her husband? What happened to Yoko?"

Naoto was asked by everyone and she replied, "She has Parkinson's disease," but they didn't ask any further.

There were more than 100 participants in the alumni association, including Yojiro Nakase. When the toast started and the feast was full, Nakase came to Yoko's table, standing behind her and tapping her shoulders.

He encouraged them, "Yoko, cheer up. No illness is a match for you."

Nakase is a childhood friend of Yoko and her elementary school, and they are close to each other's house, so it seems that he was Yoko's first love.

When Yoko was hospitalized at the Roadside Hospital in Nagasaki, she found the name tag 'Nakase' in the men's room on the same third floor.

When the nurse asked, "What's your husband's name?" Yoko answered, "Yojiro."

The nurse was surprised when she said that. "Didn't you say Yamamoto before?"

Yoko seems to have had a considerable amount of disorientation (a disorder in which she cannot correctly recognize time, place, person, etc., which is one of the dementias) from around this time, but this behavior may have been unexpectedly caused by Yoko's true intentions. Naoto also heard from her friend Yoko when she was in junior high school that "Yoko's first love is Yojiro Nakase."

However, Nakase also died, along with Hideki Saijo, his mother, and Yojiro Nakase, who liked Yoko. Of course, this was still a secret to Yoko.

Naoto was in the same 12-group boys, class with Nakase when he was in his third year of high school. Naoto had enrolled in Nagasaki University School of Medicine, partly because his father had a strong desire to become a doctor. However, shortly after that, his father collapsed due to a cerebral infarction, so Naoto suddenly quit college and started working at a local civil engineering and construction company. Naoto thought about becoming a barber and taking over the hairdresser in order to repay the debt of his father's hairdresser, but at that time long hair became popular and the number of customers dropped sharply, and my mother said, "The salon won't be profitable from now on. You should stop doing it," and gave up on becoming a barber.

However, when he joined a construction company, he was surprised at the difference between the starting salary of university graduates and high school graduates, so he decided to leave the university again and attended the Faculty of Economics for four years.

After graduating from the National Defense Academy, Nakase joined the Maritime Self-Defense Force and became the captain of the escort ship 'Yamagiri'.

At that time, his place of work was Yokosuka, and his official residence was in Musashi Nakahara next to Musashi Kosugi, so he often went out with Yoko and their children.

Actually, at this time, five classmates who were close friends in Ume lived near Tokyo, Kawasaki, and Yokohama. Oddly, the five wives were also classmates in Umechu, so ten people were often gathered. These were Naoto and Yoko, Nakase Yojiro and Sumiko, Hayada Daimasu and Noriko, Honda Yusuke and Toshiko, and Doi Hiroshi and Hiroko.

Hayada was the same Marunouchi corporate group as Naoto, Marunouchi Kako Construction, and Honda was a composer of theme songs such as TV dramas, and was a strange person who was a long-distance truck driver to become a composer.

When Naoto asked why Nakase did trucking, he said, "Because long-haul truck drivers can listen to their favorite music all day long."

Honda seems to have composed the theme music for the TV drama Furuhata Ninzaburo. He also seems to have composed many theme songs for famous TV anime.

Doi was in Nihonbashi and ran a snack shop for office workers and a Nagasaki Champon shop. He also recently opened a barbecue specialty store nearby. As soon as he graduated from high school, he moved to Tokyo, engaged in night business such as bartender at Nihonbashi, and was a hard worker who started businesses one after another with his own vitality, a race completely different from bureaucrats and company people. He was a man with a strong vitality.

At one point, the five men played golf at the Atsugi Country Club with the president of Shigeno Sushi.

The president had a nickname for each of them: Naoto was 'Ministry of Finance' (currently the Financial Services Agency) and Nakase was 'Defense Agency' (currently the Ministry of Defense).

The president always shouted "Ministry of Finance" at the time of billing and called Naoto. Also, at the start of golf, Nakase was angry, saying, "Defense Agency, hit early, late. That's why Japan lost the war." Since then, he had been intimately associated with the president of Shigeno Sushi.

For reference, Shigeno Sushi has its head office in Nihonbashi and branches in Shibuya and Miyazakidai on the Tokyu Denentoshi Line. Since I am intimate with the president, I always eat delicious sushi cheaply.

Nakase once invited four people, Hayada's wife and eldest son Shuhei, Yoko and second son Tsubame, when the escort ship "Yamagiri" arrived in Yokosuka.

On that day, Tsubame came home with great joy and longed for Captain Nakase's coolness. He remembered it as if it were yesterday, his son was so excited to declare, "I'm going to join the Maritime Self-Defense Force one day!"

Also, at one point, we gathered at Hayada's house in Yokohama without his wives and held a banquet. When everyone got liquor, they were fighting for all-you-can-eat discussions.

In the meantime, the topic became each other's wife, and Nakase got involved with Naoto. "Hey, Yamamoto, you have to manage Kami more properly. If it's laid on her ass, it's related to the Japanese boy's ticket."

Naoto also argued against Nakase's remarks with the momentum of sake. "Hey, Nakase, I feel sorry for Kami-san in Kampaku, the host like you. You should be kinder to Kami-san."

After such a dispute, Nakase finally got really angry. "That's why you can't do it. Become a more hostess Kampaku!"

"Because the couple's style is ten people and ten colors, you shouldn't force the hostess Kampaku like you. Your girlfriend may just be patient even if you really want to argue."

In the end, the discussion of this host, Kampaku, was inconclusive and was carried over to the next time. However, everyone became too busy after that. Naoto was looking forward to the next rematch with Nakase, but it never happened.

It's a shame that such a strong man couldn't beat lung cancer.

Naoto was relieved to hear from Mrs. Nakase that his children were already independent, but she was worried that his wife would be quite lonely without Nakase.

Naoto asked his wife about her husband at Nakase's house. She said that he hadn't expected. "At home he was a kind husband who helped me with housework."

Naoto heard that and she was relieved that Nakase was really kind. However, at the very early farewell of 66 years old, Naoto thought, 'Well, we're at that time,' and at the same time, it was a fun time when ten people gathered again like those days. He couldn't help feeling lonely when it came to nostalgic and distant memories.

And another classmate of Naoto was at Nagasaki Road Station Hospital where Yoko was hospitalized.

One day Naoto went to Nagasaki Roadside Station Hospital to help Yoko as usual, he happened to meet Masahiko Shirai, a classmate in Umechu, in the elevator. He was his classmate in the third year of junior high school and was a white, slender and gentle boy that was still fair and thin.

"Shirai? It's been decades. It's been 45 years since the last class reunion was held five or six years after graduating from junior high school."

Shirai also answered with a surprised look. "Mr. Yamamoto, how are you doing after all this time?"

Naoto saw Shirai's clothes and soon realized that he was hospitalized. "Shirai, are you hospitalized here? What's wrong?"

"It's schizophrenia (a mental illness that causes delusions, hallucinations, thought disorders, etc. and affects one in 100 people). I've been hospitalized here for six years now. What happened to Mr. Yamamoto? What's wrong?"

Naoto replied, "No, it's not me. My wife has Parkinson's disease so I've been here for about a year now."

"That's tough. I'm still single, so no one comes to visit me. My parents and sister died young, and I'm left lonely."

"Well, Shirai must have had a lot of trouble. Let's get

well quickly and go to Doza (the downtown area at night) for a drink."

"That's right. Let's get better as soon as possible. Thank you for your cooperation."

Shirai got off the elevator on the 8th floor. The eighth floor was the floor where patients with schizophrenia received long-term treatment. Naoto thought, 'What a small world,' and at the same time, 'How many people are out there suffering from schizophrenia?'

The next day, Naoto stopped by on the 8th floor to visit Shirai before going to Yoko's hospital room. When he got off on the 8th floor, he heard a loud scream.

"Kill me, let me die already!" Shirai was being held down by two male nurses.

Naoto rushed over. "Shirai, what are you talking about, be firm. Remember when you were in junior high school. You weren't the guy who made such a soft noise. Seeing your friends being bullied, you fought at the forefront. Where did Shirai go at that time?"

Shirai looked up at Naoto from below and said between sobs, "Mr. Yamamoto, please help me. It's no good anymore."

"What are you talking about? Life is just around the corner. There are lots of fun things to do in the future. I really regret it if I don't get rid of my illness quickly."

Shirai stood up and said 'thank you' before going back to

his room.

Naoto asked the nurse, "Does this happen often?"

"Unfortunately, yes. We're in trouble from the lack of manpower. I was saved today. Are you a friend of Mr. Shirai?"

"Yes, he was my classmate in junior high school. I bumped into him the other day in the elevator."

"So Mr. Shirai must have also felt that sense of nostalgia for his friends, and he felt calm. Thank you."

When Naoto was about to head up the elevator, Dr. Ueki, Yoko's doctor, stepped out. "What happened to you, Mr. Yamamoto?"

Naoto talked about being a junior high school classmate with Shirai and having met by chance the other day.

Ueki told Naoto, "I was informed that Mr. Shirai was rampaging, and I rushed in, but thanks to Mr. Yamamoto, he seems to have calmed down. As you can see, Mr. Shirai has schizophrenia, but the cause is not just loneliness. He doesn't have leukemia (blood cancer) in his second generation. I think that's probably the reason why schizophrenia doesn't go away."

"That's right. Poor Shirai is also hard. Teacher, thank you for your cooperation."


A week later, after 7 am on Monday morning, a hearse came into the back of the hospital and stopped. Naoto was doing his calisthenics at the front door of the hospital as usual, when Dr. Ueki rushed up to him.

"Mr. Yamamoto, I'm sorry but Mr. Shirai died last night. Recently, he was having difficulty breathing at night. The leukemia was too much for him."

Naoto had been visiting Shirai almost every day since the outburst he had seen. Shirai listened to Naoto's old tales with nostalgia, and sometimes clapping his hands and laughing. He looked so fine, but he just acted well with care for me. Did Shirai finally die by being called to heaven?

Naoto was later called to Dr. Ueki's office. The doctor had a grim face and an envelope in his hand. "This is a suicide note addressed to you, from Mr. Shirai. There's also 500,000 yen in cash here addressed to you."

Naoto remembered that Shirai had said the other day that he was lonely for the rest of his life. When he opened the final letter, it said:

Naoto Yamamoto,

It was my last blessing to meet you again at this hospital. It's about my time to be picked up from heaven. I'm very sorry to Mr. Yamamoto, but could you give me a funeral with this money? Thank you.

Please place my remains in the Shirai family grave in Daionji Temple in Teramachi. I'm really sorry for the difficult part of caring for my wife, but thank you.

I enjoyed listening to old tales every day in the hospital room, and I missed the most enjoyable time in his life when he was in junior high school. I can finally go home at that time. I'm really thankful to you.

Masahiko Shirai

The next day, Naoto held a funeral for Shirai, who had no relatives, by himself, and a few days later he completed the ossuary.

Naoto was worried that it might be his turn next, because his classmates Shirai and Nakase had died in quick succession. However, for Yoko's sake, he just prayed to God to put that off until later.

Later, when he was carrying out home care in Kawasaki, a visiting doctor, Dr. Obayashi, asked Naoto a question. "How do you keep going with long-term care? There are quite a lot of caregivers who get depressed from the mental stress. Do you have any secrets?"

Naoto replied after a moment of thought. "I started volunteering to change my mood. I think life is always connected to someone and I think I'm never alone."

Obayashi nodded along. "Well, I still have a lot to learn."

# Chapter 1  Aspiration Pneumonia

---

Two months had passed since they returned to Kawasaki and began settling into the home-care routine. In the early morning on January 31st, 2020, Naoto noticed Yoko's face was a little red–her temperature was over 40 degrees Celsius (104 degrees Fahrenheit). Naoto heeded Yuko's advice from last time and took off her blankets to release the heat. After a while, he measured it again, and it was still over 40 degrees.

It was only 7 o'clock in the morning, and the outpatient reception at Sakuradamon Hospital didn't open until 8 o'clock. He finished up using the respirator and walked to the hospital to get her a patient registration ticket ahead of time. He asked the receptionist, "My wife is usually in the neurology department, but her fever is over 40 degrees. I think she may have a cold, could she get a medical examination right away?"

"Internal medicine is busy as usual. She'd have to wait till 10 o'clock at the earliest."

"If there's no other option, then I'll bring her to wait here."

When Naoto returned home and checked on Yoko, she was still burning up and her breathing seemed labored. He needed to hurry, so he called up their friends, the Onoyamas.

He asked Mrs. Onoyama to come and watch after Yoko while he went to the hospital to try and get her in earlier.

"Of course, I'll be right there."

Naoto tried to transfer Yoko to her wheelchair, but Yoko didn't have enough strength to use her legs to help him. With Mrs. Onoyama's help they got her into the wheelchair, but it seemed too dangerous for them to get Yoko all the way down to the front door by themselves. Mrs. Onoyama suggested they should call an ambulance, and Naoto hurriedly called '119'. When he told the operator about her fever (the coronavirus infection wasn't yet in full swing), they sent over an ambulance within a few minutes. Three EMTs carried Yoko to the ambulance.

"Which hospital?" one of the emergency personnel asked, and Naoto told them he had alerted Sakuradamon Hospital earlier in the day. The ambulance arrived there in less than three minutes, but from there, nothing went as Naoto had expected.

One of the doctors from internal medicine rushed over to them. He asked Naoto, "What happened? Who is your doctor here?"

Naoto replied, "She has a fever over 40 degrees, she's usually with Dr. Sugiyama."

The physician instructed the nurse to contact Dr. Sugiyama immediately.

From the facial expression and attitude of this physician,

it seemed like he was wondering, 'Why would you use an ambulance just to see your regular doctor?'

After that, Naoto went to his doctor and Sugiyama asked, "Why did you use an ambulance?" This only worsened his opinion of the man.

Yoko received an IV drip right away and was put on standby in the emergency room for about an hour. In the meantime, Naoto completed all of the hospital paperwork and handed it off to the billing department.

She asked, "Would you like a private room or a larger one with a couple other patients?"

"The large room is fine," Naoto replied.

Yet, he was told, "We actually don't have any vacant beds right now," and had to wait in the emergency room for over two hours. Finally they were taken to Room 302 in the annex, a quadruple room with only one other patient. Had all of the beds really been full?

Naoto rushed home and came back with the essentials, such as underwear, pajamas, diapers, toothbrushes, toiletries, medication, and gastrostomy equipment.

Thankfully, after receiving the drip for about two hours, Yoko's fever dropped to 38 degrees Celsius. It seemed she was indeed sick, and Naoto had been too late again.

After that, Yoko underwent various examinations such as blood tests, urine tests, an X-ray, and an electrocardiogram.

While Naoto was waiting in the room for these examinations to finish, the chief nurse and the nurse in charge came to greet him.

"I'm Yamagishi, the chief nurse. Doctor Sugiyama, will be here in a moment to give a rundown."

"I'm Kawada, the nurse in charge of your wife."

The nurses worked in teams of three, and Kawada seemed to be one of the leaders, even though they were young.

Naoto passed by the nurse station on his way to Yoko's room, and he was surprised to see so many young nurses–it seemed like a nursing school rather than a hospital. It seemed like the average age was around five or six years younger than the employees at the hospital in Nagasaki.

Around 3 in the afternoon, Dr. Sugiyama finally came to check on their situation. "Mr. Yamamoto, maybe next time evaluate whether an ambulance is truly needed. Her fever dropped to 38, and there were no particular problems with her breathing. We'll continue to infuse antibiotics for about a week."

After that, Dr. Sugiyama gave a detailed explanation of Yoko's medical condition in the conference room next door. In addition to Sugiyama, there was a female doctor in charge, a social worker, a chief nurse, and the nurse in charge of Yoko that sat in for the meeting.

Sugiyama spoke first, "Mr. Yamamoto, your wife has

aspiration pneumonia. That may be the cause of her fever. Has she had any problems lately?"

"Every day, after doing exercises at noon, I'd give her a sip or two of juice or her favorite yogurt. She didn't have any particular problems…"

"Well for the time being, drinking is prohibited. Please note that your wife's illness impairs muscle function, so her swallowing function will inevitably worsen and she'll be prone to aspiration pneumonia."

Naoto asked, "Will the fever go away quickly with just a single infusion of antibiotics?"

"Has your wife had a fever for a few days?"

"No, I measure her temperature, blood pressure, and pulse three times a day, every morning, noon, and evening."

Before Yoko had a gastrostomy at Kibogaoka Hospital in Nagasaki, she had a similar fever and was unable to have the operation until later. The X-ray at the time led them to suspect aspiration pneumonia as well. At that time, Naoto was given a detailed explanation while the physician, Yamazaki, showed him Yoko's X-ray. "This shadow is pneumonia, but it was a long time ago. This time it's not aspiration pneumonia, it might just be a cold. Her immune system is weak, so even a normal cold could give her a high fever."

Naoto listened to this explanation and asked Yamazaki a question. "How can you tell if the pneumonia is new or old?"

"That's easy. You can judge from the darkness of the shadow. The lighter shadow is older, it's a sign of inflammation, such as pneumonia or tuberculosis, from the past."

Naoto looked at the X-ray picture shown by Dr. Sugiyama of Sakurada Gate Hospital. There was indeed a shadow, but it was fairly faint. He asked Sugiyama, "Could that mark be a sign of pneumonia from a long time ago?"

"How do you know that?" Sugiyama asked in surprise.

Naoto told him about his time with veteran doctor Yamazaki at the hospital in Nagasaki.

"There are cases where you can say that," the doctor explained, "but it's difficult even for a veteran doctor to judge whether the shadow is new or old. This one appears new."

Naoto was not convinced. Yamazaki, a physician, and Sugiyama, a neurologist, were quite different in age and experience. Yamazaki, who is reticent, had an overwhelming sense of dependability compared to Sugiyama.

Two weeks had passed since then. Yoko's fever went away completely and her IV drip came off. Naoto always came to the hospital at 11 o'clock when visiting hours started, but that day he went to the Miyamae Ward Office and couldn't get to the hospital until after 2 o'clock.

When he entered the hospital room, Yoko was receiving

nutrition through her gastrostomy. Naoto thought it was a little late for lunch, so he asked the nurse.

"No, this is her breakfast."

"So she still hasn't taken her morning medications?"

The nurse replied apologetically, "That's right. I was held up by another patient, I apologize."

Naoto knew she had to be referring to the next-door patient who was always pushing the 'call' button and tersely commanded the nurse, 'toilet', 'move up the bed', or 'need a walk'.

Yoko couldn't press the call button, so she didn't put a burden on her nurse.

Naoto was dismayed at such a response to Yoko, an honor student, and asked a slightly mean question. "So do you just administer all of her medications at once in the evening?"

The nurse answered with a troubled expression, "Since it's not possible to administer three doses at once, we won't administer her morning and noon doses today."

"Will that be alright?"

"It should be fine."

"How often does this happen?"

"This is the first time it's happened with me. I apologize."

"Is this same thing happening with other nurses?"

"I can't say anything for sure."

"Nutrition and drug administration should be recorded

properly in the patient's record." Naoto wiped the sweat from his brow. "Have the nurses been writing down her records truthfully?"

Two days later came their decisive moment.

A new nurse came into the hospital room and was preparing for the nutritional administration by Yoko's gastrostomy, not greeting Naoto in particular. Naoto was implicitly watching the situation, but the nurse began to administer nutrition directly with a syringe.

"Is that okay to do?" Naoto commented. "It's 400 cc, so it takes about an hour and a half to administer. When did they change the administration method?"

"This is fine. Don't worry, it's okay. It's faster," the nurse said with a bite to her tone, injecting 400 cc of nutrition all at once with a syringe.

As expected, Naoto got angry and couldn't help his gruff tone. "Please go check with the doctor whether this is really okay."

The nurse finally realized that Naoto was frustrated and jumped up to get the doctor. A few minutes later, the nurse returned with the doctor. "I'm sorry. I misunderstood it as a nasal administration (a method of administering nutrition through the nostrils with a syringe)."

Sugiyama, the attending physician, couldn't make any

excuses this time and had to deeply apologize.

Naoto was worried about what was happening with the nurses at this hospital, and decided to take Yoko home early. These incidents only further convinced him that no hospital could provide what home care could.

Naoto confirmed all of the conditions for discharge with Doctor Sugiyama: no fever, protein levels normal on the blood test, and no signs of pneumonia on the X-ray.

Naoto asked if Yoko could be discharged tomorrow since she cleared all of the conditions.

"Well Mr. Yamamoto, I was only able to take in your wife because we happened to have a vacant bed, but you need to realize that most of the time we can't hospitalize patients willy-nilly. So, I suggest she stay another month to ensure everything is completely healed, and this won't happen again. We're already arranging the next hospital room, there won't be a fee this time."

"Doctor, what are you talking about? She's cleared the conditions for discharge, and I think home care is better for my wife. I also heard there was a shortage of nurses for the number of patients. And what do you mean, would the hospital bed usually cost us? It should be covered fully by the national health insurance! Especially since it's a quadruple room."

"Didn't they explain this all when you signed in? Your wife's room would be near the nurse's station and a washing center, so even a quadruple room would cost an extra fee of 1,500 yen every day. You must have signed the consent form."

"I may have signed it, but I didn't receive any explanation beforehand. I was asked if she'd like a private or shared room, that's all."

Naoto wasn't convinced by this answer, but he didn't know what else to do–he didn't want to be labeled as a person who only made unreasonable complaints.

The following month, Yoko underwent gastrostomy replacement surgery at the same hospital, but the doctor didn't show his face until after the surgery. It was hard to ignore the cold reception Naoto got whenever he visited Yoko, and he got her discharged as soon as possible. Right after being discharged, the coronavirus began to spread and hospital visits were completely banned. It had been a close call. Naoto was instantly reassured by his decision and thanked God they were safe at home.

# Chapter 2  Professional Ethics

One day, while Yoko was preparing for her gastrostomy nutrition after a bath, she suddenly had a coughing fit. There were two potential causes for this: the inability to swallow saliva or a buildup of phlegm. He checked for both, and then measured her temperature just in case, but everything seemed fine.

However, Yoko's breathing was faster than usual. Naoto had never measured Yoko's respiratory rate before, but it was 36 times a minute now. He wasn't sure if this was normal, so he looked at the nurses' records.

Most of the respiratory rates during the visiting-bathing were noted as 18 to 20 times a minute–this was almost twice that rate. But soon Yoko's facial expression grew calm, so he put the notes aside for later.

The next day, he asked Yuko Motoyama, the visiting nurse from the Miyamae Care Center, about the respiratory rate, and she answered professionally. "Mr. Yamamoto, when measuring the respiratory rate, the nurse puts on a stethoscope at the same time and measures it while observing various things, such as whether there is an abnormality in the sound of the patient's lungs and whether the breathing is shallow. I don't think a high rate is a problem in itself, only if it's accompanied by other symptoms. A normal person's respiratory rate is generally 18 to 20 bpm, so I think it's a little more for Yoko. However, if something else is wrong, the nurse will notice it. You don't have to worry so much."

Her explanation put his worries at ease for the moment.

However, it happened again. After Naoto finished her visit-bathing, he posted a report of her visit-bathing measurement records to her daily record book as usual.

The report included the respiratory rates of Yoko before and after her bathing today, which was a whopping 36 and 39 bpm. Considering that Motoyama said the general number of times was 18 to 20 bpm, Yoko's numbers seemed bad.

If it was more than double the normal number, the nurse in charge today would say something to Naoto, but she didn't report anything.

Naoto was a little worried, and looked back at her past records. Then he measured Yoko's respiratory rate at 30 bpm. Therefore, she must not have particularly thought her breathing rate was unusual today, and she probably didn't say anything to Naoto.

Naoto asked her manager about this after the next day's visit-bathing. They said they would get back to him with an answer, but after a while of no response, Naoto had forgotten he had asked.

About two weeks later, the nurse suddenly apologized to Naoto for not reporting anything about Yoko's recent respiratory rate. "Mr. Yamamoto, I'm very sorry the other day. I should have reported that her respiratory rate was a little high. I will measure and report it properly today. I'm sorry."

Naoto wondered if her manager had warned her, "If you think her breathing rate is a little strange, please report it to your husband."

However, after she measured her respiratory rate, she apologized to Naoto. "Yoko's respiratory rate is 36 bpm no matter how many times I measure it. I can't put a false number in the report, so I'll put in the honest 36. I'm sorry."

Her apology seemed genuine, she couldn't have been lying.

Naoto tried to measure Yoko's breathing rate himself after the bathing was over. After all, both times were in the high 30s.

He implicitly observed how the nurses were measuring the respiratory rate. All four nurses counted for 20 seconds and then tripled the number. Therefore, the respiratory rate should have been a multiple of three, but the measurements of the three other nurses were sixteen, seventeen, nineteen, and twenty. Perhaps they needed to count for one minute.

Naoto was also well aware that, as Nurse Motoyama taught, it was a misleading idea to only take the respiratory rate as a warning sign.

Naoto apologized when she came next time, saying, "I was suspicious, I'm sorry." The nurse also apologized to Naoto for her fib.

Perhaps the other nurses began to measure the respiratory rate more carefully after this incident, and most of the numbers were in the 30s now. Except he didn't understand why the veteran nurse's respiratory rate was still only 18 to 20 bpm, which was a standard respiratory rate. However, when Naoto watched the behavior of the veteran nurse carefully, he gradually became aware of the cause.

The veteran nurse immediately included in her report Yoko's body temperature and blood pressure before taking a bath. This is because these two items were the conditions that determined whether a bath was safe. The veteran nurse's numbers were so different from the others because she did all of the post-bath work by herself, taking her much longer.

It wasn't the only problem. The same thing happened when measuring pulse rate by palpation. An inappropriate response to pulse rate caused a great deal of trouble.

These improper acts may have started as an easy way to finish the work early, but this continued for a year and nine months–missing out on the chance to discover Yoko's frequent arrhythmias and extrasystoles. The reality of delaying the discovery of Yoko's arrhythmia from their light hearts could never be overlooked. Naoto couldn't help resenting the fact that veteran nurses were still doing this.

"The next choice would be to build a 'gastric fistula' and wear a ventilator. This issue is due to the stiffness of the throat and respiratory muscles, which inevitably causes swallowing and respiratory function. Please think carefully in advance what to do in that case. Once the ventilator is attached, it cannot be removed."

Naoto was worried about when this risk would become apparent, and was overwhelmed by the results of his home-visit medical care and home-visit nursing vital checks. Naoto thought that it was out of the question to doubt the numbers measured by the professionals. He could never forgive it.

However, at this time, there was still a sense of calmness that this problem should not be disturbed and the relationship of trust that had been built up until now should not be broken. So he decided to propose a realistic solution to his manager. "It's not realistic for nurses to spend time measuring their respiratory rate during a busy home-visit-bathing operation, isn't it? Instead of measuring their respiratory rate, oxygen concentration with a pulse oximeter. How about an alternative method of measuring?"

If the oxygen concentration was normal, the respiratory rate wouldn't be a problem. It was two birds with one stone that led to the efficiency of visiting-bathing work and the peace of mind of customers. Naoto asked the visiting nurse Motoyama about this change plan in advance, and now, even in visiting nursing and home-visit medical care, he is trying to improve efficiency by measuring the oxygen concentration with a pulse oximeter instead of the respiratory rate.

However, although the manager agreed to measure the oxygen concentration, he responded that he would continue to measure the respiratory rate as in the company's regulations.

Therefore, the measurement of respiratory rate continued after this without any change. Naoto finally set out for the next operation. According to the measured report, it seems that the strategy was also incorrect for the pulse rate, which is measured by palpation without using a device as well.

Naoto examined all the records from December 1st, 2019, when the visiting-bathing appointments had started. For about a year after, this veteran nurse was in charge of almost one person, and the respiratory rate was 18 to 20 bpm, and the pulse rate was 60 to 66 bpm, which is almost a fixed number.

After that, two dispatched nurses were put into Yoko's visiting-bathing work, and the other day's honest nurse joined as a temporary nurse. In other words, the number of nurses in charge had changed from one to four.

When all these were measured by these four people, a surprising fact was found.

- The measured numbers of the two dispatched nurses were 18 bpm for respiratory rate and 60 bpm for pulse rate, which were almost the same as the measured numbers from the veteran nurse until Naoto pointed out an abnormality to the manager. However, after Naoto pointed out the abnormality, the measured numbers of the two dispatched nurses were 30 bpm and 50 bpm pulse rate, both of which were different from before.

- Of the four nurses, only the honest nurse had a respiratory rate of 30 bpm and a pulse rate of 50 bpm.

- Under these circumstances, on March 14, a dispatched nurse discovered Yoko's arrhythmia. The pulse rate recorded 40 bpm for the first time. Since then, the pulse rate had been in the range of 40 to 50 bpm.

Estimating from these facts, it must be said that the number of veteran nurses measured in the first year lacks credibility by any means. The two dispatched nurses would have taken care of her so as not to deviate from the number measured by this veteran nurse.

Naoto asked the care manager, it seems that visiting bathers have been in trouble due to a shortage of nurses for some time. The importance of veteran nurses in the company and the widespread use within the company can be seen from the fact that the two dispatched nurses were enthusiastic about these veteran nurses.

However, in such a situation, only an honest nurse continued to keep her professional ethics as a nurse without being influenced by other nurses. She was a good nurse.

In any case, the respiratory rate and pulse rate measured by these four people had a big difference that could not be thought of as the values of the same user. There was a dilemma that if someone thought it was right, others were obviously wrong.

Therefore, Naoto investigated what happened to the law and professional ethics of nurses as a national qualification in the first place.

[Article 14 of the Nurse Code of Ethics]
"If there is an act that impairs the dignity of a nurse, the Minister of Health, Labor and Welfare may take the following dispositions.

1. Reminder
2. Suspension of business within a few years
3. Cancellation of license"

[Nurse Code of Ethics]
"Nurses are responsible for explaining their own nursing, judgment, and taking responsibility for the actions and results."

[Guidelines for Nursing Records]

"First, this guideline shows the ideal way of creating records and the handling of those records for all nursing staff."

"Second, a nursing record was a record of a series of processes of all nursing practices that are practiced everywhere."

"Third, in order to ensure the accuracy of nursing records, it is necessary to pay attention to the following points.

- Describe the facts accurately
- Leave the date and time stated and the name of the individual stated
- hen correcting the description, make sure that the person who made the correction, the content, and the date and time are known.

    Records must not be tampered with. Falsification of a record means intentionally rewriting all or part of the record with contents that are different from the facts. Falsification of nursing records is not only contrary to the fact that nurses build a relationship of trust with the target people and provide nursing based on that relationship of trust, but also legally criminal liability and punishment."

Professional ethics required nurses to clear many hurdles, with penalties stipulated if they failed to. Depending on how you think about it, nurses were required to have higher professional ethics than doctors, and it was unlikely that nurses with such obligations and responsibilities would do inappropriate acts.

Naoto has asked her doctor Ueki several times, because Yoko had had bradycardia (arrhythmia that slows her pulse) since she was admitted to the Roadside Station Hospital in Nagasaki.

"Doctor, I have been diagnosed with bradycardia before, but Yoko also has bradycardia, and sometimes there are arrhythmias where her pulse increases. It is usually in the 50s, but sometimes 40s. If you're not good at it, you may have thirty units. Does this need to be treated?"

Ueki replied, "If it's in the 50s, it doesn't matter so much, but if 40s, especially 30s, occur frequently, I think it's necessary to find out the cause and treat it."

However, from the time he returned to Kawasaki and started visiting bathing, the number of pulse measurements by veteran nurses was recorded in the 60s each time, so Naoto clearly said that Yoko's bradycardia had improved. With that in mind, he had completely forgotten about arrhythmias and bradycardia.

Meanwhile, on March 14, a dispatched nurse found Yoko's arrhythmia. Naoto immediately asked Dr. Obayashi, who visited the clinic, to perform an ECG test for 24 hours.

The result was more serious than Naoto had expected. Extrasystoles (a phenomenon in which the heart beats regularly through a normal electric circuit, but electrical excitement is generated from an abnormal circuit and the heart contracts earlier than the normal pulse) had occurred more than 20,000 times in a single day.

Naoto also had such extrasystoles before his heart surgery, but even so, out of 100,000 heart rates a day, the number of arrhythmias was only 10,000, which was only 10%.

Dr. Obayashi seemed to be at a loss for the test results and left it up to Naoto to decide what to do. "I think that extrasystoles occur more than 20,000 times a day, so I think it is necessary to find out the cause and treat it. The same thing is stated in the test result report. I think it's better to have a detailed examination at Sakuradamon Hospital, please consult with Dr. Sugiyama."

Naoto heard Dr. Sugiyama of Sakuradamon Hospital and immediately rejected the idea. "I haven't talked to Dr. Sugiyama for almost two years now. The examination is to see the patient, isn't it? You wouldn't look at your computer. He has always ignored Yoko and barely shown any interest in his patients. The two of us are hated by Dr. Sugiyama. Besides, if she is hospitalized for a test when the coronavirus infection is so widespread, we won't be able to visit. Yoko's symptoms, which have improved so much, will come back at once."

Mr. Obayashi nodded and said no more.

In the end, it is true that the discovery of arrhythmia due

to Yoko's extrasystoles was delayed due to improper behavior that would have started with a slight off feeling from the visiting bathing nurse.

In the unlikely event that the next ECG test yielded even worse results, Naoto decided to thoroughly condemn these inappropriate behaviors and asked Nurse Motoyama implicitly, "I was skeptical about the big difference between the measured values of respiratory rate and pulse rate between the four nurses who visited the bath, and I examined the reports so far in detail. There was a point that didn't make sense. I can't think of it as the measured value of the same user."

She pondered it for a moment. "But even if you say that the number is wrong, I think it's difficult to prove it unless the nurse admits it was inappropriate."

"That's what it is. The motive for why such an inappropriate act was taken is clear. In other words, the visiting bathing work was tight and time-consuming, and I just cut corners. There is no motivation for a nurse to do such a thing. The role of a visiting bathing nurse is just to judge whether or not you can take a bath, and since you are busy measuring, you feel so guilty even if you skip a little."

"Nurses are involved in life-threatening work for patients, and strict professional ethics are required. They should be trustworthy."

Naoto was told so by his trusted Motoyama and lost his

fighting spirit. Fortunately, his second examination showed a lower number of extrasystoles and concluded that it didn't interfere with daily life.

Naoto thought that if there was an inappropriate act that he suspected, a nurse with a high level of professional ethics would apologize. The fact that he still had no apology had to mean that there was no improper conduct. Naoto prayed this was the case.

# Chapter 3 Corticobasal Degeneration

The story goes back to when Yoko was hospitalized at "Roadside Station Hospital" in Nagasaki, and she became unable to walk independently after a year of repeated hospitalizations and discharges at Roadside Station Hospital.

Around this time, all of her muscles began to contract, perhaps because of tension. Perhaps because of that, her left leg couldn't stretch straight, and her left hand was squeezed tight and her fingers couldn't open. These anomalies were concentrated in her left half of her body.

Naoto asked her doctor, Dr. Ueki. "It seems that the muscle rigidity is concentrated on the left half of her body. Why is this?"

"I think this is also accompanied by corticobasal degeneration. Parkinson's disease and dementia are all diseases that occur due to abnormalities in the brain. The cause is atrophy or hollowing out of the brain. Corticobasal degeneration is a Parkinson's symptom that causes motor dysfunction such as muscle rigidity and walking, and the hand becomes immobile or awkward as expected on either the left or right side of the body. It's a disease that causes strong cerebral cortex disorders at the same time."

"Well, by the way, Yoko's left hand is often bent or she can't open it herself by squeezing her fingers. In addition, her left foot is always bent. Therefore, even if she uses the rehabilitation bicycle, her left foot does not reach the pedals."

"That's right. After all, there was a strong suspicion of corticobasal degeneration. Why don't you take a detailed examination at Tozai Hospital once?"

"Well, I understand. Can I apply for an examination at Tozai Hospital?"

"No problem, we can handle it today."

This detailed examination revealed that Yoko had developed corticobasal degeneration in addition to Parkinson's disease. However, it was not Parkinson's disease in reality, but it is a disease called "progressive supranuclear palsy" in which symptoms similar to Parkinson's symptoms appear in the early stage, but then the muscles gradually become rigid.

One day, Yoko beckoned Naoto from her hospital bed. She whispered in his ear, "I have to tell you something, close the curtain."

"What is it?" Naoto asked, eyeing her serious expression. "You're not going to say you want to go back to Kawasaki again, are you?"

Yoko shook her head from side to side and said, "Naoto, I'm simply waiting out death here. I'm not afraid to die anymore."

Her words took a minute to register and he struggled for a reply. "Everyone is waiting to die, because someday we'll all die."

Yoko continued, "No. I'm about to die here. I'm waiting for it."

Naoto was frantic while Yoko sat there calmly. However, she said something like this shortly afterwards. "I'm going to Mr. Iguchi's melon shops

"This is Nagasaki. Isn't Mr. Iguchi's melon shop in Kawasaki?"

Yoko continued to try and get up in silence.

Perhaps Yoko had become mentally calm after returning to Kawasaki, she became less nervous and her muscles were less rigid, and she began to listen to Naoto's story. She sometimes came to follow Naoto's instructions. When she had her eyes open, she became more sensitive to human voices, especially children's voices.

Naoto compared the early records of his care with the present to see what is causing these improvements. And it turned out that the most unusual thing was in the three hours immediately after he got up.

&lt;Early days&gt;

5:30 Get up, take out garbage, open windows, prepare for long-term care (boiler, medicine, diapers, etc.)

6:00 Change diapers, clean hot water, treat pressure ulcers (apply Aznol)

6:30 Nutritional administration by gastrostomy (Morinaga CZHI 267 M, milk 350 M, soy milk 125 M)

7:30 Medications (dopamine, dops, donepezil, cilostazol, magnesium oxide)

7:40 Dental care

8:30 Aspiration, eye drops, nasal drops, aspirator cleaning


&lt;Current&gt;

4:00 Wake up, take out garbage, open windows, prepare for long-term care (boiler, medicine, diapers, etc.)

4:30 Massage, stretch to relieve rigidity of limbs, disimpaction (scraping stool), hot water cleaning, pressure ulcer prevention (Aznol application), diaper change, hip joint exercise

5:00 Brushing teeth (using 10 toothbrushes and electric toothbrush), brushing (using 10), oral care (plaque removal, stimulation with a specialized pharyngeal brush)

6:00 Aspiration, eye drops, nasal drops, toothbrush, aspirator cleaning

7:00 Nutrition administration by gastrostomy (Morinaga CZHI 267 M, milk 350 M, soy milk 125 M)

8:00 Drug administration (dopamine, dops, donepezil, cilostazol, magnesium oxide)

The biggest changes were getting up an hour and a half earlier, a massage to loosen the muscles right after waking up, putting the aspirator first thing in the morning, and making the disimpaction a priority. He also made more time for her oral hygiene.

In other words, the morning routine was exactly the same as that of a healthy person, and before breakfast. He made it look like he couldn't wait to see Yoko in the morning.

With this change, about a month later, her voice could be heard, her eye opening time was further extended, and her fingers could be moved smoothly to grab something. Her left leg, which had been rigid, began to stretch little by little, and the time for the tension in the hands and feet to be released increased. Yoko's home care had entered the second stage of activating her brain through wheelchair exercises and oral care, no more of the first stage of increasing her weight and improving her physical strength.

Naoto first massaged and stretched her rigid limbs and shoulders after waking up. He massaged both hands and feet that were tense while sleeping. Then he did the disimpaction (scraping the stool with fingers) and used hot water to wipe with a towel. Diapers were changed  four times a day, morning, noon, evening, and before bedtime. If home-visit nursing or home-visit-bathing was included in the meantime, the number of visits would be added.

After that, he put her legs upright and shook her knees slowly to the left and right for fifty rotations, and added exercises to make her hip joints more flexible. This was inspired by Yoko's favorite exercise in the rehabilitation room of the Roadside Station Hospital, where she had tumbled around while lying on her back on a mat.

This was a way to reactivate her muscles that were no longer in use due to the rigidity of her muscles. Naoto thought that perhaps Yoko liked these movements herself because it felt good.

Starting in August 2021, he asked a visiting doctor to give Yoko an acupuncture and moxibustion massage. Acupuncture and moxibustion massage was covered by medical insurance and required instructions from your doctor. The purpose was to eliminate the rigidity of the muscles caused by Parkinson's disease. Certainly Yoko started to move her shoulders better after this procedure.

The next focus was oral hygiene. This was also taught to him by a dental hygienist teacher at the Roadside Station

Hospital in Nagasaki. She came to Yoko's room for oral care every day. Naoto had Yoko sit in her wheelchair, supporting her so that her head wouldn't fall, and observed her oral care every day to learn how to do it.

First, she prepared ten toothbrushes and one electric toothbrush, and brushed with a mouthwash called Neosterin. The most important part here was that she removed all plaque that had accumulated in her mouth.

Yoko could no longer gargle, so removing bacteria was a very important process. Before the pandemic, she gargled after she ate and could swallow juice and yogurt little by little at noon. However, she had to avoid hospitalization for aspiration pneumonia, so she was currently not allowed to drink water except for through the gastrostomy.

After this, the next step was brushing with 10 interdental brushes. It was important to note that the interdental brush could deteriorate and break with the tip in between the teeth. He had made these mistakes several times in the past and it had been a hard time getting rid of them.

After brushing with the toothbrush, a special brush removed residual plaque, stimulated her throat, and completed oral care.

The last part of the morning routine was removing any phlegm with the aspirator. This was an indispensable task before feeding by gastrostomy.

Previously, Yoko didn't open her mouth easily, so she used to suck through her nasal passages, but she recently started to open her mouth.

These morning routines had an incredible effect on Yoko.

First, Yoko began to keep her eyes open for more than 30 minutes in a row. This was evidence that information from the eyes was essential for brain activation. Perhaps this had a synergistic effect.

Next, Yoko couldn't swallow saliva until then, and often suffocated or choked, but this occurred also much less. It was speculated that this might be due to the activation of the muscles that were previously tense and rigid through three hours of care in the early morning.

And the last effect was her speech. Until then, when listening to music, her mouth sometimes moved as if she was humming the lyrics, but recently, she made a few vocal noises. Naoto told this to the speech therapist and seized this opportunity for new vocal training.

Maybe it would be possible to communicate in the near future. In that case, Yoko would be able to express her intentions, so further improvement could be expected. All of this hope came from the visiting rehabilitation teachers.

Naoto often talked to Yoko about this while she was in

the hospital in Nagasaki. "Yoko, there's no one to really help us anymore, so we have to do our best together."

However, those days were no more. "Yoko, we've finally reached this point with the help of so many people. I'm really looking forward to seeing what kind of helpers will bless us next. Maybe someone that can cure your illness completely."

When Naoto said so, Yoko squeezed Naoto's hand and smiled as much as she could.

Naoto usually tried not to remember the past, but he allowed himself to remember all of their happy moments, and squeezed Yoko's hand one hundred times tighter.

# Chapter 4 The Stress of Long-term Care

Naoto had recently wondered if he was growing more impatient. It was probably a natural experience for everyone as they aged, but he couldn't bring himself to admit it. Especially as a long-term caregiver, he was often overwhelmed and his patience grew thin. His sense of justice had grown slightly out of control–if he thought the other person was in the wrong, he would go at them relentlessly.

It's been almost three years since he was able to 'talk' to Yoko. Perhaps because of that, when Naoto has a chance to talk to someone, he often couldn't stop talking. The same was true for email. Occasionally, when someone sent him an email, the reply text was always long, no matter who the receiver was.

When Yoko was in the Nagasaki hospital, he had the opportunity to talk at least daily with her doctor, nurse, caregiver, dental hygienist, rehabilitation teacher, and hospitalized patients.

He had only learned about long-term care stress as a concept recently. It all revolved around a lack of socialization. He looked back on the factors that had begun to wear at his mental health.

Naoto began to take care of Yoko when she first developed the intractable disease and repeatedly fell.

However, at that time, there were no major changes compared to their life up until that point, and to put it bluntly, it took a little longer for Yoko to accompany him when they went out. Yoko was also able to have a normal conversation at this time, so sometimes they quarreled because they didn't agree with each other.

Such a normal life changed completely when Yoko's self-harm began. After returning to Nagasaki, he accompanied Yoko at all times to prevent her from self-harming. He even timed his bathroom use for after Yoko fell asleep.

Around this time, Yoko went to a nearby day service at 9 o'clock and Naoto had to do all the laundry, cleaning, shopping, cooking, walking the dog, etc. in 6 hours before she returned at 3 o'clock. Every day, it passed in the blink of an eye. However, this day service did not last for more than a month.

Looking back, Naoto felt that Yoko's nursing care was the most difficult at that time.

Therefore, when the inpatient medical treatment at the Nagasaki hospital started after this, life grew easier for Naoto. When Naoto finished his visit and stepped out of the hospital, he felt sorry for Yoko, but he also felt a sense of liberation. However, on the contrary, that time may have been painful for

Yoko.

Naoto continued to be an unofficial long-term care worker at the hospital for nearly two years, where he had two incidents of heart issues and two cardiac surgeries.

Naoto had a strong goal at this time to get rid of Yoko's intractable disease, and was absorbed in the nursing care.

However, when Yoko's true illness was revealed, her doctor said, "It is impossible to cure completely and I can only do my best to maintain the status quo."

Despite this set back, the long-sought home-care was actualized. But it was nothing like Naoto had expected, and after Yoko fell asleep, he thanked God every day that she had done nothing that day. Perhaps this tension was the driving force behind the continuation of home care.

However, by the time a year passed, he had become accustomed to it, and the problems involved became glaringly apparent. Such a pile of difficult adversities may have triggered Naoto's dormant sense of justice. It was a fight for Yoko's sake, but he also had to care for her and it took more than double the time to do anything.

The side effect that appeared was probably 'long-term care stress'. It was a warning from Naoto's body in the face of the harsh reality of how to overcome these challenges in a world without any help.

【Government office】

When Naoto went to the Miyamae Ward Office for the moving paperwork, the staff member he consulted said, "First, please submit the move-in notification and complete the resident's card registration."

Then, with the new resident card, he went through the address change procedure, such as the social security card, health insurance card, specific medical certificate designated for intractable diseases, disability certificate, and registration of the second generation of the atomic bomb survivors.

However, the reception desks were on different floors, and in some cases, they went back and forth between the floors many times. Each time, his reception number card was drawn at his window, and in the end, he fell into a vicious circle of waiting for a long, long time.

When they were finally completed, he went to the Miyamae police station to change the address on his driver's license. Naoto thought he could return home soon, but it took more than half a day to complete the procedure.

Naoto wanted to propose to the Miyamae Ward Office as a Kawasaki citizen. He wanted to establish a new window that gave priority to vulnerable people, such as home caregivers and the physically handicapped, so that all procedures could be done at once.

What was even more troublesome was the procedure for

renewing the Certificate of Recipient of Specified Medical Expenses Designated for Intractable Diseases (certificate of income exemption of medical expenses if the intractable disease designated by the government was applicable). Before returning to Kawasaki, Naoto went to Nagasaki City Hall many times to complete this renewal procedure with his doctor's diagnostic questionnaire and salary certificate, and finally completed it. However, he was told in Kawasaki that this renewal procedure was necessary again.

When Naoto asked them why, the staff member replied, "The format of the application form for the specific medical expenses beneficiary certificate designated for intractable diseases differs depending on the local government. Furthermore, the doctor's diagnostic questionnaire must be prepared by the doctor of the hospital or clinic in the area where you apply."

Naoto argued head-on. "The system for designating intractable diseases is based on the Act on Medical Care for Patients with Intractable Diseases, the national policy that the national government is implementing to reduce the cost burden on patients and their families? Isn't it inflexible between local governments? Isn't it strange that the procedures cannot be unified? Why do you impose such a burden on the vulnerable people? Why can't a local government, who is familiar with the business and problems in contact with them, appeal to the national government to change this procedure, saying, 'This procedure should be unified nationwide promptly'?"

The official replied, "This is the procedure that has been used in the past and cannot be changed."

Next, Naoto applied to the Miyamae Ward Office to subsidize the installation cost so he could install an elevator at the entrance of his house immediately after moving. During this procedure, all six parties involved, including the person at the counter of the government office, the investigator of the application content, the manufacturer of the equipment, the mediator of the long-term care and welfare equipment, and the applicant, completed the procedure. A government official told him that everyone had to get together at least three times to complete.

As a result, it took time to adjust the schedule, and it took half a year from the application to the approval. By the time this application was approved, the coronavirus infection had spread, and they couldn't go out in the first place, so with the elevator installed, it had only been used once so far.

Even more mysterious was the exemption system established for the purpose of reducing the financial burden on persons with disabilities.

First, there was a reduction or exemption system for "water charges". This was a system that partially exempts individual water charges such as those with physical disabilities, but it has little effect on those who were bedridden or had first-class living vulnerabilities, such as Yoko.

Because it was the basic charge and its consumption tax were exempted, the basic charge was only 16 cubic meters (1420 yen) in two months.

The average two-month water charge for a family of four was 4000-500 yen. In households with bedridden, disabled people, the amount of tap water used for visiting bathing and aspiration was large, and it cost 10,000 yen or more on average in two months. It would be more effective to reduce the royalties by half than that.

Next was the NHM consultation fee reduction and exemption system. When they returned to Kawasaki for the first time in two years, a staff member who was entrusted by NHM said on the intercom, "Please sign up for the TV consultation fee."

Naoto told the staff, "We don't have a TV, we care for the first-class family of disabled people at home, and the disabled people should be exempt from the consultation fee."

The staff member argued, "Do you really not have a TV? Can I go inside and check?"

"It won't be that much. Will the disabled be fully exempt?"

"That's right, but it requires an application for exemption. You have to pay the consultation fee until the approval is given."

"I was helping my wife, so I can't just drop that."

"Well this is my job too."

"OK, just please wait until I'm finished with the aspirator. But when you see that there's no TV, I expect an apology."

"You can watch TV on your phone now," the employee explained wearily, "even if you don't have a physical TV."

"And I'm telling you I've never used my phone for that. I don't have time in my day to watch TV."

After all, when he went to the entrance, the staff was gone. Naoto couldn't get rid of his frustration for the rest of the day.


When Naoto went to the office, he was often stunned by how many staff members there were. There were times when there were more staff in the office than people in the waiting room.

Shouldn't the government office think more efficiently about its personnel? The salaries and bonuses paid to employees came from the taxes of the local residents.


【Pharmacy】

Naoto had Yoko's medicine prescribed by a visiting doctor every month, taking the prescription to the pharmacy in front of the station, and having it delivered to his home a few days later. This was because there were seven boxes and 140 packs of Lacol, a nutritional supplement, which was too much to be carried by one person on foot.

However, one day he gave a prescription to reception, the employee asked, "Does she have a long-term care insurance policy?"

Naoto had never been asked for a long-term care insurance certificate at a pharmacy. "Sorry, I always bring my medical insurance card," he listed off, "health insurance card, intractable disease designation management card, disability certificate, disability insurance card, medicine certificate, etc. together, but I've never brought my long-term care insurance card. It's somewhere…"

"I need the long-term care insurance certificate. Please bring it next time," she repeated in a monotone.

Naoto became more and more angry, and spat out, "Why do you need a long-term care insurance certificate?"

She dodged the question. "Please bring it properly next time."

"I'm not bringing anything until you answer my question! What's the purpose?"

In the end, she didn't reveal why she needed a long-term care insurance certificate. Naoto thought that it was probably to confirm that the degree of long-term care had not changed, but the patient with bedridden long-term care 5 who was designated as an intractable disease. Everyone should know whether or not the level of long-term care would increase.

One day he asked the pharmacy manager about the side effects of the medicine. "My wife has been taking medicines for Parkinson's disease and dementia for four years, but the doctor in charge of the hospital in Nagasaki told me there's no medicine specifically for progressive supranuclear palsy. I've been advised to try these, since there were cases where it has improved by taking a combination. However, my wife doesn't seem to have any particular improvement with this drug. Also, I've been taking cilostazol as a preventive drug for bradycardia, but recently I've had tachycardia (arrhythmia that makes the pulse faster), so I think it is better to stop this drug. If I continue to take the same medicine for four years, I'm more worried about the side effects caused by it, so I'd like to reduce or discontinue the amount of the medicine. What is your expert opinion?"

"I'll talk with the visiting doctor," but there hadn't been an answer for over a month.

Naoto asked the same question to Dr. Obayashi, who visited the clinic, and Obayashi replied, "The medicine your wife is taking is certainly a treatment for Parkinson's disease, but progressive supranuclear palsy has the same symptoms as Parkinson's disease, so I think these medicines are necessary. It's a medicine that supplements the dopamine that you are doing, so you don't have to worry about side effects."

Naoto remembered what the doctor said at a hospital in Nagasaki and tried to tell Obayashi. "I was told at a hospital in Nagasaki, 'There is no medicine for progressive supranuclear palsy so far', and I asked, 'Then, does it mean that there is no effect if I stop all the medicines?'" And the doctor said that's one of the options. Which advice should I follow?"

In the end, Obayashi couldn't tell him which was correct, "If you want to stop the drug, you can stop it while gradually reducing the amount. It is up to you to decide."

How could doctors in the same neurology department have such different opinions?

【Home-visit nursing and rehabilitation】

In home-visit nursing and home-visit rehabilitation, when there was a change in time, troubles often occurred due to the fact that the changed time was not thoroughly enforced. If you hadn't been notified of the change in advance and the appointment time was delayed by more than an hour, it would domino into further problems.

Furthermore, in cases where it was necessary to change the schedule due to the circumstances of the other party, irresponsible responses, such as putting it all on the home caregiver, was never allowed.

In addition, there were some businesses that couldn't contact the person in charge directly due to problems with personal information and had to go through the reception desk of the office. So it sometimes took extra time to communicate. Often troubles occurred because of this. A company whose boss had a cell phone but didn't allow the person in charge to have a cell phone cannot survive the corporate competition that requires speed in the future.

Furthermore, in all long-term care services named home-visit, such as home-visit care, home-visit rehabilitation, home-visit medical care, and home-visit-bathing, the mysterious commonality was the 'first question' when visiting patients.

The first question was always, "Were there any changes for your wife in the past week?"

This would be a very convenient and meaningful question for long-term care service providers, but how often would patients and their families answer 'there was a change' when asked? Almost all the answers would be 'No, there was no particular change'.

Naoto thought that every time he received this question, they should ask more specifically about the symptoms. For example, 'Are you sleeping well lately?', 'Do you have a daily routine?', 'What has your phlegm output been like these days?'.

When asked specifically like this, patients and their families would probably give more accurate answers. Doctors, nurses and specialists needed to think a little more from the standpoint of patients and their families.

【Visiting Medical Care】

On August 6, 2021 Naoto had to renew the 'Specified Medical Expenses Recipient Certificate' designated for anyone with an intractable diseases. The deadline was at the end of September. He asked Dr. Obayashi for a 'diagnosis questionnaire'.

But Dr. Obayashi said, 'The name of her disease needs to be changed from 'Parkinson's Disease' to 'Parkinson's Syndrome', and you'll need to reapply."

Naoto was surprised and remembered telling Obayashi the same thing before. "Please wait a moment. As I said before, as a result of a detailed examination at the Tozai Hospital in Nagasaki, the name of my wife's disease changed to 'progressive supranuclear palsy'. However, at that time, I asked her doctor, Dr. Asai, if it was necessary to change the name of the disease when I was applying. The doctor who diagnosed 'progressive supranuclear palsy' said that it wasn't necessary to change the disease name in the intractable disease designation application, so isn't it fine?"

Obayashi also seemed to have a strong sense of justice as a doctor, and argued against Naoto. "If you leave this as it is, the statistical data of patients designated by the Ministry of Health, Labor and Welfare will be incorrect. For me, changing to the correct disease name is the correct decision as the doctor in charge."

"I see, I can appreciate your moral obligation as a doctor. Then, at the next renewal procedure, I will apply with the correct disease name. However, there is only one condition. Promise that the change will not incur any costs or administrative burden on us and won't delay the renewal process. Then I accept the change."

Obayashi was in a dilemma. If the name of the disease was changed, a new detailed examination would be required, and a certain amount of cost would be incurred. Since it will be treated as a new disease, it would take time for the examination, and it was expected that the renewal procedure would be delayed.

"Doctor, we live on the edge of life and death every day," Naoto continued. "So I don't want you to increase our burden anymore just to make the country's stats correct. I think that there are currently hundreds of thousands of patients applying for Parkinson's disease under the correct name, but probably there are quite a few patients with Parkinson's syndrome like my wife. Correcting us alone will not make the statistical data more reliable. If you really want to make the statistical data accurate, shouldn't the Ministry of Health, Labor and Welfare take the lead in treating a large-scale re-examination mechanism and making a fundamental review?"

Finally, Obayashi seemed to have given up. "Okay. Let's

continue the renewal procedure under 'Parkinson's disease'."

Naoto asked one more question. "I heard that Yoko will be vaccinated to prevent coronavirus infection, but can I also be vaccinated here as a home caregiver?"

"I'm afraid not, it's limited to only patients who are eligible for home visits."

"I thought this vaccination was available for all elderly people over the age of 65. I'm not convinced that it is limited to those who are eligible for home-visit medical care. I'm taking care of my wife at home for 24 hours. Of course, it's a good idea to think of them as one. At the time of influenza vaccination last year, Kawasaki citizens were originally free, but they were charged because the teacher's clinic is located in Yokohama. This is also a strange story, isn't it? Kawasaki City bears all the costs of influenza vaccination for Kawasaki citizens, right? If so, wouldn't it be a good idea for this clinic to charge Kawasaki City for vaccination costs for Kawasaki citizens? Kawasaki citizens could get vaccinated for free."

Obayashi nodded and did not argue against it.

# Chapter 5  Socially Disadvantaged People

It had become an even more difficult world for 'socially vulnerable people' (people with social disadvantages, such as the elderly and disabled people).

On August 23, 2021, around five in the afternoon, after the visiting-bath staff finished as usual, the three staff members washed their hands in the washroom on the second floor.

Naoto waved them off at the front door, then went to handle Yoko's gastrostomy, finishing their routine around 6 in the evening.

Brushing his teeth, he noticed that the washbasin wasn't draining at all. The drain was packed with pieces of cement. Naoto had used the shower that morning, so it must have happened between then and now

Naoto picked out a dozen pieces of cement and asked a plumber to check on it.

The specialist claimed, "It's odd that such a piece of cement would come out of the pipe leading to the drain. Perhaps this piece of cement was washed away from somewhere else. Who was the last person to use this washroom? Check with them."

The next day, the manager came to his home and reported, "I checked with my three staff members, but they didn't remember anything. I believe them. I've been working with them for a long time."

Naoto argued, "Any boss would trust his subordinates. I did, too. That said, the bathroom drain had cement in it. When I asked a plumber, they said it hadn't come out of the water pipe. Could you ask them again?"

The manager looked at Naoto like he was out of his mind. "The answer is the same no matter how many times I check. I can't forgive this kind of suspicion."

That night, Naoto regretted that he had come on too strongly to the administrator, and apologized to him by email. Naoto was afraid that if the investigation was prolonged, Yoko's long-term care service would be affected. However, despite Naoto's apology, the manager listened to the opinions of all the staff and told him they were canceling their service.

While looking for a replacement service, on the morning of August 31st, an email came from the administrator. "There are no plans for the visit-bathing service after today. Yesterday was the last visit-bathing service. This was decided after hearing the opinions of all the staff. I will bring the cancellation application documents at a later date."

Naoto couldn't control his anger at last.

Naoto was not afraid to submit this cancellation request

document, but before that he did, he demanded that the manager's boss explain how they could pick and choose their customers.

A few days later, the manager in charge of the branch office contacted him on September 13, "The head office will handle this matter from here."

After waiting for more than two months, there was no contact from the head office. Naoto's anger did not subside. He would have to fight using the law.

Naoto hurriedly created two petitions, asking to crack down on the illegal activities of this office. One was addressed to Mayor Kawasaki and the other to the Minister of Health, Labor and Welfare.

However, as expected, he never got a reply, so he called for confirmation. First, the city officials who answered the phone avoided their responsibilities as usual. "Mr. Yamamoto, this is a place to guide home-visit care providers, not a place to arbitrate troubles between users and businesses."

Naoto quickly responded, "Then I would like to ask you, but Article 21 of the contract for visiting-bathing has a provision that it is an intermediary of a third-party organization, and the administrative authorities must mediate it. As you said, the government office is in charge of instructing the business operator and is not in a position to arbitrate the trouble. If so, shouldn't we instruct the person in charge to clearly include the phrase 'the government office is not involved in the trouble between the user and the business operator' in the usage contract created by the business operator?"

The employee stammered. "Anyway, please discuss the minor troubles related to visiting bathing with the people concerned."

Minor trouble? "How is this considered minor trouble? For vulnerable people, this is a matter of life or death. Did you read the petition I submitted? If so, you should know what you are complaining about. I am pointing out that the notice of unilateral cancellation of the usage contract due to the convenience of the business operator is "Designated Visiting Bathing Care Business" in Article 9 of the Ministry of Health and Welfare Ordinance No. 37. Persons must not refuse to provide designated home-visit-bathing care without good reason. "I have pointed out the problem of breach of law that may be in breach of the law. Isn't it the original job to crack down on violations?"

The person on the other line was silent before Naoto hung up in anger.


He then called a MHLW representative, but the staff member who answered the phone said, "Currently, we are working remotely due to the coronavirus, and the person in charge is not at work today, so please call back at a later date."

"Can't you contact the person in charge? I'll call them, so please tell me their phone number."

"The phone number of the person in charge is personal information, so I can't tell you. The person in charge will be at work the day after tomorrow, so I ask you to call back."

Naoto couldn't help refuting this excuse. "I submitted a petition to the Minister of Health, Labor and Welfare the other day. Two weeks have passed since then, but I haven't heard from him, so I'm calling for confirmation. Will work from home instead of going to the office as a corona infection prevention measure. If so, put in a system to transfer to the person in charge's home or you can talk on behalf of the person in charge. Shouldn't we ask? Who are the civil servants working for?"

Naoto was amazed at the fact that this office was using the pandemic as an excuse. As usual, the constitution of the government office did not improve at all.


However, it didn't end there. Later, when he contacted the person in charge to confirm the petition, the person in charge gave another useless reply. "The contact point for the petition is not the Administrative Counseling Room, General Affairs Division, Minister of Health, Labor and Welfare, but the Complaint Counseling Room, General Affairs Division, Health and Welfare Bureau, Ministry of Health, Labor and Welfare."

Even so, maybe Naoto's protest against the city hall was successful, and a few days later, the manager in charge of the branch office of the visiting bathing service contacted him for the first time in three months, saying, "I want to have a meeting."

On January 22nd, 2021, the branch managers, section managers, business managers, managers, care managers, and community-based comprehensive support for the branch offices that have jurisdiction over the business establishments gathered at Naoto's home.

After three months of silence, the branch manager started talking normally as if nothing had happened. "I received a report from the person in charge of the business office that Mr. Yamamoto wanted to cancel our visit-bathing due to trouble with the staff, and instructed him to accept the cancellation request. It was said that the cancellation was unilaterally notified from here. I recognized that this was just a cancellation request from the user's family."

"Branch manager, you're claiming you're not doing anything wrong. So why did you just have to keep me waiting for three months? Isn't it stated in the usage contract that we will respond promptly to complaints from the user side? In other words, because we violated the law of unilateral cancellation notice, we could not explain it. Haven't you been a month late? If so, your first voice today should start with an apology. In the first place, branch manager, did you forget that the job of visiting bathing service is a long-term care business? Did you forget that the target users are not 'healthy people' but rather 'disabled people'? My wife has an incurable illness and is a first-class disabled person who has been bedridden for more than five years. You have unilaterally notified that you cannot provide a home-visit-bathing service from today, but do you think it is as good as abusive behavior against the physically challenged?"

The branch manager suddenly bowed to Naoto and apologized, perhaps because he had finally regained his decency as a human being. "Sir, I'm really sorry that I postponed the response for three months due to this situation."

"Now you know that your job isn't aimed at customers such as the average consumer, but at bedridden disabled people. I know. My parents have taught me since I was little that a person needs to apologize when they make a mistake. It took me three months, but he apologized properly. I appreciate that. I regretted and apologized that day when I wondered if I had overpowered the administrator to investigate when the washbasin trouble that started this problem occurred."

However, the manager and manager of the business office did not try to apologize silently even though the branch manager apologized in front of him. So Naoto realized something was wrong with it and asked them a question. "You look like you haven't done anything wrong yet, but the one-sided cancellation notice says that you can't do it from today, even though you've been providing a home-visit-bathing service until yesterday. Do you say no?"

This time, they both looked like they had argued something, but they remained silent. At that time, the person in charge of the Regional Comprehensive Center made an unexpected statement that was completely different from the previous issues. "If such a problem occurs, the care manager in charge will listen carefully to both parties and enter into arbitration. How did the care manager respond this time?"

"I was surprised at the response of the business operator when I heard the situation from my husband. After that, I urged the manager of the business office to talk with my husband many times."

Naoto did not overlook the care manager's remarks that the manager and manager of the establishment had a suspicious look. Naoto gradually began to see the cause of the trouble.

Naoto managed to get the manager and his boss to tell the truth. "The one-sided cancellation notification email sent by the administrator to me is, of course, a response with the consent of the person in charge, that is, the person in charge gave the final go-ahead, right?"

The person in charge finally opened his mouth. "Because

I heard from the care manager that Mr. Yamamoto will ask the next alternative company to do it, I understood that I would send an email." Finally, the truth became clear.

Naoto once said from the manager, "All interactions with the user regarding visiting bathing are reported to the care manager and with her consent. If the care manager glares at us, we will not be able to work. I remember hearing that. Then, I found out why the trusted and honest administrator was able to send a one-sided cancellation notification email to Naoto. The care manager was effectively giving a go-ahead. However, it is true that Naoto made a fuss and the manager closed his mouth with the care manager. In the end, they all hid the truth, even though they knew the cause of the trouble. If I apologized immediately at that point, I wouldn't have been so confused. Humans are creatures that make mistakes. That's why you should apologize immediately if you find that you're wrong. However, not all three were ill-intentioned. For Yoko, she may have tried to solve it as comfortably as possible. Naoto wanted to believe that.

Meanwhile, he received a phone call from Nurse Motoyama. "Mr. Yamamoto, in fact, my husband has been transferred to Shizuoka, and the whole family has moved to Shizuoka. Thank you very much for your help for the past two years."

"Well, is that so? Congratulations on your husband's prosperity. It is very disappointing and lonely for me that Mr. Motoyama will no longer be able to come to home-visit nursing. I will continue to work in home-visit nursing in Shizuoka. You can do it. Please do your best there as well." Naoto told Motoyama about the series of troubles in this home-visit-bathing care, and he received this advice from Motoyama:

"Mr. Yamamoto has already overtaken our nursing level in less than two years. It's the same situation in rehabilitation. Perhaps he knows his wife better than the visiting doctor. I wonder if you're here. From Mr. Yamamoto's point of view, I think everyone's poor and bad points can't be helped. You probably came to the company in the same way. However, I think that the line of sight that Mr. Yamamoto considers to pass is extremely high for ordinary people. From now on, I think it's better to lower your eyes a little more and live slowly. This shouldn't be something that a third party like me, other than his wife, should say"

Naoto took his hat off to Motoyama's insight. That's exactly because Naoto had just guessed that he had to reflect on him lately.

After all, she may really be the reincarnation of his younger sister, Yuko, just as Naoto thought.

# Epilogue Volunteering

Naoto thought about volunteering to help with the long-term stress from his home-care tasks.

He asked Yoko, "I want to start volunteering, where should I start?"

Yoko slowly opened her closed eyes and blinked twice, "Jesus."

"Will you be OK on your own while I'm volunteering?"

Yoko, who couldn't speak, took her right hand out of the blanket and gave a thumbs-up.

Naoto applied to volunteer the next day. The female employee who answered the phone responded, "Currently, we're not accepting volunteer activities due to the spread of coronavirus infection. We are sorry, please apply again later. Oh, wait a moment. There is one volunteer activity we are looking for. It's for children in need of financial support with single-mother families. The volunteer would help them study, play with them, and watch over the kids until the moms return from work."

It was called 'Asunaro child support'.

Asunaro was an evergreen tree of the Cupressaceae family, which was smaller than a cypress, but also stood as a metaphor for children growing bigger each day. Naoto participated there every Tuesday and Thursday from 4 to 7 o'clock.

In fact, about 15 years ago, Yoko was registered as a volunteer to take care of foreign students from all over the world at the Kawasaki International Center. Yoko has a sociable personality and makes friends with anyone immediately, so this volunteer was perfect for her.

They first took in three German working international students–Weinstein, Schultz, and Becker. All three young men worked for a well-known German company, and were scheduled to stay overnight at their home on the last day of the factory tour.

Yoko seemed to have a pretty good impression of those three young people, and every year she wanted the person in charge of the exchange center to accept the participants from this same German organization. Naoto was in charge of preparing the Japanese food and liquor, but they always quickly ran out.

At night, Yoko took an international student to a nearby Bon Odori festival. She prepared a 'jinbei', a type of kimono for men, and she gave them as a gift.

"Is this a traditional Japanese kimono?" He asked Yoko.

Yoko tells them, "Yes…" However, she couldn't explain the details.

Naoto had taken German in college, and she managed to explain the difference.

Naoto had the impression that Yoko was happiest when sharing her culture and hosting interesting people. After that, the next international student was Nick, an Australian high school student that towered over them. Nick wanted to be a pilot in the future. He was a big eater, and on his way home from the Japanese language school in Takadanobaba, he would always stop at KFC on the way home, but still be hungry for dinner.

Yoko accepted international students from various countries, such as the United States, France, Canada, Italy, Greece, Spain, Portugal, Lithuania, Hong Kong, China, South Korea, Thailand and Indonesia. They always thanked Yoko for various foods and local specialties.

Naoto had confided with Yoko about his retirement plans, "When we retire, let's travel around the world together and visit the countries of every international student who came to our house."

Yoko was very much looking forward to it, but this plan was never realized in any country.


Naoto started his volunteering that August, in Musashi Kosugi, where he used to live.

There were 17 children in total, most of them in the 5th

and 6th grade. Naoto always arrived at 3:30 in the afternoon and helped with the prep work at the meeting place. Then he taught homework and drill problems, played dodgeball and soccer together in a nearby park, played cards and games together, and finally the mothers came to pick them up.

However, there were some children whose mothers could not come pick them up for various reasons, and those children were sent home by car after 7 o'clock by the staff.

The children were all honest and brighter than he expected. At first, he had a hard time remembering their names. But after a month, he gradually learned their various personalities, and came up with an idea. The meals they bought for the kids were never very delicious. So, Naoto decided to make and bring curry rice, to show off his cooking skills that started after Yoko developed dysgeusia.

"Mr. Yamamoto, do you have a license as a cook? With COVID-19 restrictions, we have to be very careful about what we give the children. I'm sorry, but I don't think we can serve this."

"There are many mothers who volunteer to provide rice balls, etc., as well as volunteers who prepare meals in the event of an emergency. Do you ask those volunteers if they have a license as a cook? Coronavirus doesn't adhere to foods, does it? If that happened, all the restaurants and cafeterias that are open only for takeout would be closed."

He was outvoted at that time. However, when he brought food for just the staff at another date, they complimented it and asked for his recipe.

Naoto was forbidden to bring in curry, so he secretly thought about delivering some to the children and their families on Sundays, so he asked a child where they lived.

The child, who had been having fun talking with Naoto until then, suddenly became silent. For the first time, Naoto realized that these children might not have the best home situations.

Another day, he noticed one child yawning a lot, and asked when they went to bed.

"I went to bed at 9 and woke up at 5," said the child.

"That's pretty early!"

"Mom goes to bed late and wakes up even earlier than me in the morning."

"That's hard, since she has to cook everyone's meals."

"Mom doesn't always cook breakfast. Sometimes I just have bread."

Naoto regretted having pried into the child's home life. Another time when one of his students was refusing to do his math homework, a staff member called Naoto aside. He wondered what was going on and headed to another room with her.

"Mr. Yamamoto, it's best not to force the children too much, because they're from single-parent families, they're not always up to speed."

Naoto argued before he could stop himself. "Isn't that just your prejudice?"

"You're a new volunteer, so trust our experience."

Naoto wanted to help these children gain confidence now, or else they might be bullied when they were older.

One day, a boy named Kurt, who seemed to be in junior high school, came to their club.

"Hello," Naoto called out. "Did you used to come here? What grade are you in now?"

"I used to go here since I was in third grade, and now I'm in the ninth grade."

Kurt was suddenly surrounded by the younger students, all clambering for his attention. He had two younger siblings there and did his homework with them.

"If there's anything you don't understand, I'll teach you so come and listen," Naoto told him.

"Thank you." Kurt bowed politely.

Eventually, Naoto asked the boy what he wanted to be when he grew up. Kurt's answer surprised him.

"It doesn't matter what kind of profession really, but I want to get a job that earns a lot of money. I want to take care of my mom when I'm older."

Naoto felt a sense of relief–if all of these students could grow up like Kurt, he had nothing to worry about.

Naoto had previously thought that his life would be dedicated to Yoko, children with incurable diseases, and the orphans left behind from a parent's early death. This didn't mean just donating money. He wanted to provide his own efforts.

By helping the children of Kawasaki City, where Naoto and Yoko had spent half of their lives together, made Naoto's sense of mission even stronger. He felt as if he was directly affecting the future of his home.

# Part 4
# Family Volume
## (Familial Bonds)

# Prologue  Mysterious Events

**\<Getting His Name\>**

He was born on February 10, 1953, and three days later, he was named 'Naoto'.

Naoto's father was descended from Ryutsuki, the creator of fortune-telling in Omuta, Fukuoka. "When a boy is born, think of five names you want and write them down. Offer them to your at-home shrine for a day, then cut off each of the five names, fold them into small pieces, and put them in a bowl. Shake the bowl five times and keep the name that appears most often."

His father did exactly that and had his mother shake the bowl. 'Naoto' came out the first two times. "If you shake it again and Naoto appears, that'll be it."

His mother hoped it would. And it did. She was elated, but asked for his father to try shaking it as well. Both times, 'Naoto' came out.

Naoto heard this story from his mother when he was in his second year of junior high school, and calculated the probability that 'Naoto' would have come out.

"The probability that the one with Naoto appears five times out of five, out of five pieces of paper, is nearly impossible," teenage Naoto told his mother.

"But that's the reality. After all, you may have been named Naoto from the beginning."

**\<Lost Child\>**

Naoto seemed to be able to walk less than a year after he was born.

His father's foster family, the Yamamoto, was wealthy and once ran the famous restaurant 'Kagetsu' in Nagasaki–the one where Ryoma Sakamoto had gotten drunk and left a mark on a pillar with his sword. One day, my father had asked his foster mother to watch Naoto while he went to the hairdresser.

The haircut took him about an hour, but when he left the hairdresser, his father swore he heard baby Naoto's voice say, "Dah-dah." He whipped around and Naoto was standing alone there. His father assumed his mother had brought Naoto here, but she was nowhere to be seen. So he took Naoto to Maruyama Park and let him play for about an hour before returning home.

"Oh, did you bring Naoto to the Maruyamas' house?" His grandfather asked.

"Dad, what are you talking about? I thought Mom had him!"

When they asked his grandmother, she hadn't taken Naoto either–the toddler might have walked to the Maruyama's parents' house alone.

However, my father had some doubts. The distance from the barber shop to theirs was more than a kilometer, and it took about 15 minutes for adults and 30 minutes for children. Plus, the road was filled with bikes and cars. However, Naoto must have chased his father, 'Dad-dah', all the way there.

### <Penmanship Class>

Naoto's mother had her children learn calligraphy. Naoto was about five years old when his two older sisters were elementary school students. Both of them went to a penmanship class from 4 to 6 o'clock every Monday, Wednesday, and Friday.

One day, Sachiko took Naoto to the penmanship class with her. He was so happy that he ran around the classroom in circles. Mr. Tateishi was a strict teacher and scolded Naoto to be quiet. Naoto immediately shut up and watched his sister write. When she looked away, Naoto grabbed the brush himself. At that time, his sister had written 'blue sky' in calligraphy. If the students' calligraphy passed the teacher's harsh criticism, he would write 'OK' on the bottom corner and those students were able to go home early.

That day, Sachiko couldn't get that 'OK' and was stuck there until the end. So, she tried bringing Naoto's writing to the teacher–it got the 'OK'.

At one point, his mother was called by Professor Tateishi

and asked if Naoto should participate in the upcoming elementary school penmanship competition hosted by the Nagasaki Newspaper.

His mother didn't want Naoto to participate with students much older than him, so the teacher set up a 'kindergarten' category. Naoto received the first prize. His mother thought, 'Naoto must have been a calligrapher in his previous life'. Naoto continued to attend the Tateishi penmanship class for two years. His mother kept five of his Chinese character pieces that she thought were the prettiest: Divine Punishment, Buddhist Paradise, Discipline, Underworld, and Fulfillment.

### <Father's Regrets>

His father worked with his mother every day, from morning till night, to grow their hairdressing business. The number of employees they hired had increased from two to five, and their name was growing.

However, soon his father was involved in a terrible incident.

One day, a friend in the same industry as his father came to ask if he could be a guarantor for a loan he needed. His father of course wanted to help any of his friends in need. However, he kept this a secret from Naoto's mother.

Less than three months after that, his friend went missing. Debt collectors came to the hairdresser frequently to collect the money, so his dad couldn't come to work. The Yamamotos decided to pay off the 3 million yen with their life's savings. He couldn't forgive his friend, and every night after work, he kept a knife in his pocket and walked by his friend's house. One night, he ran into his former friend, and his father attacked the man like a bat out of hell. While chasing his friend, he heard Naoto screaming somewhere in the distance. He dropped the knife and ran back home.

His mother was surprised to see him burst in and said to him, "Naoto was yelling something about 'Dad, stop'. I thought he was sleep-talking so I came out here."

"I heard him from down the street," his father said, stunned.

The next morning, when his mother asked Naoto if he remembered sleep-talking, he shook his head. However, he did have a cut on his face and blood on his futon that had not been there the night prior.

### \<The Landslide\>

When Naoto enrolled in Nagasaki's local Umegasaki Junior High School, he joined the basketball club and practiced every day.

One Sunday when he was heading to school for a practice match, there was a big stone wall just before the school that was under construction. Naoto went to school every day past this big stone wall, but always stepped a little faster past the loose rocks. No one else was on the road since it was so early on the weekend.

However, when he was about to cross the stone wall this time, something terrible happened. Naoto was distracted thinking about various strategies for today's game, but someone stopped him, crying out, "Naoto, Naoto!"

Naoto stopped and looked back, but there was no one behind him. There was a strange smell, and the cliff collapsed, sending big rocks everywhere

Naoto jumped back in surprise. The rocks had missed him by only a hair. If he hadn't stopped, he would have been under the rubble.

Who had called him? The voice had been so faint. Several police officers rushed up and one of them asked Naoto, "Are you alright? Was anyone walking in front of you? Were there any cars under the cliff?"

Naoto managed to remember something in front of him when he was walking. No one had been walking in front of Naoto, but he felt like there had been a car stopped. Naoto closed his eyes and tried to remember what happened at that time–two people in a car, one was a child. Naoto told the police officer in a hurry.

The police officer arranged the emergency vehicles, and the removal of the large falling rocks began. As Naoto had said, a car was discovered, and there was a parent and child in it, and both were rescued. Naoto learned from the news that evening that the rescued parent and child were fortunately only slightly injured, nothing life-threatening.

That night, he still wondered who was calling out to him from behind.

But that night, Naoto dreamed of Tsuki, his father's birth-mother, whom he had only met once. Tsuki laughed and said to him, "Naoto, what are you in such a hurry? Your life is yet to come. You don't have to hurry so much."

### \<Neighborhood Events\>

The president and his wife of a precision machinery company in Ota Ward lived across the street from Yoko and Naoto. Yoko was on good terms with the president, but one day smoke was pouring out of the neighbor's bathroom window. At that time, Aki, their golden retriever, put her paws up on the glass and started howling. Yoko stopped what she was doing to look out the window, and immediately called '119'. Three fire engines rushed in, and the fire was immediately extinguished– the president and his wife were rescued safely.

Aki was commended by the Miyamae Fire Department. Because of this, the president and his wife became close friends with the Yamamotos. Since they were already in their 90s, soon after that, they decided to move into a luxury nursing home in

Tamaplaza. Right after, the wife died and the president was left alone. Yoko was worried about the man all alone, so she often visited the nursing home with her favorite sake as a souvenir.

His broken heart might have been too much for him, because two months later, he died and followed his wife to heaven. A few days later, in the middle of the night, Naoto dreamed of the president and his wife returning home and waving up at him from their balcony. Naoto woke up with a jolt and ran to the window, but no one was there.

Yoko said every time she visited the president, he said he wanted to go home with his wife, where he had lived for many years.

One month later, the old woman next to the president's house died. She lived with her disabled daughter, who always took out the trash in the morning and greeted Yoko. Now, the daughter was left behind.

One night, when Naoto took Aki for a walk, she barked at something in front of the old lady's house. Naoto also felt something strange at that time. But he saw nothing. After he entered the house, he peeked out at the house and saw the old woman who should have been dead in the garden beckoning him.

The next morning he told Yoko about this, and Yoko said, "I haven't seen the girl across the street lately."

Naoto told the situation at the nearby police box and asked

if he could look inside the house, but they refused. However, even one week after that, the daughter still did not show up. He went to the police box again, and they finally went. They found the daughter was barely breathing in her bedroom. The old lady must have been beckoning to inform Naoto of her daughter's illness. He hoped her daughter was still alive, she must have been the same age as Yoko.

# Chapter 1  A Mother-in-law's Promise

Yoko used to have to use the aspirator five or six times a day, often in the middle of the night, but nowadays it was typically only once before bed. Naoto no longer had to wake up in the middle of the night and could sleep soundly until about five in the morning. Perhaps this peaceful sleep triggered Naoto's newly frequent dreams of his parents. Not only them, but Yoko's parents as well.

Naoto's mother, Aiko, died at the age of 94 on October 5, 2018 in Kawasaki. At that time, Naoto was in the middle of taking Yoko back to Nagasaki, so their eldest daughter, Kumi, who lived in Yokohama, went to Tamaplaza's nursing home every week in Naoto's stead. On the day Aiko died, Kumi called him and could barely say anything. He went to Kawasaki that very afternoon and the next day had his mother cremated.

Naoto took her remains back to Nagasaki and laid them at the Yamamotos' grave, next to his father in Kawakami Machi, a short walk from their apartment. Naoto's father had died on May 25, 2004, waiting nearly fifteen years for his wife to join him in heaven.

Naoto took a copy of his mother's death certificate to

the Miyamae Ward Office, and saw a detailed record of his mother's birth for the first time. His mother was born on September 1, 1924, as the eldest daughter of her father, Sueki Takeshita, and her mother, Yoshinoe, in Kumamoto Prefecture. She was also the adopted daughter of his maternal grandfather, Dohei Matsumoto, and his grandmother, Tatsu Matsumoto.

When Naoto was little, he had heard about his spirited grandmother from his mother many times. Grandma Tatsu had a chronic valvular heart disease that Naoto likely inherited.

Naoto's father, Masao, was born on March 1, 1915, the second son of his father, Ryuichi, and his birth-mother, Tsuki, in Fukuoka Prefecture. The following year, on May 9, 1916, he was adopted at one year old by a man who ran a geisha house in Maruyama, Nagasaki. The Yamamoto family was wealthy and once ran the famous restaurant 'Kagetsu' in Nagasaki–the one where Ryoma Sakamoto had gotten drunk and left a mark on a pillar with his sword.

Meanwhile, Yoko's mother, Suma Yamashita, died at the Showakai Hospital near her home on December 7, 2019, at the age of 95. Suma was born on October 13, 1924 as the fourth daughter of her father, Toraichi Hayashida, and mother, Fuku, in Nagasaki Prefecture. She was the adopted daughter of her foster mother.

Yoko's father, Makoto Hanzawa, was born on June 30, 1924, as the third son of his father, Masaharu Hanzawa, and his mother, Masa, in Miyagi Prefecture. He was adopted by the Yamashita family on February 17th, 1947. Makoto died on April 1, 2004 at the age of 79.

Naoto saw her parents' birth and death certificates and found it strange. First of all, all four were born in different prefectures. Naoto's father in Fukuoka, his mother in Kumamoto, Yoko's mother in Nagasaki, and his father in Miyagi prefecture. Also, all four were adopted by other families. Was adoption a normal practice at that time? Furthermore both of their fathers had died in 2004 and both of their mothers around 2019. Naoto's father was 89 years old and his mother was 94 years old. Yoko's father died at the age of 79, and her mother at the age of 95. It could be said that all of them lived out their natural lifespans.

Finally, they each had four children: one son and three daughters.

Of these, Naoto's younger sister, Yuko, and Yoko's older sister, Kumi, both died at a young age. It was a series of odd coincidences. The truly strange thing was that these similarities happened not only in their parents' generation, but also for each of their four children.

Naoto's birthday and Yoko's sister Kumi's birthday were both February 10. Naoto had suggested the name 'Kumi' for their eldest daughter, even though he had never heard of Yoko's dead sister with the same name.

Yoko's older sister Kumi's death date was September 17th, the same as Naoto's younger sister, Yuko's death anniversary. Past lives, present lives, and the afterlife–were they all connected by the red thread of fate?

Yoko's mother, Suma, seemed to have the most spectacular and turbulent life of all of them. She was born as the fourth daughter of the Hayashida family, but was adopted by the Yamashita family next door when she was two years old. The Yamashita family was wealthy, but never blessed with children. Suma took over the Yamashitas' dressmaking classes after she graduated from Nagasaki Prefectural High School for Girls. Later, Suma welcomed Makoto Hanzawa as her first son-in-law, though it appeared to be a 'shotgun wedding'.

Suma was in Suwa-cho near the atomic bomb's hypocenter when in dropped on Nagasaki on August 9, 1945. Luckily, she had been on a tram at the time and wasn't hit directly by the blast–this saved her life.

However, her eldest daughter, Kumi, who was born a year and a half after the bomb, died at the young age of 24 because of one of the after effects of the nuclear bombs, hydrocephalus. Kayo, her second daughter, was born on November 29, 1948, the year after Kumi. Yoko was born as the third daughter on August 31, 1952, four years later. Finally, three years later, on May 13, 1955, the eldest son was born.

Suma's husband, Makoto Hanzawa, came to Nagasaki after graduating from the veterinary school of Tohoku University and got a job at the Nagasaki Prefectural Government. Yet, he fell into an affair with a woman at work and lived separately from Suma for nearly 40 years until her death. During that time, she raised four children by herself.

Kumi, the eldest daughter, was hospitalized for a long time in a psychiatric hospital after the age of 20. Suma continued her dressmaking class all while taking care of her Kumi, and her other three children.

However, life wore Suma down and she attempted suicide twice. Yoko could see her mother's anguish even from a young age, and always stayed close to her side.

Her first child, Kumi, passed away at the early age of 24. Both Kayo and Yoko went on to work at hospitals, while her youngest child and only son, Yu, became a dental technician in Tokyo.

At that time, Yu often came to visit Naoto at the company housing in Musashi Kosugi. Yoko had been planning to share an apartment with her younger brother, to help around the house. Back then, Naoto was working too many hours to spend quality time with either of them.

Suma seems to have relied on Yoko the most out of her children, and visited their Kawasaki house many times. She of course came to celebrate late into the night when their eldest daughter, Kumi, was born.

Every time Suma came to Kawasaki, she repeatedly said that if Naoto quit his bank job, she would pay his tuition to go to medical school at Nagasaki University–she had always wanted Yoko to be a doctor's wife. For a period of time, Naoto seriously considered the offer when he was frustrated with his job. However, going back to school for nearly ten years with three children was not something he looked forward to.

For Suma, this time in Kawasaki with Yoko and her grandchildren may have been the happiest of her life. By the time she died, she had come to Kawasaki more than 20 times in total, but the last time she came was in April 2014, when Naoto's mother was also visiting.

At this time, there were four people, Naoto, Yoko, Aiko, and Suma, inside the house, so it was always lively. Suma stayed for nearly two months, but sadly after she returned to Nagasaki, the dementia began to set in.

Kayo, the second daughter, had not been blessed with her marriage. Kayo had refused to date a promising employee at Nagasaki Prefectural Government, who her father recommended, simply because he was shorter than her. Instead, she married Ikuo Muto, who worked at the same department store as her. The Muto family was a wealthy family in Fukuoka, and Kayo had hoped that she could become the president's wife of their company one day. However, the Muto family's company went to the wayside due to the subsequent recession.

Ikuo had loved gambling, such as mahjong, pachinko, and racing, since college, and when he got married to Kayo, he already had a large amount of debt. Kayo often snuck out valuables from Suma's house and pawned them off. It seems that Suma knew, and would go to the pawn shop to buy it back each time.

There was also a big quarrel between the sisters. Yoko claimed that Kayo withdrew the money Naoto had sent to Suma. In January 2009, Suma gave Naoto a mission–to find out how much debt Kayo's husband, Ikuo, was actually in. Through Naoto's investigation, he found that Ikuo had a debt of nearly 30,000,000 yen, most of which was at a high interest rate.

Ikuo was barely keeping afloat by getting more and more loans to pay off the ones he already owed. Naoto urged Ikuo to file for bankruptcy since that amount was not repayable, but it seems that he couldn't even do that because most of the debts were from gambling. The previously wealthy man refused to admit how much debt he was truly in.

Eventually, Ikuo was seized from his home by Sasebo City and a financial guarantee company, and his possessions were auctioned off.

Therefore, Kayo relentlessly urged Suma to give her the promised inheritance property to her early, and Suma, who had developed dementia, seemed to have given in to her daughter.

After that, Suma died on December 7, 2019, when her dementia took a turn for the worse. From there, the fierce inheritance battle between her second daughter Kayo and her eldest son began.

Suma once told Naoto when he came to visit her at her facility, "Isn't Kayo pitiful? I heard that all she did with the inheritance money I gave her early was deal with her husband's debts. That money came from my father's survivor's pension, his national pension and the A-bomb survivor's allowance, plus many of my stocks. If there's any more problems after I die, I want you to handle it."

Naoto was entrusted with Suma's will, so he went into arbitration many times to try to reconcile her eldest son and second daughter. However, the gap between them was too deep and it didn't go well.

But he was determined–Naoto owed Suma a great debt for his marriage to Yoko. It started when he was working at the Fukuoka branch and was just a family friend. At that time, Yoko was working at a hospital in Tokyo with a friend of Suma's, but she returned to Nagasaki during the holidays and introduced her family to Saduly–a young man dispatched from

Saudi Arabia to the Nagasaki Shipyard of Marunouchi Heavy Industries.

Yoko told Suma that she was dating him as a potential marriage candidate. Suma asked Naoto what he thought about Saduly, and Naoto said he seemed like a polite, hard worker. Naoto didn't notice at the time how Suma was pushing Yoko to marry Naoto.

About half a year later, Yoko contacted Naoto with a dilemma–Saduly would have to return to Saudi Arabia soon, so if she wanted to marry him, Suma would have to give them her blessing that very weekend. However, Suma was going on a hunger-strike to protest their relationship.

Naoto met Saduly at the coffee shop 'Umino' that Sunday, explained the parent-child quarrel between Yoko and Suma, and tried to gauge how seriously he was thinking about marrying Yoko.

"Mr. Yamamoto, do you know anything about polygamy? In Saudi Arabia, the polygamy system allows a man to have up to four wives. Actually, I already have a fiance in Saudi Arabia, but I also like Yoko."

Naoto asked immediately, "Would Yoko be the first wife or second wife?"

He answered honestly, "Yoko would be my second wife."

"Does Yoko know that?"

"I haven't talked to her about it yet."

Naoto couldn't believe this selfish thought process. "We don't have legal polygamy in Japan. Yoko is Japanese, so naturally polygamy is a new concept for her. The first step would be to explain all this to Yoko."

"Alright, I'll do that."

Saduly and Yoko talked and the marriage was quickly out of the question. Soon after, Saduly had to leave Japan and return to Saudi Arabia alone.

Suma was elated, and advised Yoko to marry Naoto. However, the next marriage proposal came rolling in soon after. This time, Yoko's father brought a promising young man, his subordinate at the Nagasaki Prefectural Office, and they began to date.

However, Suma didn't like that her husband, who was separated from her, was the one to introduce them in the first place. So, there was another hunger-strike.

Three years later, after Naoto had moved to Tokyo, he met Yoko again at the hospital she worked at.

Yoko seemed to have given up on marrying anyone after she was overwhelmed by Suma's opposition. In other words, Suma created an opportunity for Naoto and Yoko to get married. Therefore, Naoto owed Suma big time, and entered into arbitration for the inheritance dispute between Yoko's siblings to try to repay her.

From the time Naoto returned to Kawasaki with Yoko

and started taking care of her at home, her brother-in-law from Nagasaki began calling him for advice almost every night. The relationship between the siblings still hadn't been mended during the year of arguments, so they applied for mediation in September 2020.

"Naoto, yesterday I received an inquiry from the Nagasaki Taxation Office, what should I do?"

Naoto asked him, "Are there any documents from the tax office?"

"I received some documents, but I didn't think I needed to submit them, so I left them alone. Does that have anything to do with this?"

Naoto contemplated the situation–the tax office received reports of withheld taxes on transactions conducted by taxpayers from financial institutions and securities companies, and had a certain degree of understanding of the taxpayer's assets. Therefore, the tax office sent an inheritance tax questionnaire to heirs who are likely to incur inheritance tax in advance. The person in charge at the Nagasaki Tax Office was probably alerted that Yu hadn't answered the questionnaire.

Therefore, Naoto contacted the person in charge at the Nagasaki Taxation Office on his behalf. "Hello, is this the Property Tax Division? My name is Naoto Yamamoto. I'm Yu Yamashita's brother-in-law. He contacted me about the inheritance tax filing the other day. I'd just like to confirm some things."

The person on the other line sighed. "What do you want to check?"

"I heard that my brother-in-law was told by the tax office to file an inheritance tax, but is it really necessary to file an inheritance tax if the inheritance property is within the basic deduction of 48,000,000 yen? The buildings and securities would cost 32,000,000 alone."

"My brother-in-law said that if someone received a gift of more than 80 million yen in inheritance before the person died, they would have to file an inheritance tax. By law, when calculating inheritance property, that advancement would be added back to the inherited property as a special beneficiary, right?"

"That's the calculation method when sharing inherited property among multiple heirs. The inheritance tax declaration is judged based on the amount of property that exists at the time of the start of inheritance, the day the person dies."

Naoto had some knowledge of inheritance tax, so he could understand what the tax office staff was saying, but he had no idea what they were saying to his brother-in-law, and he needed to file an inheritance tax.

In the first place, the tax office was as tense as the police station was for general taxpayers. Naoto wished that the tax office staff would be able to explain everything on a beginner-level.

"Then I ask you, do you think that the money given to the heir during their lifetime is included in the inheritance property in the inheritance tax filing? It may be an extreme analogy, but if the property owner dies after having their money stolen, does the heir need to file an inheritance tax for that stolen amount of money?"

The tax office staff answered Naoto's question as follows, "Of course, the inheritance tax filing is based on the property at the time the decedent died, so the large amount of money stolen before the death is not included in the inheritance tax filing."

Naoto double-checked. "Then, it's fine for my brother-in-law to not file an inheritance tax."

"That's right, but the gift tax will be levied to the older sister who received her advancement."

Naoto nodded to himself. "By the way, I was taken care of by a special investigator named Kenichi Kato of the Tokyo National Tax Bureau at my previous workplace?"

"You know Kenichi Kato? Actually, I attended the National Tax College and he was a teacher there. He has a tax accountant office in Ningyocho. Should I contact him?"

"Please do."

It really was a small world. Mr. Kato apparently had been promoted to the Chief of the Investigation Department of the Tokyo National Tax Bureau, and retired after serving as the

Chief of the Investigation Department for two years.

Naoto immediately called Kato, "Hello, this is Yamamoto. Is this the Kato Tax Accountant Office?"

"Is this Yamamoto from Marunouchi Bank? It's been a while."

Naoto told Kato the situation at the tax office in Nagasaki.

"You have a lot of people relying on you still. By the way, where are you working now?"

"Actually, my wife has an incurable disease and I've been taking care of her at home."

"How is she? Home care can be difficult."

Naoto answered honestly. "Well, I can't go anywhere anyway because of the coronavirus lockdown, so it doesn't matter too much."

"That's true, but make sure not to over-do it." Kato changed the subject. "When I was appointed Chief of the Investigation Department of the Tokyo National Tax Bureau, I was also in charge of the Tokyo Marunouchi Mitsuwa Bank. You had a hard time back then asking the Commissioner of the National Tax Agency to cancel the consolidated tax payment, but somehow the deputy director in charge brought an application to reapply it."

"What did the deputy director say?"

"He said, 'The Tokyo National Taxation Bureau will be in trouble because the number of companies applying consolidated tax payments will not increase easily. We'll reapply for the application of consolidated tax payments and cooperate with them'. The deputy director did not seem to know why Mr. Yamamoto and his colleagues had to cancel the consolidated tax payment in the past. I told him, 'Study up and then come back'."

"At that time, without your advice, I would not have been able to cancel the consolidated tax payment, and the 2 trillion yen loss would have been carried forward by Mitsuwa Bank. I'm really thankful to you."

"That's not the case. It was Mr. Yamamoto's enthusiasm that moved the NTA Commissioner. I myself didn't honestly think that the Commissioner would take that much risk and approve your application. It wasn't very acceptable to apply for a change in the tax system that was selectively applied in two years. I wanted the deputy director to have the same enthusiasm, honesty, and humility as you did. Any organization, large or small, has people who work steadily every day under the hood. The corporate motto of the Marunouchi corporate group is 'organization is a person', and I have become a person who is now separated from the organization, but we can tell from the humility and sincerity of that person whether we are human beings who have survived hard in such an organization. It will be difficult for you to take care of yourself, but you should continue to survive like you always do."

Naoto had completely forgotten a question he had wanted to ask. "Mr. Kato, I'm actually in trouble because I'm involved in an inheritance battle with my relatives. When my mother-in-law died and my eldest brother-in-law examined the heritage, it was reduced to one-third of what it was. It seems that my sister-in-law received a gift from her mother-in-law to repay her husband's large debt. However, her sister-in-law insists that she has not received her advancement, and has been arguing with her brother-in-law in mediation at the family court. My sister-in-law argues that my brother-in-law should give evidence of her advancement, but since it was a parent-child gift, he cannot easily prove it. Is there any good way?"

"When I was in the inspection department of the Tokyo National Tax Bureau, I also investigated tax evasion cases involving 'gift tax'. The first way to detect tax evasion at that time was an odd amount. Did you have any doubts? The more questions you have, the more chances you have of finding evidence of tax evasion. The stage of the inheritance battle will be banks and securities companies. I bet it'd be easy for you. I wish you luck."

Kato left him motivated as usual. He had a faint idea for a solution–to overturn the allegation that her second daughter, Kayo, had not received a gift during her lifetime, with evidence on a case-by-case basis.

Naoto immediately started to collect this evidence. There

was only one truth, and the evidence should reveal it.

Finally, it was time to settle a score for his mother-in-law.

# Chapter 2  Inheritance Arbitration

Naoto received advice from Kato, a former special investigator at the Tokyo National Tax Bureau, about these inheritance issues.

First of all, the biggest hurdle would be the notarial will created by Suma. She prepared her first notarial will on March 31, 2011. It said that the land and buildings (a market value of about 28 million yen at that time) went to the eldest son's Yu, the securities through Gekko Securities (also a market value of about 28 million yen at that time) went to the second daughter Kayo. Then the securities entrusted to Nonomura Securities (a similar market value of about 28 million yen at that time) would go to Yoko, the third daughter. Any deposits and savings would be divided evenly among the three heirs.

Furthermore, the executor, who has all the authority to carry out the inheritance procedure, was designated to Yu, who had been living with Suma. This notarial will clearly intended that everything be inherited equally, so that the three would not argue.

However, for some reason, Suma only gave a copy of this will to Kayo, leaving Yoko and Yu were completely unaware of the contents. Mysteriously, that notarial will was withdrawn on

January 19, 2015, four years later, and a new one was created. The original content was changed in three places, changes that only benefitted Kayo.

The first change was that half of the Nonomura Securities investments would now go to Kayo, instead of Yoko. The second change was that all of the deposits and savings also went to Kayo, instead of being distributed evenly. Finally, the executor was changed from Yu to Kayo.

Once again, only Kayo had a copy of this will, and the other two siblings had no idea of the contents. Yet, that notarial will was withdrawn again on June 10, 2015, just five months later.

By creating a notarial act, Suma should have successfully prevented the three from fighting over the inheritance, but in the end, the battle still started.

All of these changes were strange, and Naoto was reminded of the last time Suma had visited Kawasaki, back before Yoko was sick. They had been discussing whether Kayo should get a divorce.

"I don't have an opinion on the matter, that's up to you to decide." Yoko told her mother. "It's your property, but if you give it to them during your lifetime, all of the money will go to her husband's debts, and Kayo won't see any of it. If you don't want that to happen, wait until they possibly get divorced."

"Yeah, that's a good point. I'll talk to Kayo when I get

home."

Perhaps Suma made it a condition that if Kayo lived with her after her divorce, she would change her notarial will to Kayo's favor and have her as executor. Yet at the very end, Kayo refused to divorse her husband, Ikuo. By then most of the property had already been donated to Kayo during Suma's lifetime, to cover their many debts.

It's probably true that Suma withdrew her notarial will, fearing that her remaining property would be taken by Kayo and her husband, and Kayo must have known this. One of the few things Suma had left was the life insurance that was meant to go to Yoko, but Kayo requested that the insurance company change the beneficiary to herself. This was later revealed by a document from the insurance company while Suma was hospitalized.

Naoto thoroughly cross-examined the transaction data with Suma's banks and securities companies, and found parts of Kayo's plan.

First, all the Gekko Securities, which was to be inherited by Kayo according to the first will, were sold by February 9, 2015, and the account was canceled. What should be noted was the fact that the first notarial will was changed on March 31, 2015, immediately after this.

Kayo took out everything from Suma's room, including her cash, passbook, and cash card, so that Yu couldn't confirm his heritage. Kayo continued to refuse to give the items back.

In the inheritance procedure, the first step was of course to determine the total amount of inheritance available as of December 7, 2019, when Suma died, but they couldn't find any information.

Yu went around to all of the banks and securities companies that Suma would have been trading with, and confirmed the existence of transactions. He found transactions with Hachijuni Bank, Shinwa Bank, Tokyo Marunouchi Mitsuwa Bank, and Inaho Bank, but all of the balances were about 1,000 yen or less. In addition, although there was a transaction between Gekko Securities and Nonomura Securities, the Gekko Securities account had been canceled in February 2015 and the Nonomura Securities account had a peak balance in 2010, but even that was only 15 million yen, when each child's inheritance had originally been 28 million yen.

Yu reported these facts to the court. Kayo admitted that the securities deposited at the securities company had been sold and transferred to the bank, but denied that she was the one to withdraw them.

The biggest problem was that Yu couldn't find any convincing evidence that Kayo had received an 80 million yen 'gift' from Suma when she was still alive. Kayo claimed, "Mother had a bank passbook, seal and card, but she wasn't in a situation where she could withdraw the money."

Kayo's motive was clear–her husband had many, many gambling debts to pay off. Even so, nothing could be done without hard evidence.

That was until Naoto went over Kayo's claims in court. She clearly stated that Suma had made some transactions in January 2016. He flipped back to find that the period when cash was withdrawn the most was between 2014 and 2015. He also found evidence of Kayo's husband applying for 'debt settlement' in 2015. That debt settlement system allowed some repayments to be reduced if a person's income over five years was under a certain amount.

Naoto called up his brother-in-law with this information.

"Like I've said before," Yu told him, "my mother had developed Alzheimer's disease around 2013 and had been seen at several hospitals. I've been thinking of asking a doctor for a medical certificate to prove that. And there is one more thing I would like to confirm–city hall investigators came every year to inspect the level of care given to Suma. I wonder if that information could be helpful if disclosed."

"If we can get that information, new facts may be revealed."

About two weeks later, one day, Yu called again. "I got the information disclosure material. There are about 90 pages in total. I found some surprising information from the 2013 to 2015 inspections."

Naoto grabbed a pen to write all of it down.

March 7, 2013: Suma handles her own money and goes to the bank alone.

March 7, 2014: Suma manages her own shares,

March 7, 2015: Most money is managed by the second daughter. Suma had given out her money freely and quickly ran out, so she was deemed unable to manage most of her funds.

He noticed that the time when Kayo kept the bankbook, seal, card, etc. from her mother was different from the time described in the interview by the investigator.

According to the hearing, Kayo was supposed to have already kept the bankbook, seal, card, etc. from Suma in 2014. That would mean Kayo could have only withdrawn cash frequently from the banks from 2014 to 2015. The total amount of cash withdrawn from the bank in those two years was 21.31 million yen, which couldn't have been withdrawn by anyone other than Kayo.

Finally, there was definitive proof. Plus, the store number listed was from the Fukuoka branch, different from the Nagasaki branch used by Suma.

At the court mediation on November 10, 2021, the

presiding judge told Kayo, "Please live more honestly from now on."

With this, he was finally able to pay back his mother-in-law. Yet Naoto couldn't help but be angry with the outcome. Suma raised four children almost entirely on her own, and she has struggled to build her fortune over many years. Her property was something she wanted to leave to her four children, not to repay the gambling debt of a deadbeat husband. Naoto could never forgive Kayo for continuing fueling her husband's pachinko-filled life without even an apology.

It was scary how gambling could even break family ties. For Kayo, her sister Yoko was suffering from an incurable illness, but her husband's mistakes made her turn into a person obsessed with money without a conscience.

# Chapter 3  Guardian of an Adult

However, this inheritance struggle didn't end there. Kayo refused to accept the results of the mediation, leading to the whole arbitration unraveling. Yu couldn't contain his anger and filed a lawsuit seeking a refund of the money Kayo had arbitrarily withdrawn while Suma had been hospitalized. Yu asked Naoto to stand in for Yoko, to protect her inheritance rights–to legally be her guardian, as a person with an incurable illness and a lack in cognition. This process included the necessary contracts and managing all property. Naoto immediately investigated this system, prepared the necessary documents, and applied to the Kawasaki branch of the Yokohama Family Court.

About a week after that, he was given an interview date, to determine if Naoto was appropriate as Yoko's guardian.

Naoto was nervous, but he simply explained to the interviewer why this was all necessary, and they didn't ask any difficult questions. A few days later, he received the notice in the mail that he was Yoko's appointed guardian.

However, Naoto soon realized how truly ridiculous the whole process after reading the documents distributed by the court:

- After being appointed, the guardian must submit a 'property inventory list' and 'guardianship plan' to the family court within one month.
- The guardian must be aware that the management of the person's assets is separate, even if said person is family, etc. The property of the guardian and the property of their ward must be clearly distinguished and managed.
- The guardian is given heavy responsibility because of the importance of their duties. If the guardian causes harm to their ward or acts against their best interests, the guardian will be liable for a civil suit. If there is malicious intent, the guardian will be held criminally liable for embezzlement.
- The guardian must keep a monetary account book every time income or an expenditure is generated and submit it to the court as needed.

"I'm caring for my wife's intractable illness at home 24/7," Naoto told the country clerk, "but now I'm also required to do these additional jobs as her guardian? I did this all in order to protect my wife's inheritance. Is it possible for me just to be her guardian for this legal aspect?"

"I'm sorry, but a legal guardian cannot pick and choose which responsibilities to uphold."

Naoto sighed deeply. "So, I need to manage her income and expenditures and report to the court on a regular basis." The clerk nodded, and Naoto continued. "But we're husband and wife who have managed both of our finances as one entity for many years. Even so, you want me to now handle all of my wife's property separately?"

"That's correct."

"Then, when I become an adult guardian, are we no longer seen as a married couple? If that's the case, should I be reimbursed for the home care? In fact, the other day, I asked my visiting staff how much it would cost if I had to employ people to do my workload, in case of an emergency. Since 24-hour care isn't covered by insurance, it would cost about 160,000 yen a day. If I was working as a separate entity from my wife, she would never be able to afford that. Isn't there something wrong with all this?"

"Well," the clerk started nervously, "Mr. Yamamoto's case is special."

"But our situation won't be treated any differently, as stipulated by the law. How will this problem work given our aging society? This law seems to have been put in place to protect award from being taken advantage of, but shouldn't we review this design if it's between an already married couple?"

The clerk nodded slowly, clearly at his wits' end.

# Chapter 4  A Mother's Miscalculation

Naoto urged his own mother, Aiko, who lived alone in Nagasaki to come live with him in Kawasaki numerous times. Yet, she always refused, saying that she was fine living alone.

However, at the beginning of the New Year in 2014, she suddenly got in touch with Naoto. "I've been thinking it over a lot, if I should come live with you."

Naoto wanted to ask what had changed her mind, after years insisting she wanted to live by herself. "Of course, you're always welcome. I'll send Yoko to help you pack."

"Thank you. I think it will take a couple of months to prepare, but is Yoko really okay to travel all the way here?"

"It's fine, I think it'd make Yoko happy too."

From March 25, 2014, Aiko got to enjoy life in the Tokyo area. She was amazed at the size of her son's three-story house. She especially liked that she could see Mt. Fuji from the third floor, and would sit at the window every day with her hands folded.

Naoto bought a stairlift for his mother, but it didn't get much use since Aiko moved into a nursing home in Tamaplaza six months later. The lift proved useful later, once Yoko could no longer walk up the stairs either.

Naoto asked his mother why she had changed her mind about a month after she moved to Kawasaki.

She laughed and said, "Recently, your father has been beckoning me from beyond. So, I thought I'd spent some time with you before that."

His mother was 88 years old at that time. She spent more than six years in Kawasaki before she died at age 94.

When Naoto was going through her things after her death, he found a note labeled, 'funeral plans' in her purse. In it, she wrote all of the arrangements in detail, such as a contact list and a request for the 'Buddhist priest of the Jodo Shinshu Otani sect'. It seemed like this note had been written years ago. His mother had miscalculated–she had thought she only had a year left, but she actually had six. As proof of that, after three years of moving to Kawasaki, his mother asked him to sell her Nagasaki condominium to raise money. She ended up paying more than 23 million yen for the six years she was at the Elderly Housing with Care at Tamaplaza.

Naoto had a 'heritage division agreement' so that when his father died in May 2004 his mother could inherit both real estate properties owned by his father. The agreement was created and the inheritance was registered. At that time, he had a hard time getting the signatures he needed from his sister Sachiko, who had immigrated to Canada.

When his mother died, he was wondering what to do with the inheritance registration of the real estate in Aioi-cho, which she had rented, but with Yoko's long-term care, he postponed the decision.

However, recently, a person who wanted to buy the property appeared, and the fact that this inheritance registration had not been made yet became a real problem.

In the previous inheritance registration, his father's inheritance heirs were his wife, Naoto, and his two daughters. But now, Naoto's two older sisters had already died, so the five of their children were also the heirs.

However, one of the kids lived in Canada and another lived in the United Kingdom, and due to COVID-19, international mail had slowed dramatically. Naoto was surprised at the complexity of the inheritance registration forms.

First, he needed his mother's death certificate, the family registry, and a list of any changed addresses. It was difficult to update the family registry after the death of his sisters. Then, the six heirs needed a copy of the family registry, their personal seal, and a residence card.

Since the two people living overseas no longer had a residence card, they had to sign the 'heritage division agreement' in front of the local Japanese consulate. In the end, it took more than three months to complete all the documents, and arrange the travel.

As an aside, a bill that put penalties around this inheritance process was passed by the Diet in October 2021 and will come into effect two years later. Inheritance registration is expected to be a heavy administrative burden considering Japan's aging society in the future. For that reason, there is a concern that the business will not turn around unless the procedure is simplified by making the best use of IT, such as confirming the intention of the person. Perhaps the number of jobs for lawyers and judicial scriveners will increase rapidly.

There had been another large miscalculation brought forth from his mother's death.

It was a dispute with her younger brother over the Wakamatsu land in Kitakyushu, which her mother's adoptive father gave to her to protect the property from the yakuza. After inheriting the land, his mother married his father and lived in Nagasaki for more than sixty years. Meanwhile, her younger brother, who lived in Wakamatsu, started building a house on his mother's land without permission.

When his mother learned about this, she gave her brother the land where he built the house, so she repeatedly asked her brother to return her land title, but she stubbornly asked for it. At last, his younger brother died at the age of 78, leaving the conflict as it was.

So his mother filed a lawsuit in the Kokura District Court

to reclaim the land.

Naoto took his mother from Kawasaki to Nagasaki to the court in Kokura more than ten times. His mother could walk with her cane in the beginning, but eventually she needed a wheelchair. She was 82 years old at this time.

Eventually Aiko won the case, but she couldn't get rid of her younger brother's wife, who lived there at the time.

In the end, the land could not be surrendered during his mother's lifetime, nor could she sell the land like she had hoped to. Instead Naoto inherited this land via his mother's notarial will.

Aiko said this to Naoto during her lifetime, "I wanted to figure out this land problem for myself, but I couldn't finish it in the end. I have to ask you to complete it in my stead. Don't make the same mistakes with your family and squabble over petty things."

It was his mother's biggest regret. She was a smart, courageous and foresighted woman, one who learned how to use a smartphone even after she was eighty years old. Naoto finalized the two real estate issues all while continuing Yoko's long-term care, so he could fulfill his mother's last wish. As he watched over Yoko, his thoughts would wander, 'What is the most important thing in life? How could a family who used to be so close to each other, through joy and sadness, break that bond over a small fortune?'

# Chapter 5  Naoto's Genetics

Naoto's father often said he went to Shanghai, China twice during the Pacific War–as a Chinese and Russian interpreter, not an ordinary soldier. He also told stories about how he helped many Chinese locals. He said that he brought back the remains of a Chinese man without a family to Nagasaki and put them in the Yamamoto family grave. Naoto cleaned said grave when his father died, and found an urn with many Chinese names written on it. His father had been telling the truth.

Curious, Naoto ordered a copy of his father's records. When and where did his father learn Chinese and Russian?

His father was born in Omuta City, Fukuoka Prefecture in 1915, the second son of his father, Ryuichi and his mother, Tsuki. The following year, he was adopted by a man who ran a geisha house in Maruyama, Nagasaki. The Yamamoto family was wealthy and once ran the famous restaurant 'Kagetsu' in Nagasaki–the one where Ryoma Sakamoto had gotten drunk and left a mark on a pillar with his sword.

He couldn't have studied Chinese and Russian at school because his father had only attended elementary school. Perhaps he was self-taught, but he couldn't have become fluent like that. When he looked up his paternal grandparent's last name, it seemed that it was common in Fukuoka and Saga prefectures in Kyushu. His ancestors came from a wealthy clan with power in the northwestern part of Kyushu

When he got drunk, his father always said, 'Our ancestors were the Ryuzoji clan, who served the Nabeshima clan in Saga'. There was also a theory that the Ryuzoji clan were pirates. If so, they must have had interactions in the sea of China. Maybe his father spoke Chinese in a previous life.

But that didn't explain the Russian. His father used to bring back Russian passengers to entertain whenever their ship arrived in Nagasaki. Certainly his father was speaking Russian to these friends.

Next was Tsuki, his father's birth mother. Naoto had only met his grandmother once when he was little. She was dressed up like a shaman and made a living fortune-telling. His grandmother once saw Naoto and told his father, "This child inherited my blood." Naoto wondered if he and Kumi had gotten their sixth sense from Tsuki.

However, when he first met Yuko Motoyama, the visiting nurse, he was overwhelmed with the sense that he had known her in a past life.

Since then, Naoto has been wondering where this feeling came from, only beginning to understand it later in life. Naoto and Yuko Motoyama may be descendants of the same ancestors, maybe sharing the same genes.

Naoto often heard from his father who heard it from his mother, "A person will encounter three non-family members with the same genes as their ancestors in their lifetime." Naoto thought Yuko Motoyama was one of his three, with her last name also tracing back to western Kyushu.

Humans have over 6 billion genes. He had met two other people in his lifetime that he thought shared some of those genes.

One was Takeshi Terada, who died on February 17, 2020 when he was hit by a train on the Sobu Line. Terada was originally from Kyoto, but he could likely trace ancestors back to the Ryuzoji clan too.

The other was Masaru Ishida, who was next in line to be the president of Tokyo Marunouchi Mitsuwa Bank, but died before he could fulfill that dream. When he drank with Ishida one night, he heard that the man's maternal ancestor was a pirate who was territorial in the rough seas of the Genkai Sea in northern Kyushu. Ishida was an extremely talented subordinate who had worked with Naoto for more than 10 years.

One day, Ishida called Naoto, who had retired from the bank and was working at the Foundation. "Mr. Yamamoto, it's been a long time. It seems that you're doing a great job at your new position. I think most companies will join the Foundation. It's been hard without you at the bank, I've been feeling nostalgic for the days where we toiled during the Lehman shock."

Naoto remembered when he and Ishida worked on the negotiations to establish a joint company to rescue Morgan Stanley Securities in the United States, which was rumored to be the next bankruptcy case.

The Lehman shock happened in September 2008 when the Lehman Brothers, one of the major investment banks in the United States, collapsed due to the sharp drop in the price of subprime mortgages in the housing bubble. It was a financial crisis that made stock prices plummet worldwide.

Morgan Stanley Securities had sought relief from Tokyo Marunouchi Mitsuwa Bank, which had a lot of momentum in Japan at that time.

Tokyo Marunouchi Mitsuwa Bank was excited at the possibility of taking over one of the three big investment banks in the United States, so the two companies had started negotiations right away.

The negotiations continued for about a month, so they rented out rooms in a famous hotel, where Ishida consulted with Naoto. "Deputy Director Yamamoto, I know that the joint investment plan is a trap, but I can't figure out any concrete way to prove it."

Naoto carefully read the proposal from Morgan Stanley. The plan was to make the joint venture company a subsidiary of the bank, with Tokyo Marunouchi Mitsuwa Bank at 51 percent and Morgan Stanley Securities at 49 percent. It seemed like a good deal until he looked at the contents of each other's investment–the bank would need to invest in cash, while the other party invested labor. Ishida had sensed this problem in his gut.

Naoto thought for a while. "Mr. Ishida, the other party's proposal is constructed with perfect logic, I cannot argue with it as an amateur. However, considering Morgan Stanley's plight, they should be making more concessions."

Thus, the joint investment was postponed and Ishida kept the bank from falling into a sticky situation.


One day, Ishida called Naoto seemingly out of the blue. "I can't help myself anymore. I miss the times when I was crazy about my work, I'd want to go back to that time if I could."

"Hey, Ishida, you're still in your early fifties, you have plenty of time. I thought you were striving to become president, what happened?"

"Nothing is exciting anymore, we're a top bank and all of the mergers are settled. I called you with the intention of getting some of your know-how, learning how to take decisive actions and cut down the competition."

"Woah, woah, I don't remember being that good." Naoto laughed. "I've been out of the game for a while, but I can still say one thing. You shouldn't put 120 percent effort into every job. You'll never do a good job if you don't have any energy left."

"You may be right. But I don't know how to work less."

"That's exactly how I was. You may have inherited the same Ryuzoji blood as I did. Mr. Ishida, work continues on until you die. If you put so much effort on your shoulders at once, you'll never make it to the finish line. I regret not taking more time for myself and my family."

"Thank you, I'll figure out a way. Hearing Mr. Yamamoto's voice made me relax a little. It'll be fine"

Naoto felt a little uncomfortable with Ishida's 'I'll be fine'. Thinking back to it, Ishida may have wanted to actually say, "I'm already at my limit."

"Mr. Ishida, life continues to be an uphill climb, so be careful and take your time."

"I understand. Thank you very much."

This call was the last conversation with Ishida. Three days after this call, Ishida ended his own life at only fifty-four years old. It was another premature death of a corporate warrior.


Naoto was reminded of that last phone call again and was filled with regret. All of the stress had deteriorated Ishida's mental state, even when he tried to reach out.

Ishida was the best subordinate in the 24 years Naoto was in the Planning Department. Perhaps he was one of the few people to become president in the future and lead the bank in the right direction.

When he thought about Ishida with his shared genes no longer being in this world, Naoto was overwhelmed by the feeling of loss. It was an indescribable pain, like the loss of a family member.

Five years later, in April 2021, Koichi Tazawa was appointed as the president of Tokyo Marunouchi Mitsuwa Bank. No one could say when or how their fate might change. Tazawa could easily realize Ishida's unfulfilled dream.

# Chapter 6  A Member of the Family

When Yoko was hospitalized at the Roadside Station Hospital in Nagasaki, she would often point to a large tree outside the window and say, "Naoto, Banana is waiting in the tree over there. Did you give him any bread today?"

'Banana' was a baby crow that had fallen from a large ginkgo tree in front of Miyazakidai station in the spring of 2004, back when Yoko was still healthy. A lot of people had gathered around, wondering what the loud squawk had been. Yoko squeezed through the crowd, plopped the crow chick in the hat she was wearing and took the bird home.

Yoko named the animal 'Banana'. When Naoto asked why, she said it was because Japanese crows were 'jungle crows' with thick beaks in the shape of a banana.

Parent crows apparently would no longer raise their chicks if they were touched by humans. Yoko put Banana in a large cardboard box on their third floor balcony, feeding it bread and water. After three months had passed, Banana was ready to leave the nest. Yoko threw Banana from the veranda, rejoicing as her child tried to take flight.

However, Banana still couldn't spread its wings well and lost control and crashed into the schoolyard nearby. Yoko ran over and asked the front staff, "I'm sorry, my Banana fell into your yard, could I pop back and grab it?"

"A banana?" one of the staff asked. "Did it slip when you were trying to eat it?"

"Oh no, not the fruit, Banana is our pet crow."

"Your pet?" the woman asked, surprised. "Do you keep a crow at home?"

"That's right. Today was its first flight."

The staff made a dismayed face and raised one hand as if to say 'do whatever you want' and gestured to Yoko to go out back.

Yoko went outside and called out, "Come here Banana!"

Eventually Banana jumped out of a bush. Yoko quickly caught it in her hands.

The staff member peeking out from the door gasped and shouted, "You just caught a crow with your bare hands!"

For about a week after that, Yoko had flying practice with Banana on the balcony every day.

Finally, the second fledging ceremony had begun.

Yoko carefully picked up Banana and lifted it up to the sky. Perhaps the week of practice had paid off. Banana spread its wings and leapt high in the sky brilliantly. Yoko seemed relieved to see it, but she also looked a little lonely.

"Oh, I'm finally saying goodbye to Banana. I'm relieved."

However, within an hour, Aki and Great began barking

from the front yard. Naoto wondered if someone had visited and popped his head out on the balcony. Banana had landed on the roof of the dogs' kennel, tilting its head side-to-side at the two dogs, almost as if to say, "Take care of her for me."

Banana stopped again at the balcony railing. Yoko laughed with delight when she saw it, but said, "Go on to see your friends, don't come back here."

However, Banana refused to leave its balcony for too long. One day, Yoko brought home a big birdcage from a pet shop in Saginuma.

"No way," Naoto started. "It's not right to keep Banana caged in the house."

Yoko shook her head. "No, I'm taking Banana far away and letting it go. Then it won't be able to come back home anymore and will live free."

Yoko called a rural taxi the next evening, wrapped Banana in the birdcage, and got into the car. "Driver, please go to Todoroki Green Space Park in Musashi Kosugi."

Yoko came back two hours later with a sad face. After she let Banana go, she hid in a nearby bush for a while to watch it. She thought she was finally able to say goodbye to Banana.

After four or five days without the crow returning, Yoko was relieved that Banana was able to become independent.

However, the next morning, Naoto casually looked out the balcony and noticed Banana perched on the railing. Banana was wandering around outside the house, as if it was looking for its mother. Naoto hurriedly called Yoko, "Banana is back."

Yoko came into the room surprised, but with an excited smile. "Banana is so smart, how did it find us?" She offered Banana the sausage bread she had bought at the bakery in front of the station.

Banana gladly took it and flew off toward the roof of the condominium.

In this way, Banana has inhabited the nearby forest, but still came to their balcony a couple of times every day to get sausage bread from Yoko. Eventually, Banana became a member of the Yamamoto family and became friends with their two dogs.

However, Naoto wondered if crows were a lot smarter than dogs, since Banana always seemed to outsmart them when they played. Even if the two animals cooperated to chase after Banana, the crow easily escaped and teased them every time. The pet dogs also learned to cling to Yoko when Banana came in hopes of sausage, but Yoko never gave it to them–the dogs were obese and needed to go on a diet.

Yoko always took the sausage bread on her morning walk with the dogs. Banana would watch from a distance and fly low until Yoko tossed some of the food into the air.

This lifestyle continued for about two years, but then

Banana suddenly stopped coming. Perhaps Banana had found another crow and moved on. Every time Yoko saw crows, she would call out, "Banana, Banana, sausage bread!" in case it ever came back.

One day, Yoko's friend came to visit. They both sat on the third floor with a view of the balcony, chatting. Then her friend suddenly shouted, "Yoko, there's a huge crow on the balcony. Chase it away before it calls its friends!"

"Banana, you know better than to come when there's other visitors."

"Yoko, have you been keeping a crow? You're going to get complaints from your neighbors."

"It's fine, since Banana is smart and listens to instructions." With that said, Yoko went out to the balcony.

"Yoko, it's dangerous to get too close, it might attack you."

"It's fine, it's fine," she said and went up to pet Banana lightly. "Banana, aren't you getting a little fat? It's time to get some diet bread."

Her friend was stunned. "What's going on with this house? Yoko is acting like a witch."

After that, they had to move to Nagasaki for Yoko's treatment, far away from their Kawasaki home. When they came back years later, Banana showed up a few days after they unpacked their boxes. The crow had grown surprisingly large and its black coat had turned slightly gray. In addition, there were two younger crows following behind it.

"Banana, you're a girl! You've become a mother. Thank you for showing me your children."

Yoko got Naoto to bring up three of the sausage breads she always kept in the fridge. When the children watched their mother eat from Yoko's hand, they quickly followed suit.

Naoto thought back to the day before they left Kawasaki for good. Yoko had said to Banana, "We're going to Nagasaki on the 24th of this month. I'm afraid nobody's going to be at this house anymore. Do you understand?" She stroked the bird's feathers as it ate from her hand. The crow used to take off with the sausage bread, but that time it seemed like Banana was saying farewell, just like Banana did with her babies now.

For two years and four months, the Kawasaki house had sat empty. When Yoko came back bedridden, Naoto would call out to any crow nearby, "Banana, Banana!" Yet neither Yoko or the birds would respond. Every day he still hoped the crow would fly over and caw enough to catch Yoko's attention and make her smile.

# Epilogue  The Joys and Sorrows of Life

It had been one year and nine months since they started nursing care at their old home in Kawasaki. During that time, Yoko's weight increased by 20 kilograms, from 38 kilograms to 58, and was almost at the same level as a healthy person, even with a blood test once every two months.

Her renewed physical strength even made her coughing and sneezing louder. They owed so much to the staff of the visit-bathing, home-visit nursing, home-visit rehabilitation, and home-visit massage business.

However, with all of the new restrictions due to the coronavirus, Yoko could no longer eat ice cream or yogurt, just in case it led to aspiration pneumonia and she couldn't be hospitalized.

Naoto sometimes worried that Yoko would lose her ability to eat and drink again. Her stay at the Roadside Station Hospital in Nagasaki when she'd barely been able to snack on strawberries and kiwis didn't feel that long ago.

Once Naoto got used to the home-care, his mind was finally free to focus on other things–though sometimes he just found new things to worry about. Yoko was bedridden, she couldn't eat what she loved anymore, and her cognitive function didn't quite recover as expected. Was Yoko really happy? Was there anything left that she enjoyed?

Before she developed this illness, Yoko loved to cook and would often say, "If I couldn't eat, I'd be better off dead."

Recalling this always brought up mixed feelings in his gut. Whenever that happened he would turn to the words of Chief Nurse Takegami, who had helped him when Yoko was admitted to the Nagasaki Tozai Hospital for exams: "Yoko is going through the toughest period now. After a little more time, I'm sure it'll be easier and the ray of light at the end of the long tunnel will shine through. We just need a little more patience."

Naoto thought she only said that to comfort him at that time. However, when comparing Yoko now to the Yoko from that time, the difference was indeed clear.

Naoto asked his doctor, Dr. Ueki, many times. "Why does Yoko always have such a pained, rugged appearance?"

Ueki simply replied, "It's because of her illness." However, after spending 24 hours with Yoko for home care after a year and nine months, Naoto realized that wasn't the case.

He was convinced that Yoko's outer appearance reflected her mental state. Before, she hadn't wanted to keep living. But now, she kept a calm expression.

Sometimes they no longer feel like a married couple, but

rather a father-daughter relationship. Perhaps because it now felt like they were connected by blood.

Naoto would have to thank the chief nurse, Takegami, more. At the Roadside Station Hospital, Yoko was restrained and forced to wear mittens on her hands in order to be hospitalized. At that time, Naoto had signed the consent form because Yoko had repeatedly tried to hurt herself.

However, a few days after she was transferred to Tozai Hospital, Chief Nurse Takegami said, "Mr. Yamamoto, why don't we try taking off your wife's restraints? We can watch over her properly. I'll also put an alarm mat under the bed. In the unlikely event that she gets off the bed, the alarm will sound and a nurse will rush in immediately."

Naoto couldn't believe it. "Can you really do that?"

"Yes, I think the belt and mittens are causing her more mental strife. With your consent, I'll remove them."

Whenever Naoto would try to return to the hospital room after Yoko's walking or wheelchair exercises, Yoko would put her feet on the ground, refusing to let the wheelchair move. He hated it. Sometimes he had to ask a nurse or two to take her back.

After all, it must have been a great pain for Yoko to be restrained all the time, deprived of use of her hands or fingers by mittens. Naoto stalled as much as he could, but he had to return Yoko to her room by dinner.

At the suggestion of Chief Nurse Takegami, Yoko's restraints were removed the next day and her facial expression was noticeably calmer.

Takegami was a saint that put the patient first, without considering the risks to herself.

However, when she returned after her examination at Tozai Hospital, she returned to the life of the restraints and mittens. Naoto told the chief nurse that Yoko had been fine without the restraints at Tozai Hospital. But the next day, he found Yoko on the floor next to the bed.

Naoto asked the chief nurse why she was on the floor, and the chief nurse replied, "Mr. Yamamoto, we thought about how to prevent the risk of your wife falling, and we came to the conclusion that it would be best to have her sleep on the floor."

"Yes, that eliminates the risk of falling, but for heaven's sake, I basically take care of her all by myself from 8 to 5 every day! I take her to the cafeteria or toilet in her wheelchair. I take her to the rehab room, dentist, and barber by myself. I can transfer her from the bed to the wheelchair alone, but not from the floor to the wheelchair. Certainly you can get someone to stay watch overnight to make sure she doesn't fall off the bed!"

Her face fell. "Sir, we're having a hard time due to the lack of manpower. It's impossible to have someone stay in the hospital room."

"Then just remove the belt and mittens and use an alarm mat or a monitoring system, like Tozai Hospital! I assist you every day from 8 to 5, so you don't need as many staff members then, right?"

The chief nurse reluctantly agreed.

The hospital was using their labor shortage as an excuse to treat patients as less than human, all while covering their own skins.


Whenever Yoko was in Naoto's dreams, she was always healthy, like she was years ago. Maybe Naoto's brain still couldn't accept the current reality. As Yoko's illness progressed, Naoto woke up every morning and repeatedly wished that all of it was a dream. But the harsh reality always shattered that wish.

A friend often told Naoto that nursing care had to take the future into account. But, Naoto didn't want to look ahead, he was busy focusing on each moment. His motto for his long-term care life was, "If there is something you can do now, even if it is one hour ahead, one day ahead, one month ahead, or one year ahead, do it now." Because there was no guarantee that these peaceful days would continue tomorrow.

Naoto hadn't yet found the answer to his biggest fear, that his atrial fibrillation would recur and hospitalize him. If that happened, Yoko would be forced to fend for herself at a hospital as well.

There were three possible options.

The first was to have a visiting nurse or visiting caregiver come to their house for nursing care on his behalf. The labor that Naoto does himself would cost 160,000 yen a day, about 5,000,000 yen a month, and about 60,000,000 yen a year. It was not an amount two retirees could pay. The next possible option, again unrealistic, would be to ask someone in their family to take care of Yoko. But all of their children had their own busy, independent lives.

The last option was to go to heaven together. Yoko might probably choose this last option.

Amidst his worrying thoughts, Naoto received a letter from Masayuki Hiratsuka. He had forgotten that he had written to his old friend and described his new everyday life.

He opened the letter, and the contents were hard to believe:

Naoto,

You're living a really fulfilling long-term care life. After reading your recent report, I thought I'd make my own.

Actually, half a year ago, I was diagnosed with a "spinal cord infarction" (a disease that clogs the blood vessels that pass through the spinal cord and damages nerves), and was paralyzed from the waist down. Now I'm in a wheelchair every day. Thanks to my continued rehabilitation, I can manage walking a short distance if I use a walker. Fortunately, my upper body is functioning fine, so with my wife's support, I go about my daily life without many problems. The biggest problem is of course using the bathroom. In the hospital, I had to use a diaper and a catheter. But with special training from my physiotherapist and occupational therapist, I can now use a wheelchair to go to the toilet alone, giving me back some freedom.

Compared to the hardships of Yoko's nursing care, it doesn't feel like a big deal anymore. You and Yoko may continue to struggle in the future, but I'm supporting you from afar.

Let's continue to do our best together and fight these illnesses!

Naoto read this letter over and over again. He really couldn't believe that Hiratsuka was in a wheelchair. Even so, he was impressed by how strong his spirit was. He wouldn't be able to think as positively as Hiratsuka if he suddenly couldn't walk. Checking Yoko's schedule, Naoto decided he could visit Hiratsuka the next day.

After visiting rehabilitation in the morning and visiting-bathing in the afternoon, Naoto would go shopping at the store every three days, but hadn't seen people for a while due to

COVID-19. He had about 3 hours free–the trip to Hiratsuka's home was an hour each way, leaving him only an hour to actually talk.

The next day, he finished Yoko's morning schedule early and left the house at one o'clock to get to Hiratsuka's right at 2 o'clock. When he pressed the chime at their front door, Hiratsuka came out in a wheelchair. "Oh, it's been a long time. You're punctual as always."

Hiratsuka looked brighter and more energetic than he expected.

At that time, Ai came out and told Naoto, "I'm sorry we haven't been able to visit you for more than half a year."

"No, it's completely understandable, we've been busy too."

"I wanted to reach out, but my husband here told me not to bother you while you were hard at work on your home-care."

"That's not the case, we would have loved to hear from you."

Hiratsuka explained his illness in detail, as if he were talking about someone else. "One night, when I was sleeping, my legs started to get stiff, so I got up and sat on the couch. But then my legs and hips started to get numb and I couldn't stand. I called an ambulance right away and underwent a detailed examination at the hospital. They diagnosed the 'spinal cord infarction' and after two long months of rehabilitation, I was finally able to move using a walker. It's a lot of work, but with the support of my wife, I can manage to live a normal life."

Ai explained further, "My husband is tall and weighs 80 kilograms, so it's hard to support him. He has to go on a diet soon."

"Hey, I lost more than 10 kilos while I was in the hospital, so I'm already less than 80 kilos. A diet is just overkill."

Naoto was envious of this kind of daily conversation between the Hiratsuka couple. However, where did Hiratsuka's strength and brightness come from? Naoto was once again impressed by the strength of Hiratsuka's spirit– if he were in Hiratsuka's position, he would not behave as cheerfully.

Naoto changed the topic and asked Hiratsuka a question. "By the way, it may be strange to ask this kind of thing now, but Hiratsuka is from Saga and Ai is from Nagasaki. I had thought you two first met at the same hospital Yoko worked at, but didn't Hiratsuka actually know Ai before that?"

"Yamamoto, that's some sharp intuition. That's right. Actually, we were at Kyushu University together. We met through the archery club."

"I always thought it was odd how quickly you got married after you 'met for the first time'."

The hour of nostalgic excitement passed in a blink of an eye.

"It's time for Yoko's medicine, so I have to go home soon.

Thank you for having me, good luck with everything."

Hiratsuka guided him out and asked Naoto, "Hey Yamamoto. How can you continue to care for Yoko so much? If I were in your position, I wouldn't be able to do all that. How do you stay motivated?"

"Hiratsuka, long-term care isn't something that 'can or can't be done'. I have no choice but to do it. I've been fighting for  Yoko for over 40 years. She's my comrade."

Naoto read the letter from Hiratsuka yesterday, and worried that his friend might be depressed. When he handed the envelope containing his reply to Hiratsuka, Naoto said, "Hiratsuka, my secret for long-term care is in the envelope. After I leave, read it and then give it to Ai. I'll come see you again soon."

After Naoto went home, Hiratsuka opened the envelope. Inside were Naoto's vows from their wedding.


To Yoko:


In sickness or in health,


Joy or sadness,


Rich or poor,

We will love, respect, and comfort each other, help each other,

As long as we're alive, I will do my best to protect you,

Until the two of us set out for that distant world,

I swear to continue walking together.

Naoto

The End

This work is a novel based on the author's own life, but the events also include fiction. Personal names and company names are pseudonyms and have nothing to do with any real-life counterparts.

## *About the author*

### Katsumi Yamaguchi

Born in Nagasaki Prefecture in 1953, he is a graduate of Nagasaki University. He joined a major metropolitan bank in 1976, and after working at the Fukuoka branch and the Motosumiyoshi branch, he was transferred to the Planning Department of the bank for a quarter of a century. During that time, he served under eight different presidents, liberalized interest rates, helped end the convoy system, listed on the New York Stock Exchange, BIS capital ratio regulation, financial big bang, bubble burst, bad debt problem, FSA inspection, bank collapse, management Experience the turbulent period of banks such as integration and Lehman shock. After he retired from the bank, he was the secretary general of the Accounting Education Foundation, and he focused on rebuilding the foundation, promoting accounting education, and fostering younger generations. He then devoted himself to home care to care for his wife, who suffered from his intractable disease.

著者プロフィール

## 山口 勝美 （やまぐち かつみ）

1953年長崎県生まれ。長崎大学卒。1976年に大手都市銀行に入行し福
岡支店、元住吉支店を経て四半世紀にわたり、同行企画部に在籍。その
間、八人の頭取に仕え、金利の自由化、護送船団方式の終焉、ニューヨ
ーク証券取引所上場、BIS 自己資本比率規制、金融ビッグバン、バブ
ル崩壊、不良債権問題、金融庁検査、銀行破綻、経営統合、リーマンシ
ョックなどまさに銀行の激動期を身をもって体験。銀行退職後は教育財
団の事務局長として、財団の再建、会計教育および後進の育成に注力し
た。その後、難病に罹った妻を介護するため、在宅勤務に専念。

翻訳者プロフィール

## Harley Emmons （ハーレイ エモンス）

（Japanease to English Translation & Localization）
I have done freelance work for various companies, such as Amazon,
Honda, Mizuho Bank, and numerous medical suppliers and IT companies,
for over six years.

## Giving Back One-Hundred-Fold Volume2

Humanity The Joys and Sorrows of Life （人生の百倍返し 英訳版２）

2023年７月15日 初版第１刷発行

著　者　YAMAGUCHI Katsumi
発行者　瓜谷 綱延
発行所　株式会社文芸社
　　　　〒160-0022 東京都新宿区新宿1－10－1
　　　　　　　　電話 03-5369-3060 （代表）
　　　　　　　　　　　03-5369-2299 （販売）

印刷所　株式会社晃陽社

ISBN978-4-286-24485-3

郵 便 は が き

料金受取人払郵便

新宿局承認

7553

差出有効期間
2024年1月
31日まで
（切手不要）

160-8791

141

東京都新宿区新宿1－10－1

**㈱文芸社**

愛読者カード係 行

IIılı·IIı·ılIı·ıIIIı·II·ıIıı·ıIı·ıIıIı·ıIı·ıIıIı·Iı·ıIı·Iı·Iı

| ふりがな<br>お名前 | | 明治　大正<br>昭和　平成　年生　歳 | |
|---|---|---|---|
| ふりがな<br>ご住所 | □□□-□□□□ | 性別<br>男・女 | |
| お電話<br>番　号 | （書籍ご注文の際に必要です） | ご職業 | |
| E-mail | | | |
| ご購読雑誌（複数可） | | ご購読新聞 | 新聞 |

最近読んでおもしろかった本や今後、とりあげてほしいテーマをお教えください。

ご自分の研究成果や経験、お考え等を出版してみたいというお気持ちはありますか。

ある　　　　ない　　　　内容・テーマ（　　　　　　　　　　　　　　　　　）

現在完成した作品をお持ちですか。

ある　　　　ない　　　　ジャンル・原稿量（　　　　　　　　　　　　　　　）

| 書　名 | | | | | | |
|---|---|---|---|---|---|---|
| お買上<br>書　店 | 都道<br>府県 | 市区<br>郡 | 書店名 | | | 書店 |
| | | | ご購入日 | 年 | 月 | 日 |

本書をどこでお知りになりましたか?
　　1.書店店頭　2.知人にすすめられて　3.インターネット(サイト名
　　4.DMハガキ　5.広告、記事を見て(新聞、雑誌名

上の質問に関連して、ご購入の決め手となったのは?
　　1.タイトル　2.著者　3.内容　4.カバーデザイン　5.帯
　　その他ご自由にお書きください。

本書についてのご意見、ご感想をお聞かせください。
①内容について



②カバー、タイトル、帯について


弊社Webサイトからもご意見、ご感想をお寄せいただけます。